She could lose everything she valued if she spent much more time around this man.

Hazel swallowed and tried to shift her gaze elsewhere, tried to pretend that she was really in charge—and wished she were as strong as she pretended to be.

Guy looked up at her, his eyes so somber and soft with promise that Hazel's breath caught. "I don't know who hurt you so badly you think you can't have something I can see you want, but let me in and I won't hurt you. Ever. You can trust me with anything you care to share with me. Your worries, your body, your heart, your love. And if it comes to the point you need to run away, I won't want you to go, but I'll survive."

"But I might not." The admission surprised her; she hadn't intended to say anything.

Dear Reader,

As always, Intimate Moments offers you six terrific books to fill your reading time, starting with Terese Ramin's *Her Guardian Agent*. For FBI agent Hazel Youvella, the case that took her back to revisit her Native American roots was a very personal one. For not only did she find the hero of her heart in Native American tracker Guy Levoie, she discovered the truth about the missing child she was seeking. This wasn't just any child—this was *her* child.

If you enjoyed last month's introduction to our FIRSTBORN SONS in-line continuity, you won't want to miss the second installment. Carla Cassidy's *Born of Passion* will grip you from the first page and leave you longing for the rest of these wonderful linked books. Valerie Parv takes a side trip from Silhouette Romance to debut in Intimate Moments with a stunner of a reunion romance called *Interrupted Lullaby*. Karen Templeton begins a new miniseries called HOW TO MARRY A MONARCH with *Plain-Jane Princess,* and Linda Winstead Jones returns with *Hot on His Trail,* a book you should be hot on the trail of yourself. Finally, welcome Sharon Mignerey back and take a look at her newest, *Too Close for Comfort.*

And don't forget to look in the back of this book to see how Silhouette can make you a star.

Enjoy them all, and come back next month for more of the best and most exciting romance reading around.

Yours,

Leslie J. Wainger
Executive Senior Editor

Please address questions and book requests to:
Silhouette Reader Service
U.S.: 3010 Walden Ave., P.O. Box 1325, Buffalo, NY 14269
Canadian: P.O. Box 609, Fort Erie, Ont. L2A 5X3

Her Guardian Agent
TERESE RAMIN

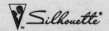

INTIMATE MOMENTS™
Published by Silhouette Books
America's Publisher of Contemporary Romance

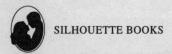 SILHOUETTE BOOKS

ISBN 0-373-27163-8

HER GUARDIAN AGENT

Copyright © 2001 by Terese daly Ramin

This edition published by arrangement with Harlequin Books S.A.

® and TM are trademarks of Harlequin Books S.A., used under license. Trademarks indicated with ® are registered in the United States Patent and Trademark Office, the Canadian Trade Marks Office and in other countries.

Visit Silhouette at www.eHarlequin.com

Printed in U.S.A.

Books by Terese Ramin

Silhouette Intimate Moments

Water from the Moon #279
Winter Beach #477
A Certain Slant of Light #634
Five Kids, One Christmas #680
An Unexpected Addition #793
Mary's Child #881
A Drive-By Wedding #981
Her Guardian Agent #1093

Silhouette Special Edition

Accompanying Alice #656

TERESE RAMIN

The granddaughter of an Irish Blarney stone kisser (who, lowered by her ankles to do so, kissed it last at the age of 96) and the oldest of eight, Terese Ramin has been surrounded by kids, chaos and storytelling all her life. At the request of her siblings she told outrageous stories late into the night, which caused a great deal of giggling among the kids and aggravation for her parents, who merely wanted them all To Go To Sleep! Terese lives in Michigan with five dogs, three cats, two kids and a husband who creates sawdust.

For my husband, Bill, my "Guy" always.

With thanks to Bill Ramin, whose contributions
to my research efforts all too frequently go, er, unbilled.
Particular thanks to author Laura Baker for finding me
books, articles, ideas and research to which I would not
otherwise have had access. Bless you! I'd also like to
acknowledge a research debt to the works of
Tom Brown, Jr. Any mistakes (for which I apologize
in advance), stretches of reality and leaps of imagination
are solely my own.

In memory of Joan Shapiro
Friend, critique partner,
soul sister, cohort. I was so lucky to have known you
and I will miss you more than I can say. I hope the
angels realize how fortunate they are to count you
among their number. Oh, and by the way, when the
dessert comes, you can have the fork with the most
chocolate, but I get the cherry.

*Take the breath of the new dawn and make it part of you.
It will give you strength.*

—Hopi saying

Chapter 1

Winslow, Arizona

Guy Levoie knew the moment he laid eyes on Hazel Youvella that he would fall in love with her.

Of course, since he also knew that he had a tendency to fall in love and love easily, the knowledge didn't surprise him in the least. Neither did the lust he experienced when he once-overed her petite but lush figure, her severely tamed black hair, her full lips, high, prominent cheekbones and thick-lashed, ink-black eyes. What surprised him was the ice-queen anger this small bundle of controlled energy, this possible love of his life, projected toward him from the instant she set foot in his brother Russ's office.

"I'm looking for a tracker by the name of Guy Levoie."

She directed the announcement at Russ, who was seated behind the black metal desk near the windows, obviously in charge. The quick once-over she sent the other four men in the office—Guy; Jeth, who was a tribal cop and another of Guy's brothers; a Coconino County Deputy Sheriff and a local FBI field agent—was filled with misgiving.

Maybe, Guy reflected, controlling a grin and considering the doubt a challenge, all that anger wasn't really directed at him personally, but at men in general. It was an unfortunate occupational hazard, an attitude developed by any number of women like her in law enforcement, who assumed—rightly or wrongly—that all men in law enforcement were gender-biased rats, who'd go out of their way to make the woman miserable until she "proved herself."

In Guy's not particularly humble, but considered, opinion, women were equally capable of making wrong assumptions and thus falling prey to the ass-u-me rule. But he would wait to point out Hazel's mistake to her until he had a chance to know her better—say perhaps the minute they were alone on this assignment. Whatever the hell it was that was important enough to pull him in from the field where he'd spent overnight trying to track the Hopi Tribal Chairman's missing daughter. Might as well begin as he meant to go on; his father hadn't named him Guyapi or "Candid" for nothing.

He shoved himself off the wall, wincing only slightly at the muscle twinges running through his right shoulder, where he'd been speared by a broken shovel handle not quite three months ago. "I'm Guy."

He didn't offer to shake hands. His grip was improving, but he'd no desire to pit it against a woman out to prove herself the way this one looked to be. He didn't need to display strength in order to have it. Hell, at six feet two inches of solid muscle, he didn't often need to display it, period.

He watched her while she took in his height, his musculature, his long loose black hair, the still-pinkish scar slashed across his forehead from the same accident, the Chakotay-from-Star-Trek-Voyager-like henna tattoo he'd let his cousin paint above his left eye and the real rattlesnake tattoo that wound around his left forearm. She offered him a look that was filled with long-suffering, eye-rolling resignation.

"Of course you are," she said.

Or, Guy decided because he'd seen the look before, what she didn't say, loosely translated, was, *Oh, God, I have to work with that? Alone? Nice bod, but can it think—and will it?*

He swallowed a grin, figuring it had to be the face thing. Acting as a walking billboard for his cousin's henna body-art studio frequently elicited similar expressions from the uninitiated. Which meant that it either had to be the henna or the memory of something Hazel Youvella would prefer to forget.

Startled by an insight his gut told him was right on, he took an almost imperceptible step backward, away from her. Falling in love with a woman was the most natural thing in the world for him. Understanding more about a woman than what made her feel good about herself—and him—was not.

"Of course I am what?" he asked, firing his comeback more by rote than design.

The glance she sent him in reply should have frozen him. Unfortunately for her, Guy liked it. This was going to be fun.

She turned to Russ. "This is your tracker?"

He nodded and sent Guy a quelling glare. "For today. You're Hazel Youvella?"

"FBI Assistant Special Agent in Charge Youvella," Hazel corrected firmly. "Phoenix. I'm here to coordinate this operation."

"The one that needs a tracker," Guy prompted. He couldn't help it. Leaving well enough alone was not his strong suit.

Hazel Youvella concentrated hard on ignoring him. Satisfied, Guy chalked a mental point in the air to him. He was getting to her. That meant there'd be plenty of sparks when he fell in love with her. And striking sparks was one of his favorite things about the man-woman-love-sex alliance.

He'd have bet money that it wasn't one of Hazel's.

He crossed his arms, cocked his head and studied her frankly. Her copper-brown complexion flared with color; her jaw squared and jutted with anger and defiance; her gaze stayed on a point to the left of his over-eye tattoo.

"So, Assistant Special Agent in Charge Youvella," he said—and stopped to peruse her, maybe bring up her color a little more. Baiting her to see how much rope she'd give him to hang himself with.

"Guy," Russ warned.

"Cheese it, bro," Guy said—and had the satisfaction of getting Hazel to look directly at him. He offered her his most disarming smile. "Anyone ever tell you you've got great cheekbones, Assistant Special Agent in Charge Youvella?" he asked.

That was it, he had her.

Passion.

Her eyes flashed, mouth tightened, nostrils flared. But she didn't give in to the reflex to strike in anger. Instead she held herself rigid until fire cooled to ice, and returned her attention to Russ. "I'd appreciate it if you'd heel your dog, Lieutenant, before I have to file a sexual harassment charge against him."

"And I'd appreciate you getting to the point of your visit, Ms. Youvella," Russ responded mildly. "I don't like calling men out before dawn on some junior *suit's* whim— and especially not my best tracker when we're in the middle of a search for a pretty little eleven-year-old who's been missing overnight.''

Hazel's jaw clenched. ''I don't do anything on a *whim,* Lieutenant—''

Judging from the stiffness of her posture, her probable age and her rank, Guy had no difficulty believing that.

''I'm here because your missing child's been upgraded to a kidnapping.''

As one, the three Levoie brothers came alert. It had been a little more than three years since their baby sister, Marcy, had died during a botched kidnapping. They never took the disappearance of any child lightly, but the disappearance of a preteen girl about the age Marcy had been was especially personal.

Particularly when the disappearance involved a kidnapping.

''A kidnapping?'' Guy's younger brother, Jeth, asked, incredulous. Marcy's death had devastated him worse than any of them because she'd died on his watch, a victim of the people who'd wanted him to cease and desist on a case he was on. He'd barely begun to recover, the last few months, with the aid of his new wife and the child she'd helped him rescue from a crack house hell. Guy didn't want to think what this might do to his brother's equilibrium if it turned out they'd missed something vital to another young girl's safety. ''Since when? There's no ransom demand, nothing to suggest—''

Hazel overrode him. ''Need-to-know, Officer. Missing child's the daughter of the Hopi tribal chairman and his wife. Let's just say the department has reason to suspect it's more than it appears.''

''You've had contact?'' Guy watched her, looking for

the signs that would betray whatever knowledge she wasn't ready to share. "There's been a demand?"

"Not yet."

"Then how—"

"My grandparents live between Keams Canyon and Polacca," Hazel snapped, giving up the information with reluctance. That she hated having to admit to the local connection was evident. "They presented a compelling argument to my superiors and requested my services. I'm here."

"In an official capacity." Guy kept his voice neutral.

"To make sure the chairman's daughter is found and returned home quickly."

"We've got 150 officers and deputy sheriffs, not to mention civilians, combing for the Poleys' daughter." Russ sounded testy. "What the hell do the Feds think some city liaison, with ties but no tribal background, is going to be able to do to speed up finding her that we aren't already doing? It's not like there's a lot of money around here to bring you up."

Guy heard the audible click of Hazel's jaw tightening and eyed her shrewdly. The woman wasn't here over an issue of wealth, he was certain. She was here for the kid, flat and unequivocally, because she didn't take kindly to people who interfered with children—and she was ferocious about it, if his instincts about her were to be believed.

On the other hand, if he was reading her correctly—and much of what he accomplished depended upon him reading not only sign but people correctly—she also didn't particularly want the bunch of *guys* in this room to see this she-bear-maternal side of her, didn't want to appear weak in front of lawmen she didn't know. Guy guessed that, like many women in the often heavily chauvinistic southwestern law enforcement systems, ASAC Youvella had already received far too many assignments based on the supposed proclivities of her gender and she didn't care for it much. And that was not to mention how poorly she took to having her authority questioned.

Especially new authority she wasn't yet confident she was prepared to handle.

"It's not about money," Hazel retorted, unwittingly confirming one of Guy's suspicions. "It's about grazing rights, tradition versus progress. The Hopi have what the Navajo traditionals want. Current BIA directives side with the Hopi. According to my information, the Poleys are afraid to make waves at this point, but my grandparents think this could be related to the land-use dispute."

"And since this is at least partially Navajo Police jurisdiction, they also think officers from this station could be involved in not finding the Poleys' daughter in a timely fashion," Guy interpreted.

Russ's anger was intense, immediate and barely controlled. He would have risen from his chair had not Guy laid a restraining hand on his older brother's shoulder.

"Are you accusing my officers of collusion in the disappearance of a child, Ms. Youvella?" Russ's question was razor-edged, a slice away from the bone.

Hazel didn't blink. Guy gave her points for courage. "It crossed my mind, yes."

"Is that why you or your office made a specific request to have you meet with me and my brothers, deputy Hogarth, and Special Agent Greene? Because we're all Indian but not Navajo? Or Hopi, either, come to that, in case this is some traditionals versus progressives argument that got out of hand?"

Hazel had the grace to appear uncomfortable without letting her eyes shift elsewhere. Her voice was crisp and unapologetic. "I have to consider everything, Lieutenant."

"Including making sure you've got political clout—"

Again Guy restrained his brother, watched ASAC Youvella. "Hopi traditionals and progressives argue all the time, but they're basically on the same side," he said calmly. "Hopi and Navajo have disputed land use for the past 150 years. Usually they take their issues to the press and the courts, not to kidnapping."

"Looks like this time might be different, Agent Levoie."

"It's 'Investigator,' Ms. Youvella," Guy corrected automatically. He hated anyone assuming he was a member of one of the other federal criminal investigation agencies, but most particularly he didn't like being considered a Fibbie. It had been machinations by the Bureau and the DEA, after all that had almost gotten Jeth, his wife, Allyn, and their toddler killed a few months ago. "I'm not a member of the Federal Bureau of Interference." The candidness, with which he'd been either blessed or cursed, let him pin Hazel with a glance. "And does that mean the five of us are here because you suspect us or because you don't—yes or no?" he asked.

There was fury in the depths of her inkwell eyes, lightning contained by will alone. "You're here because my grandparents say you're the only BIA *investigator*—" the emphasis was deliberately cutting "—they've ever trusted and because you're the best tracker in these parts." She gestured toward the others with a movement of her chin. "The rest of you are here because the Bureau gave me your names and told me to work with you, and that's all." She drew one sharp, pinched breath through her nose and huffed it out. "As to whether or not I suspect any of you of anything other than your standard gender bias remains to be seen. Now let's get down to business and see what we can do about finding this missing kid."

* * *

An hour and a half later Hazel stood in the station's washroom and blotted damp paper towels over her face and the back of her neck with trembling hands. Damn nerves. She felt ghastly. Her first case as an ASAC, and it had to bring her here. Not to mention that it could probably have been assigned to any case agent who could have come in and coordinated things—at *least* until something concrete on the kid came up one way or the other—and shouldn't have brought her out into the field.

Yet.

Particularly since she'd made her ambitious push up the administrative ladder as quickly as she could just to get out of handling assignments like this. Because in the past couple of years she'd dealt with more than enough of them. They'd started to get to her. She'd begun to take their outcomes personally. And she understood well enough from watching the agents around her that the minute that happened, you chased not only doom but you courted disaster.

Which wasn't an outstandingly smart thing to do.

She cupped her hand beneath the tap, raised it to moisten her mouth with a fistful of mineral-tasting water, grimaced and spat the taste of it into the sink. God, she hated this place. She always had.

Her conscience shifted painfully, almost noiselessly, around to stick a stiletto into her heart. Okay, almost always. But she didn't have to think of that anymore.

Wouldn't.

Yeah, right, some devil inside her mocked. *And you didn't notice the snake on your tracker's arm, either, did you?*

But she had, of course. And that damned tattoo on Guy Levoie's arm had rattled her—no pun intended—more than she'd ever expected anything to rattle her again in her life.

It was almost identical to the tattoo worn by the handsome—and, now she realized, immature—twenty-something-year-old she'd met and fallen in puppy lust with while visiting her grandparents, what was it, eleven or twelve years ago. She'd been totally out of her depth then and too-full-of-herself infatuated to know it.

He'd been the same twenty-something man with whom she'd gotten drunk for the first—and only—time in her life, and to whom she'd lost her virginity and her self-respect, her parents' and her grandparents' trust at the tender age of fifteen and a bit. Levoie was far too young to be that man—Hazel guessed he wasn't more than a year or so older than she was—far too big, and his tattoo was in the wrong place, on his arm, instead of his right pectoral. But that didn't ruin the effect the snake had on her.

Nor did it ruin the devastating effect looking at Guy Levoie—or having him look back—had on her senses.

Irritation washed through her, throttling nervous fear. So he was a handsome, wiseacre, heart-stopping devil, she thought, so what? So he was big and dangerous and safe looking all at once. So…

What?

So she could already see where he'd distract her, that was what. Not to mention that she could read the signs that said he found her attractive—if not as distracting as she'd find him, drat it—too. And since he was supposedly the best of the best available *and* a BIA Law Enforcement Services criminal investigator to boot, she had to work with him for God knew how long and there was no way out of it, that was blasted what.

Him and that doggoned rattlesnake tattoo and those too-seeing, laugh-filled, dark-brown eyes, and the muscular, masculine body that whispered ''trust me'' to hers. And she knew better than to ever do that again. Play around with him, maybe, under circumstances that were absolutely under her control and that involved no emotional substance whatever, but let herself—her body—trust him and his? Not bloody likely. After all, how could she possibly trust him when, where guys like him were concerned, she'd never learned to trust herself?

Chapter 2

She looked at herself in the washroom mirror, curled a lip humorlessly and concentrated. "Focus," she admonished herself. "The kid is all, the kid is all. Runaway or kidnappee, what happened to you will not happen to her. You will not allow it. You will not—"

The trill of her cell phone startled her.

"Damn."

For a moment she clutched the edge of the sink in panic, then calmed herself and reached into the pocket of her cream-colored linen jacket. Obviously she had to get hold of herself—and maintain hold. She was only given to swearing when she was rattled. Rattled would not get the job done here.

"Youvella."

"Assistant Special Agent in Charge Hazel Youvella of the FBI?" a heavily accented male voice inquired.

"Yes."

"Good." The voice sounded pleased. "You are working on the finding of the missing Hopi girl, Emma Poley?"

Everything inside Hazel stilled. No one but her office and the five men she'd just met knew she'd been assigned to this case. This voice didn't belong to anyone she knew from either Phoenix or here. "Who is this?"

"That is not yet important. We will get back to you with instructions."

"Instructions? What—" She was listening to dead air.

She stared at the phone, concentrating all of her energies on putting something that niggled at the back of her instincts together with the phone call. There was something about the accent that seemed familiar, something connected with—

"Hey, Youvella."

Guy Levoie rapped at the door, startling her into dropping the phone. She stooped to pick it up, muttered a jittery imprecation when the battery fell out of the unprotected instrument and a piece of the plastic casing chipped away. She'd forgotten to put the thing back in its leather case when she'd changed the battery this morning.

"Hey." The knocking increased. "You all right in there? Trail's gettin' cold. We on this thing or what?"

Hazel jammed the phone back together and snatched the door open.

And ran smack into the unyielding hunka-hunka wall of attractive beef that was Guy.

He caught her elbow to steady her. "You okay? I thought I heard something fall."

She yanked her arm out of his grasp before the whatever-it-was about him and his touch burned her senses alive. "Fine." Her voice felt hoarse and unsteady. She cleared her throat, made herself say firmly, "No problem. Dropped my cell phone."

Something in her expression or her tone must have alerted him. His eyes narrowed. "What's up?"

She glanced at his face and understood at once that he would know if she so much as fudged the truth a little, let alone flat-out lied. Probably something about the tracker in him.

Or the tongue-tied, tattooed-older-man-infatuated, almost-sixteen-year-old, guilt-ridden girl left in her.

Except Guy Levoie wasn't really older, and she was no longer a fragile, overprotected adolescent with a fascination for tattoos.

Half rankled by her own inability to prevaricate convincingly in certain situations, she swung away from him and headed down the hall toward the station's entrance.

"Think I just got a call from the kidnappers," she told him over her shoulder. "They said they'd call again with instructions. We need to get out to the Poleys' in case—"

Guy grabbed her arm and hauled her back as she reached the door. "*You* got a call from the kidnappers?"

She looked at his fingers, up at him. Something in the nature of cold fear and expectant heat washed through her. Fear of herself and the unaccustomed intensity of her desires, heat because those same desires had suffered enough at the hands of her timing and her history. She did her best to rein in both.

"Hands off, Investigator," she said tightly.

He released her without apology. His eyes were intense and seeking. "The kidnappers called *you?*" he repeated.

"Yeah."

"On your cell phone." A flat statement, soft and unadulterated, yet curiously detached.

"Yes." Hazel knew where he was going; she'd been there first.

"You don't find it strange that you've been here ninety

minutes, but after more than twelve hours of hanging on to her, the kidnappers suddenly call you?''

"What I find *strange,* Investigator Levoie," Hazel said coolly, "is that you want to stand here and discuss my phone call when, as you so aptly put it, the 'trail's gettin' cold.'"

"Fine." Guy shoved open the door and stood aside to let her pass. "We'll discuss it on the way to the Poleys'." He jerked his head at the Beemer she drove with pride. "That your car?"

Automatically offended by his apparent derision for the vehicle she'd waited a long time to buy; a vehicle that, for her, was not only a status symbol but an emotional boost that helped make her feel more confident about herself and her abilities, she snapped, "You got a problem with my vehicle, Levoie?"

"Yeah." Guy shrugged. "Pretty, but damned impractical around here. Won't make it where we're goin'." He headed down the walk toward the tan four-by-four pickup sitting at the end of the small parking lot. "C'mon. We'll take my truck."

Hazel eyed the oversize back-country tires and the high step-up into the cab with dismay. In her straight linen skirt she wasn't dressed for this. She'd known that giving in to her parents' and grandparents' emotional blackmail and accepting this assignment at the department's urging would prove a mistake. This was just one more nail in the coffin.

Obviously guessing why she hesitated, Guy—damn the man—looked at her and grinned. Then he opened the passenger door and let down the extra steps that would allow her easier access to the cab.

"Believe it or not, I date on occasion," he said. "But if you're comin' out trackin' with me, maybe you want to change before we leave? I got my gear in the bed."

Despite the provoking tone of his voice, Hazel clenched her teeth and held her peace. She wanted to say no, wanted to get on her high horse, leave him flat in the dust and never come back. But ego was not the thing that would get the Poleys' daughter back. Cooperation and magnanimity might.

"I'll get my bag out of the car," she said evenly. "That way we can get going, straight from the Poleys'."

Guy followed her to the Beemer. "You got camping gear in there?"

He was joking, right? What did he think she was here to do, sleep under the stars? Tracking kidnappers no longer meant Tom Horn and Hec Ramsey or whoever the hell those old-time trackers and bounty hunters were, nor even the likes of the contemporary master tracker, Tom Brown, Jr. It meant electronics, nice cars, clean sheets and a roof. "Camping gear?"

"Yeah. Sleeping bag, pack, food, water, practical clothes, poncho, boots, shot gun or rifle—things you'll need if we're gonna be hunting in the desert on horseback."

She paled. Had she failed to take something into consideration here? "Horseback?"

"Heck, yes."

He viewed her with some disgust—and, unfortunately for him, just a little too much innocence. Hazel narrowed her eyes and gave the modern age some thought while her tormentor continued.

"You've been here before, right? That's part of the reason they sent you? What'd you think we were going to be able to do, Hazel, track her from a comfortable motel room? 'S not the way it works out here. One, there are only two hotels anywhere near the Poleys' and they're full up. Hopis allow tourists, but don't necessarily encourage them. You're Hopi, you got to know that, right?

"Two, the Poleys' place is too small for guests, and it'd be a real impolite imposition for us to assume they could put us up and feed us on what little they've got, even if we were gonna stay in one place. We'll use the truck if we can, but I don't know if that'll be practical."

Hazel opened the trunk and motioned at the suit bag, briefcase and the usual department paraphernalia she'd brought along, torn between calling his bluff and wondering if he *was* bluffing. The fact that he considered it a nuisance that she'd ordered him in from the hunt was clear. Just how much of a nuisance it really was remained to be seen. "But my equipment—"

Guy snorted. "You think you brought me in to sit in a room and wear a headset and watch telephone equipment like they do in the movies when the Poleys don't even have a radio-phone set-up, you're mistaken. I'm a tracker, damn it. I go out, I find. If that doesn't meet with your approval, stay here and be comfortable and let me go back out and do the job your orders pulled me off this morning. And FYI, I'll get this done a sight faster without you taggin' along, slowin' me down."

Shoulders tight, nerves and temper checked, Hazel stared at him. This was his territory and he undoubtedly knew whereof he spoke. She would not, damn it, would *not* allow her ego to get in the way of this case.

But Guy Levoie didn't get to have it all, either.

"Fine," she said, and eyed him toe to head, assessing. He stared back, waiting to be believed or caught out— inviting it. Whole lot of bull could be packed into seventy-four-plus inches of man, Hazel reflected. "But first I've got to know…"

The corners of his mouth couldn't quite stay still, gave him away. *Bring it on,* something in his eyes coaxed, laughing, and Hazel was all of a sudden quite certain that he would chuckle harder at himself than he would at her.

The unexpected insight both pleased and bothered her, made her uncomfortable to press the encounter at all.

"Sure," he agreed.

"How come you guys don't use motorcycles, four-by-fours and all-terrain vehicles for tracking, the way the border patrol does?"

He grinned, far too laid-back for her tastes and not the least bit put-out that she'd called his bluff. Exactly as she'd known he wouldn't be.

"Oh, we do. And helicopters, cutting lights, infrared scopes, cell phones when we can, radios, Handie-Talkies and search *teams*." The emphasis on the word was unmistakable. "I just wanted to make sure you got the picture. We're not in L.A., and even with modern equipment, backup can be half an hour or more away. Plus we're not looking for illegal aliens in flat desert here, we're looking for one little girl in rocky desert country and the someone or someones who picked her up. They're not going to be as predictable as illegals muling marijuana across a finite length of border."

Hazel nodded, temper checked with effort. "Point taken," she said. She yanked one of the larger cases out of the trunk and passed it to him. "The kidnappers have a phone." She would not let him get to her, she would not allow him to make her feel guilty, and she would not *ever* give him the upper hand. She would *not*. "For whatever reason, however they knew I'd be the one coordinating things, they called me the first time. They call again, what's in here might help us home in on them."

"Fine, bring it." He indicated the suit bag she was picking up. "You got any practical clothes in there? Jeans, boots, anything like that?"

Suddenly feeling like the naively incompetent-though-dauntless Kathleen Turner harassed by Michael Douglas over the state of her wardrobe early in *Romancing the Stone,* she shook her head.

"Sh—" Guy bit back the expletive that was only rarely provoked from him. The same way he hardly ever carried a gun, he hardly ever carried profanity. All too often, as far as he was concerned, when push came to shove either tool was more likely to complicate a resolution than to bring about the peaceable outcome he sought. "Where does the Bureau get you people from, anyway? Blasted *suits.*"

He turned his back on her and headed for the truck. "Leave the bag and let's go. I know a place we can stop and pick up what you'll need." He opened the pickup's cap and swung the case he carried, then the rifle case she handed him, into the bed. "Hope you got your Bureau credit card along. Vila's prices won't be cheap."

Vila's prices were what the market would bear and then some. In fact, from a look she caught Guy exchanging with the Navajo proprietress, Hazel guessed they were specially inflated for the out-of-towner's benefit.

Suddenly and uncomfortably disturbed by the sense of being a tourist in her father's homeland, she picked out the gear Investigator Levoie assured her she'd require where they were likely to be going. She had to admit that he didn't urge her to purchase more than she'd physically need—or than she or, she presumed, a horse could carry. He also made sure that everything she purchased was comfortable. His point being that, despite his urgency to get back to the hunt, an uncomfortably booted and improperly clothed city Fed would only slow him down in the long run—no matter how tough she pretended to be.

All in all, tracking with Guy Levoie, Hazel suspected,

would be no worse than a bad day in boot camp. She'd
toughed that out right after high school ten years ago and
put in her time in order to get her college paid. Georgia
had been no picnic, but within six months of joining the
army, she'd been as fit as any man in her outfit and a good
deal fitter than some. She could handle whatever Levoie
might throw at her.

All except for maybe moving as quickly as he was re-
portedly able to move on a trail or facing those damned
snakes or riding a horse. And she was mighty afraid that if
confronted with any reptiles she would disgrace herself,
turn tail and run, and that the poor little girl they were
looking for would find herself out of luck when it came to
getting any help from one not-so-tough cookie Youvella.

The ride to the Poleys' was long, bumpy and strenuously
silent. It was interrupted only once at the border to Hopiland by a Hopi tribal cop who, before he recognized Guy,
informed them that the reservation was closed to visitors
indefinitely. Hazel eyed the cop, perplexed; the last time
she'd visited, the border had been open to all, always.

"How long since you been here?" the cop asked when
she questioned him.

She stared at him without response.

He shook his head. "You sure you're Hopi?"

When Hazel gave him stony, he pursed his lips, nodded
once and waved them through.

"Thought so," Guy observed.

She didn't want to appear interested in anything but the
task at hand, but she couldn't help the question mark that
lifted her incorrigible left eyebrow. Guy made a note of the
involuntary movement, pleased to have her attention.

"It's not just me, it's all men, isn't it?"

Emotion raised the color in her neck and face, tightened

her jaw. Her chin rose; he saw her bite her tongue to prevent it wagging. Silence returned. He gave her almost a full ten minutes before asking, "You ticked at me because of Vila's?"

"Ticked?" Hazel didn't bother to turn her head from the view beyond the windshield. She could see him perfectly well with her peripheral vision and, according to her blessed, blasted pulse even that minimal glimpse was more than enough. "No, I wouldn't say that. 'Ticked' is an inadequate word."

"Ah." He slid her a glance that was infuriatingly amused. "What word would be adequate?"

"One my mother taught me was impolite to use under any circumstance."

She thought he strangled a chuckle. "I see."

"No, I don't think you do," she said softly, vehemently. "I don't think you see much of anything but ways to gratify your ego at some woman's expense."

"Excuse me?"

The truck jounced through a rut, causing Hazel to bite her tongue. Like many of the other feelings that passed through her life, she refused to acknowledge the physical pain. "You heard me."

"Yeah, I did," Guy said ruefully, wincing when his shoulder hit the seat too hard. "I hoped I was wrong."

Hazel tightened her lips and swallowed the rusted metal taste of blood. "You weren't."

"That's too bad. You were much prettier when I could imagine you with an open mind."

Mouth agape and unable to help herself, Hazel stared at him. "You...you—" Words failed. The things you were confronted with when you couldn't use your gun. "You... you arrogant, self-centered, unbelievable..." Again verbal description floundered in disbelief at his temerity.

"Horse's behind?" Guy supplied helpfully. "Chauvinist pig? Dunderhead?"

"You—man!" Hazel sputtered furiously. "You smug, egotistical, gender-bigoted, cork-brained *man!* Consider yourself written up for sexual harassment the minute we're back at the station."

"Depending on how things go with the case, that could be awhile," Guy said mildly. "You'll probably have changed your opinion of me by then. Most people do."

"I will *never*—"

"Ah-ah." Guy held up a warning finger. "Never say *never*. It'll rear up and bite you in the butt every time."

Hazel clenched her fists. He had a comeback for everything. She didn't accept that from anyone, but especially not men. Or at least not the ones she worked with. Usually a frosty approach kept them at the distance where she wanted them to stay. "There's got to be someone better than you who I can work with. You are impossible."

"There's no one better than me out here, and you've got a chip on your shoulder the size of the San Francisco Peaks. Face it. You're stuck with me the same way I'm stuck with you. The only difference is—" he grinned and cast her a sideways glance "—I like the pairing. But you aren't used to most people talking back to you, so you don't."

For one brief second Hazel stared at him nonplussed by his ability to read her mind and maddeningly drawn to the same things in him that she thought she hated. But he was wrong about one thing, however. It would only swell his head if he learned she was doing her best to stop herself from liking the pairing, too.

Then she snapped her mouth closed and returned her attention grimly to the road in front of them and concentrated on trying to put Guy Levoie out of her mind once and for all.

Chapter 3

Of course, putting him out of her mind didn't work—mostly because he refused to go.

By the time they neared their destination, he had regaled her with the majority of his life history, with stories about his family—four brothers and one living sister, his parents, one sister-in-law and innumerable cousins—and with tales of some of his other cases. He was funny, easily told stories on himself that would have embarrassed Hazel if they'd happened to her, and in spite of herself, she found herself beginning to like him just a little. He made her ache to laugh.

It had been a long time since she'd wanted to laugh at anything, let alone *with* someone else.

Especially a man.

All of which made her darned glad to reach their destination when they did—and this despite her natural reluctance to see her grandparents for the first time in an embarrassing number of years. But if she'd been forced to spend any more time alone with this rudely bold but more-appealing-by-the-moment Rattlesnake Man she might have wound up snakebit.

If she wasn't already.

The very thought made her shudder—

"Hawaah!"

—until she looked up and saw her grandmother headed for the truck, that is.

"Hazel, you're here!"

The sight of Anna Youvella brought the old nausea rolling back, filled the back of her throat with the sensation of butterflies trying to escape from her stomach.

Guy opened the passenger door and let down the step. "You okay?"

Dry-mouthed, she swallowed the imaginary wings, fitted a pair of flat, black, wraparound sunglasses to her face to cover any expression in her eyes and nodded. "Fine." She smoothed damp palms over her skirt. He'd suggested she change clothes at Vila's, but she'd worn what she'd arrived in instead. Something to do with her mother's long-held idea of dressing with respect when you visited your elders. "You going to let me out of here or what?"

Something indiscernible flickered across Guy's face. Her color dulled when she noted the already available steps. Straight-faced he offered her a hand, then stepped back out of the way when she ignored it, clutched the door handle and stepped to the ground as casually as possible.

The lightest pressure of his fingers beneath her free elbow was the only tattler that she didn't achieve the illusion on her own. How could he possibly know she'd been about to stumble when she hadn't known it herself? Did he see everything?

Oh, probably. Just as well she had the sunglasses, then.

Be just her luck to get stuck with a guy who was sensitive as well as full of himself.

Guy, guy, get it?

She tightened her jaw at the silent and altogether bad pun, the nervousness that prompted it. Humor—especially bad pun-style humor—was a luxury she couldn't afford and didn't indulge in.

Get on with it, she admonished herself, drawing a pinched breath through her nose and reciting the nursery rhyme from the movie *Mary Poppins* that she'd learned and repeated as a child when staring an onerous task in the face. *Once begun is half done.*

"Grandmother." She stepped out of the shadow cast by Guy and the truck door and moved toward her grandmother, one hand outstretched.

Her grandmother disregarded Hazel's attempt to forestall the more intimate contact of a hug by simply gathering her granddaughter into her arms and embracing her. "Welcome home."

Beyond the boundaries created by Anna's embrace, Hazel heard the murmurs of derision and dissent. With as little flinching as possible she eased herself out of her grandmother's arms and straightened. The faces of a people with whom she shared ancestry but who were also foreign to her greeted her, some openly hostile, many suspicious, a few merely curious. One or two of the faces were pitying, the people behind the glances of the same age as her grandparents. They'd heard her story, she was sure, used it without her name as a warning to their children and grandchildren.

Aliksa'I or *Haliksa'I*—depending upon the mesa to which they traced their roots—she could imagine them saying, *Here is my story. A woman-child came to our village to watch the snake dance. She was taken in by an inter-loper, that useless trickster, Coyote, and...*

And then they would tell their families about her, how she'd been tricked, what had happened to her and what she'd done...

No.

Hazel tightened her jaw, squared her chin and gave them back stare for stare, swiveling her head to take them in from the darkness behind her lenses. This wasn't about her. Memories, mistakes or no, she would not let it be.

Could not let it be.

No fear, she cautioned herself. She knew all too well the telltale scent fear gave off. She'd smelled it on both herself and others often enough.

Her grandmother swept the gathering a single glance that seemed to send them melting out to the sides, present but less mob-like.

Moses and the Red Sea, Hazel thought nonsensically, long gone Methodist bible classes catching up with her.

Then Anna linked an arm through hers and tugged Hazel urgently toward the small stone house before them.

"Come inside," she said. "The Poleys are waiting."

Suddenly afraid of something she'd never admit and couldn't define, Hazel surprised herself by looking back once to make sure Guy followed. Assured that he did, she swallowed and faced forward.

Then she went where her grandmother led.

The house was as small and dark inside as it looked from without. The darkness was deliberate, cool after the heat of the Arizona midmorning sun.

"Please, sit," Dextra Poley invited in Hopi after intro-ductions were made. She extended a rough, brown hand toward the only available chairs: four old-fashioned, vinyl-covered kitchen chairs at a marble-look linoleum-topped table. Atop the table sat a platter of the rolled, blue-corn fry bread known as *piiki*. "Let me get you—"

"Thank you, no."

Impatient to get on with her task, Hazel waved the unfinished offer aside, shocking both herself and her grandmother. Sweet heavens, no. She was even more disconcerted over being here than she'd thought.

"Hazel—"

Before Anna had the name out of her mouth, Hazel was moving to right the wrong.

"Forgive me, Grandmother," she said swiftly. She turned to the woman whose daughter was missing. "Thank you, Mrs. Poley, but—"

"Yes, thank you, Mrs. Poley," Guy interrupted firmly. He swung one of the chairs around away from the table and straddled it. Hazel realized his big frame would not have fit it comfortably any other way. "A piece of that *piiki* would be great—" he eyed the blue enamel coffeepot on the stove "—especially if you've got some coffee to go with it."

"Of course."

Dextra Poley sent him a worried, tension-filled but grateful half smile and hurried to slide the *piiki* platter toward him before bringing the coffee. Her husband and Hazel's grandfather joined Guy at the table.

Ritual, Hazel remembered suddenly watching them, chagrined to have forgotten something so simple about dealing with the families of kidnap victims, was the thing that would keep them calm, make them comfortable, allow them, perhaps, to remember more than they thought they knew about what had happened to their child. She might have thought of it herself if she weren't so thrown by her return to the scene of adolescent crimes.

Ashamed of her impatience and unaccountably put out

with Guy, who looked as if he relished every mouthful of
the Hopi fry bread—and probably did, Hazel decided, wishing he'd at least appear to pay half as much attention to
the questions she'd begun to fire off the moment the amen-
ities were seen to. Why she wanted his undivided attention
she wasn't quite sure, since his attentions had only irked
her thus far, but there you had it. She wanted to impress
him with her expertise.

Blast it.

Impatiently she admonished herself that even though she
was the more experienced kidnapping expert here, he'd
probably already asked the same questions and gotten the
same answers and then some himself, if he was half the
investigator he was reputed to be.

And that was not to mention the questions—and answers—his brothers had undoubtedly thought to toss in the
moment Emma Poley was reported missing.

Hazel had seen families before—always from the outside
and as distantly as possible—but she'd seen how they
worked. Dysfunctional or well adjusted, indifferent or de-
voted, physically and emotionally abusive or protective and
supportive, a family had a flavor about it, a tie that went
beyond obvious genetic resemblances and mannerisms.
Families had a fusion, an individual ethic that could be
destructive or freeing. To her the Levoie boys looked like
a family who knew how to stimulate as well as aggravate
each other, brothers as capable of working together as they
were separately.

Not unlike the street gang families she'd had dealings
with in L.A. before her transfer—where you got one Levoie, you got 'em all…whether you wanted them all or not.

A disturbing thought if ever she'd had one.

She watched the Levoie she had with her savoring every
bite of *piiki* and sip of coffee; a series of unwelcome tickles

of expectation drenched her already-iffy nerves and her all-at-once-uncustomarily vivid imagination pictured—heck, *felt*—him enjoying her with even greater pleasure.

Hers.

Oh…geez.

Disgusted with herself and vexed by hormones she definitely wanted to disown, Hazel yanked her attention back to the moment—but not before she inadvertently shipped Guy Levoie a glance that made him arch a brow then wink—in acknowledgment or promise, Hazel shuddered to think which.

Deliberately she turned her back on him—and caught her grandmother and Dextra Poley out of the corner of her eye exchanging, sharing…something. A significant look, a cyberbyte of knowledge they kept to themselves—a fear more eloquent than words would express.

A fear that said they knew something they hadn't told anyone, about the disappearance of Dextra's daughter.

"What?" she asked sharply, and felt but didn't see Guy straighten behind her. "You know something. Tell me."

Another look passed between the older women, a rubber band stretching and straining, vibrating with tension. Then her grandmother shook her head—but not before a tattletale glance strayed to the department-enlarged picture of Emma Poley on the table before Hazel.

"No. It is nothing."

Hazel shot a quick look at the picture, trying to see through her grandmother's eyes, wondering what the elderly woman saw besides the fifth—or was she a sixth?—grade student in the Keams Canyon School photo.

"Talk to me, Grandmother. I see it in your face. It's a lot more than nothing."

"No." This time it was her grandfather who spoke.

She remembered his voice, the cadence of a language

she didn't understand trying to teach her the old ways, the old stories in a single summer.

She also remembered not wanting to listen, being too busy, too tired of her father's world and too bored with a summer of reservation life to want to learn. Which was probably why she'd gotten into trouble in the first place.

Boredom had a lot to answer for.

"Please, Grandfather," she said as gently and respectfully as she knew how, "I came to find Mrs. Poley's child. Anything might help, it doesn't matter—"

"No." Softly stern, unequivocal. "Some things only hinder when they are spoken."

"Grandfather, you brought me up here."

Her voice was rising, she could hear it. She struggled for control. This would not get away from her. It would *not*. It was always bad for a professional to get involved with family, but she hadn't been offered a choice. Which meant that all she could try to do was maintain the ice of her professionalism, because that and distance was all she had that belonged exclusively to her. Anything less—anything more—would be unacceptable.

"You must have found a way to put pressure on the Bureau to get them to send someone from our office, let alone me specifically, into a situation that until a few hours ago might not even have been within our jurisdiction. Now what haven't you—"

She didn't realize that she was leaning flat-handed and straight-armed across the table, letting emotion make ashes of her best intentions, until she felt Guy's left hand close around her upper arm. Reflex made her twist hard in a move that would have freed her from any other man.

He, of course, wasn't any other man, and he didn't even flinch, let alone let go.

"Hazel," he said quietly.

She heard him but she couldn't stop, couldn't let go now. Not when she could feel an answer, *the* answer, just beyond the end of her fingertips, almost within reach of her grasp.

Still, where she'd meant to keep ice, passion flowed. *Hee'e'wauti,* the Warrior Maiden, and the only one of the kachinas her father and grandfather had tried to teach her about with which she'd been able to identify seemed to have risen inside her, overcome her. Disrespectful of her elders or not, she would find out what these people knew that might help her reconcile the missing child with the phone call she'd received.

"Back off, Levoie."

"Not until you do," he said simply.

"This is my investigation—" Her voice shook with feeling, every nerve beneath his fingers stung, itched... wanted...

More.

Damn it.

No, damn him and all the things about her history that she could not forgive herself for.

She stared up at him, not liking the reflection she saw of herself in his eyes. He stared back, eyes full of understanding and compassion, two things she'd never wanted from anybody—especially from him.

And abruptly, infuriatingly, *except* from him.

A soft, musical trill fitted itself into the tension of the moment, startling them all. It took Hazel an instant to realize the sound came from her pocket. She yanked her phone forth, punched it on and snapped, "Youvella."

"You should treat your elders with more respect," an accented voice observed in perfect English.

Hazel glanced inadvertently at Guy who stilled and straightened at the unspoken message, then she turned and took a few steps away from her grandparents and the Poleys. Wonder of wonders, even out here in the middle of nowhere where there was no receiver transmitter, she could tell that this was not the same voice that had called her before. No, this man's English was more polished, more fluent, but the accent was almost identical.

Hellfire and brimstone, they were watching her and she didn't even have her equipment set up to attempt to trace a signal yet. And God alone knew whether or not the equipment Levoie's crew was using was sophisticated enough for the job.

Screw it, she thought. *Forget the mechanics. Keep him talking. Find the kid.*

"Do you have her?" she asked.

A loud wave of white noise crackled through the signal. Hazel held the phone away from her ear until it passed.

"So direct." The voice sounded amused even through the less-than-ideal connection. "A poor tactic, but one I admire. Unfortunately you ask the wrong question of the wrong person."

"Tell me the right one and I'll ask it." Short and peremptory and probably an attitudinal mistake. She couldn't help it; she hated being at the mercy of intelligent bad guys, hated more that every second wasted on sparring with this one meant someone else's child was endangered.

A shadow crossed her line of vision: Guy heading for the door with some equipment designed to try and get some kind of directional fix on the phone signal. He gave her a circling gesture to keep the connection open before disappearing outside.

Hazel didn't hold out much hope for success. It was, under the best of circumstances, difficult to trace calls made to cell phones. Out here, unless the kidnappers used equipment that was far less advanced than the Bureau's or the locals', which seemed an unlikely occurrence, getting a fix on the call might be downright impossible.

"First you should ask why I am calling you."

"Okay."

The voice in her ear chuckled. "That was not a question."

Hazel stiffened her jaw, asked calmly, "Why—"

"Because you are the only one who can bring me what I want in order to get back what you are not yet aware you have lost."

Baffled, she headed for the door to see how Guy was doing. "Say again?"

"Ask your grandparents," the voice suggested—and was gone.

Nerves keyed, all senses on hyper alert, attention ready to pounce at the least provocation, Hazel closed the phone and turned, with an almost military precision, back to her grandparents and the Poleys. They watched her, terrified, hopeful, wary. She dragged her tongue around the inside of her teeth, pouched it between her molars and her cheek, and regarded first the Poleys and then her grandparents tightly. *Ask your grandparents* pounded through her thoughts and blasted against her temples, vindicating her prephone-call suspicions.

Before she could formulate which questions would best pin her grandfather down first, however, Guy reentered the house. She glanced at him. He compressed his lips and shook his head.

"Nada. My guess is they're using cells and some kind of digital scrambler, too. You?"

She slid a look at her grandparents, back to Guy. "Maybe." He raised a brow. She nodded stiffly. "Different guy, same accent, more authority. Told me I wasn't asking the right questions of the right people. Said I should ask why he called me.''

Guy nodded. ''I heard. We picked up the conversation.'' His gaze on her was sharp and calculating, seeing.

Bastard, she thought, not for the first time.

She wanted to hide from him, but that would have been cowardly. He shrugged and his lips twitched slightly with some dark humor—almost, she decided, as though she'd confirmed something for him.

''What have you or the Bureau got that someone wants, Hazel?''

His voice was carefully neutral, but Hazel felt the prick of conscience anyway. Close on conscience's heels came the automatic surge of anger that *he* should accuse her of anything, the sidebar of something that resembled the rising winds of cold fury at the thought that any man intended to make her a means to his ends again.

Especially at the expense of a child.

''Better,'' Guy continued softly, carefully, holding up the picture of Emma Poley, ''what don't you know you've lost and what can your grandparents tell you about an eleven-year-old kidnap victim who looks an awful lot like you?''

Suddenly numb, Hazel stared at the photograph, looked all the way up at Guy, then focused on her grandparents and the Poleys with an abrupt and awful clarity. There had been those months after she'd…

Hazel shut her eyes, denied history access to the present. She didn't want to think about it anymore.

History trespassed anyway, forcing its way by the barriers she planted against it.

Her parents had split up briefly, disagreeing passionately, Hazel had always been sure, on exactly how to handle her thoughtless pubescent transgressions. But maybe there had been more to it, a bad patch in their marriage that Hazel had been too wrapped up in her own adolescent miseries to recognize and that had only been aggravated by her misdeeds. Something that might have caused her father to…

She shut off the thought, but not quickly enough. The sense of betrayal was slicing, acute. She clenched her fists and found her hands shook. A tremor ran through her jaw, along the muscles in her neck, settled stiffly in her shoulders and down her spine.

Her father had always wanted her raised Hopi, but her mother's work had needed the city—her mother had needed the city. Apparently her father had found his own compromise, a way to have a child of his raised by the tribe.

Briefly she wondered if her mother knew—if Dextra Poley's husband knew.

Raw as her thoughts, her gaze flicked from her grandparents to the Poley's, registered embarrassment, defiance, guilt…and something more in her grandfather. Satisfaction, perhaps? Whatever it was, it didn't matter. How could they not have told her? How could they? They'd brought her out here on some elaborate pretext and expected her to just swallow it and do her job as if it was nothing.

"It's not what you think," Anna told her quietly at the same time that Guy closed the distance separating them and laid a hand on Hazel's shoulder.

"Tell me what I think it is, grandmother," Hazel returned. Her voice held only a slight wobble underlined with passion. The weight on her shoulder was solid, warm and reassuring, oddly comforting. She shook it off; she didn't want to be comforted.

She wanted to be angry.

She'd learned a long time ago how to make good use of her anger, how to let it keep her strong. She didn't have a clue how to let a man's warmth strengthen her—especially not under circumstances like these. Sliding into a man's warmth weakened a woman, stole from her.

"Tell me how it's different," she said softly, tightly. "Tell me why you lied to me and why you had to get *me* up here to work on this. Surely someone without a history—"

"Hazel," Guy said softly. The soothing weight of his hand on her shoulder returned. Concern was clear, damning.

She looked over her shoulder at him, trying to swallow emotion, to get rid of the taste of lies.

"Talk to you outside a minute?"

It sounded like a question, but it wasn't. Gentle as it was, it was still more command than suggestion. Jaw tight, she jerked her head down once in the affirmative and preceded him out of the house.

"You all right?" he asked the minute they stepped outside.

She tried to nod, to be the ice maiden she usually played so well.

Instead she felt herself shake her head once. She wasn't all right. She hadn't been all right for a long time, but this was the wrong day to discover that and the wrong person to discover it with. The only thing to do now was to cover the admission with another lie.

She gave him a one-shoulder shrug. "I will be."

She should have known he'd never be convinced.

"If this is going to be too much for you, we need to know it now. Deal with it. Get you replaced."

If there'd been accusation in his voice, she could have reacted with anger, dealt with it in kind. Instead there was only quiet neutrality, a compassion that made her throat ache. "It's not too much."

"Liar." He said it softly.

Something in his tone forced her to look at him. She didn't want to. She was already pretty sure what she'd see. Pity. Or questions about her competence. She'd seen both often enough. She didn't need to see either one again.

Not from him.

As if he guessed not only how close she stood to the edge of her life's abyss, but also how badly she didn't need to be there and see what was in it, his mouth hardened. If she'd cared to look, she would have seen neither pity nor competency questions.

She'd also have seen that his eyes lost none of their perceptiveness, that it was only his tone that became deliberately provoking.

"Look," he said, "I can't know exactly what's going on between you and your grandparents, but it's not gettin' us any closer to this kid and that's why I'm here. You got issues about bein' back in Hopiland, take 'em up later, and let's get to work."

"What do you think I'm trying to do?" Hazel snapped. "They know something, damn it, you heard it, you saw it, I *watched* you see it. They got me out here because somebody ordered them to—they lied to me about that, damn it!—and because they think they can't trust anyone but family. That's the case, I'm family. Not the best kind, maybe, but there we are. They can damn well start trusting me."

"You always this prickly?" Guy asked, curious. "Or is it just being here? Because if I'm going to fall in love with you after we find the Poleys' daughter, I want to be able to like you and you're makin' that kinda hard."

Flabbergasted beyond belief, Hazel could only stare all the way up at him, speechless. "You...you—"

"Yeah, yeah, we did that in the truck, remember?" He smudged at something high on her cheekbone with the edge of a finger. Hazel barely stopped herself in time from inadvertently closing her eyes and leaning into the gesture. Fisted the urge to bat his hand away. To acknowledge the touch at all. He was a man—a person—for whom touching was as natural as breathing. Who would ignore the briar patch she grew around herself, not because he was oblivious to it, but because he was undaunted by the thorns. "Get past it."

"You crumb." Why were her eyes stinging? Why was her throat clogged? "If you think—"

"Yeah, I *do* think," Guy interrupted, stooping so they were at eye level. It was a long way down. Made him feel protective, but she'd hate him if she ever found that out. "I think you can't see what you're doin' here because you're too caught up in some personal history you won't let go of. I think it was a bad idea for you to come here and for them to ask for you."

He touched a fingertip to her other cheek, brought it away damp. Folded the tear into his fist before she discovered what he held.

"Mostly I think you're right," he went on, wishing he hadn't seen this side of her. A woman who cried for lost children, and didn't know it, was not what he'd bargained on when she'd stepped into Russ's office. Seducing her into letting him fall in love with her would mean taking on a whole lot more than a few months of contented pleasures and some overnight baggage. It would mean breaking down barriers she'd built to shield her from something she couldn't handle alone. And if he let himself do that, he had the gut-deep sense that the woman he found inside the walls could consume him.

Disquieted by both this new knowledge about her and his own disconcerting determination to move forward anyway rather than to back up, he went on, "Your grandparents and the Poleys are hiding something that we may need to know. You may even have guessed what it is already, but they're more afraid of telling you the secret than they are of keeping it. I think they're trying to protect you—''

He held up a finger when she would have protested. ''I know. You don't want to be protected by anyone from anything. Tough. They're doing it. And, for whatever reason, I doubt they'll tell you until they decide you're ready to hear it. In which case, we can waste time contacting your parents for possible answers or we can get productive, cover the ground, check in with Russ and pick up the trail. Whichever you choose, that's what I'm going to do. We copacetic on that?''

For the space of three heated breaths Hazel stared at him, disliking for the second time the reflection of herself that she saw in his eyes: a woman bent on running this case by her own agenda and the hell with anyone else.

She closed her eyes against an image she didn't want to live with. Then she sighed and looked at the red earth below her feet, back at him.

''Yes,'' she agreed resignedly, and let the ice-melt of her emotions soak invisibly into the red hard-pack where she hoped it would remain. ''We're copacetic—''

The shuffle of movement behind them coincided far too neatly with the buzz of the cell phone in her hand. Hazel started, but caught the current prophet of doom before she dropped it, turned to face her grandmother who had come outside even as she slanted an uneasy half glance at Guy and flipped open the phone.

''Ah, excellent,'' the accented voice said before she got out a word. This time there was no static at all, only a horrid, vibrant clarity—as though God put a punctuation point to what Hazel was about to hear. ''I see your grandmother has decided to tell you the story of your daughter.''

Chapter 4

Even as she recoiled, physically and emotionally caught off balance by the new shock, some part of Hazel recognized the ploy for what it was: a move to mess with her mind, to destroy whatever fragile equilibrium she might have attained between calls. She'd spent time in psy-ops—psychological operations—in the Army, had studied a gross of psychology with the Bureau learning how to do the same thing.

But recognizing the situation for what it was didn't help. She was still caught off guard, literally rocked off her feet and into Guy Levoie's reaching arms. Her daughter—her illegitimate daughter—had died at birth a little over eleven years ago.

Or so she'd been told.

Guy used one hand to steady Hazel, pried the phone out of her shock-tightened fingers with the other. Underneath her native bronze, her skin had taken on a milky-gray sheen he didn't like. He pinned Hazel's grandmother with watchful hawk eyes and put the phone to his ear. Whatever had been whispered in his *partner's* ear was not what she'd expected, indicated clearly that ASAC Youvella's aversion to being back on the reservation and the questions yet to be answered here went far deeper than he had imagined.

His gut clenched and tightened with premonition. "What do you want?" he said into the phone.

The static-interrupted voice on the other end laughed mockingly. "From you, Investigator Levoie?" the accented voice queried, investing Guy's title with a caricature-like emphasis. "Wait and see. For now, listen and learn."

Once again the connection went dead.

Guy plucked the instrument from his ear, shut it and tucked it into his hip pocket. If they'd been short enough, the hairs at his nape would have stood on end. The deliberate emphasis on his title was too close a mimic to Hazel's emphasis the first time she'd used it.

There was also something about the voice he knew he should recognize, a link he should remember and couldn't place at the moment.

Fury ran through him in thin, cold threads. They were being played, and he didn't like it. He would not be puppeted about like some chessboard pawn or knight errant in a game that meant a child's life.

"Hazel," he said as gently as impatience and necessity would allow. He chafed her arms, trying to pour some of his own warmth and urgency into her. "Tell me."

She opened her mouth and shook her head slightly, still too stunned to speak. Then she looked quickly once at her grandmother before averting her face and shrinking closer to Guy.

Not too close, just closer.

Nearer to the dangerous rattlesnake imprint on his arm

and away from the stoic "we lied to you because we love you" printed on Anna's face.

"Not good enough," she whispered fiercely to her grandmother's silent nonapology. "Not even half."

"Hazel," her grandmother began—only to be interrupted by a Hopi tribal officer aboard an all-terrain vehicle that blew dust through the village when he roared to a stop next to Guy.

"We found the kid's backpack," he said without formality. "Note with it says you got fifteen minutes or all bets are off. Note says it and I saw it. Looks like it's remote-rigged to blow if anyone besides ASAC Youvella tries to touch it."

There wasn't time to get anyone from a bomb squad out to the location.

Surrounded by searchers—tribal cops, county deputies, Arizona Highway Patrol and others—Guy stood near the entrance to a sandstone-cliff canyon and tried to ignore the sensation of being a rattlesnake in an inescapable sand cage during a roundup. Sign was faint and nearly nonexistent on the ground before him, just enough to suggest that it had been left deliberately, a sort of torturous joke upon them all. He took note of it, then stepped carefully around it, anyway, walked close to where Hazel hesitated over the backpack.

"No way around it," she said, as though to herself. She looked up at him. "You might want to step back, Levoie. Just in case."

He shook his head and grinned with more nonchalance than he felt. "They want me here, too. You go, we go."

"No kid needs that kind of hero, Levoie," she said sharply.

"Good thing I'm not that kind of hero, then."

Guy hunkered down beside the bit of navy blue plastic and nylon that sported pictures of TV's Buffy, the Vampire Slayer and her main squeeze, Angel, the Vampire with the Soul, and lifted his T-shirt to show her the Kevlar vest he wore beneath it. Someone tossed him a pair of riot helmets with shields, and an extra vest. He slipped on one of the helmets, handed the vest and the other helmet to Hazel. She gave him a considering look, but accepted the armor and put it on without protest.

Guy kept his relief to himself. Both items were big on her, but it wasn't as if this were a beggars-could-be-choosers moment. They both knew she wouldn't even be able to pretend to get what whoever was at the other end of the remote wanted if she wound up maimed or dead. It didn't matter. As far as he was concerned she could pretend to be a badass all she wanted on someone else's shift; he knew better. There was nothing badass about her. He knew it, and whoever wanted something from her knew it, too.

She glanced at him once, then, as though she understood his thought as clearly as if it were her own, gave him a determined "you wait and we'll see who's the badass" look. Then she unzipped the backpack without further hesitation.

There was no explosion, no sound from the men and women gathered around them at a distance, only the menacing nylon susurration of the zipper and the unmistakable crackle-sough of plastic sagging open.

Guy didn't know what he'd expected the bag to contain—a photograph of Emma Poley bound to a bed and gagged, maybe, with a clock and a newspaper to set the date and time the way it was done in the movies. Hey, so he wasn't immune to the effects of popular culture, who was?

Instead the pack held a manila envelope and a carefully

beribboned box, both addressed to Hazel, and a clear plastic sleeve of the type used to protect collectible trading cards. The sticky note attached to it said the wrapped photo inside was for him.

For a moment everything inside him stilled and every nerve that wasn't already on alert coiled then *sproinged* to attention. He took the bit of plastic from Hazel when she passed it up to him. Their fingers brushed and he found himself instinctively opening his hand to wrap his around hers, to offer comfort and understanding—to request the same from her in return. When she didn't reflexively withdraw from him as she'd done before, he looked at her and swallowed, found his worst fears shared. Without opening their respective envelopes they both knew.

What was bad enough before had just gotten very personal and immeasurably worse.

Hazel opened the envelope first.

Betrayal was a jagged, unkind cut, a fist jammed deep into her throat, a hand squeezing the life out of her lungs until the world became a red haze before her eyes and her vision spun.

"They lied to me," she said to Guy and to no one. But it was more than that.

Far more.

They'd abused her trust. Eleven-some years ago, they'd stolen a living piece of her and replaced it with the kind of grief only a mother can feel upon learning that the infant— the *daughter*—she'd just given birth to, held in her arms too briefly, but infinitely long enough to love, is dead.

And she'd believed without question because her parents had always told her the truth.

Or so she'd thought.

But it appeared she'd been even more naive at fifteen,

after she'd discovered herself pregnant by that flattering, immature twenty-something, than she'd imagined possible.

She'd thought innocence long gone by the time she'd missed her fifth period and begun to feel scared because something was moving, turning over, seemed to live in her belly and she didn't know what it was. Then it had been her father who'd recognized that certain glow, the scent of pregnancy, and pulled her aside first and asked point-blank if she was. Even then she'd denied the possibility, because all she'd really understood about pregnancy back then was that it only happened to other, more…trampish…girls, with whom she had nothing in common, and they experienced nausea every morning at first; she'd had none.

"Hazel."

She could feel him there, squatting in front of her, blocking her from view of the others the way he'd automatically done when she'd opened her envelope and sat down trying to disbelieve the truth.

Protecting her tough-guy, ice-maiden reputation from the people she was here to take charge of in this search.

Maybe she'd be able to appreciate his effort later. Right this moment she could barely take in what she held in her hands. Because here was the birth certificate she'd signed when she'd given the name Emily Claire Youvella to her baby. Beneath it was the death certificate she'd been shown two days later only a few hours after holding her beautiful living infant and basking in the excitement of her parents apparently agreeing to let her bring Emily home with her. They'd even gone so far as to arrange for a memorial service and to put a small casket in the ground….

Her breath caught and her eyes stung. Her mind was blank except for two words:

God and *why?*

Beyond numb, she sifted further into the documents. Un-

derneath the birth and death certificates were the papers her
parents had signed giving Emily Claire into her grandparents' keeping, the adoption papers the Poleys had signed,
the new birth certificate issued for Emma Dextra Poley. Her
entire family had been—was still—in league against her
learning the truth, and now some stranger had brought history back and spit the unconscionable in her face in a game
of emotional coercion. For reasons yet unknown, she'd
been dragged out here to ransom the child made hers only
by virtue of nine months of pregnancy, twenty-four hours
of labor and the months of anguish she'd undergone because of the lies afterward.

"You all right?" Guy pitched his voice low, for her ears
alone.

She hadn't wanted him to know she was vulnerable, but
she was also glad of his wall-like presence. She gave him
the slightest negative shake of her head. *How could they?
How?* was all she could think—and knew she didn't really
want to know. It was bad enough knowing that she'd lost
their trust at the tender age of fifteen without learning that
in the circumstances she should never have let them have
hers.

"Not if these papers are as real as they look."

She didn't offer and he didn't ask to read them. She
knew without doubt that he'd seen enough to understand
everything he had to. They both eyed the box.

"We gotta look," he said gently. He didn't appear any
happier about the prospect than she was.

Hazel nodded and stiffened her jaw, felt the bones click
with the strain. She hated boxes in kidnap cases. Nothing
good ever came in them. She nudged the strings with hesitant fingers, loath to do it fast and get it over with, even
knowing that it would be easiest that way. No matter what

you saw or how many times you'd experienced the seeing, there was no way to block out the initial shock.

Especially when what was inside had to do with someone who was yours.

Guy waited six long heartbeats, then grimaced and held out a hand. "Want me to do it?"

She almost said yes. Then she shook her head and steeled herself, yanked the ribbons apart and pulled the lid off the box.

It was a braid, only a braid. Long and shining, coiled atop a photograph that she couldn't see clearly because of the emotion that spilled into her eyes.

Throat clenching, stomach lurching, she dropped the box. Relief was so strong that the bile she'd tamped down against her expectation of the worst rose, and she had to scramble to her knees behind some scrub until her body quit dry heaving. Big hands held her head, a jeans-clad thigh supported her hip. Guy meant the action to be impersonal, somewhere underneath everything else, Hazel knew that. But she also recognized with some trepidation that *impersonal* wasn't part of either his vocabulary or his body language.

Everything he did was personal: his attention to her, every movement he made, every absent stroke his thumb took along the back of her head.

She also quite abruptly understood that as much as she might hate herself for it later, right now she was glad.

She sat back on her heels, and without a word he spilled water from a canteen over a bandanna and handed it to her.

The whole area shouted to Guy of the persons and things that had passed this way. He needed to study it quietly, to find the sign—both blatant and hidden—that would lead him to the people who'd deposited Emma's backpack here.

But Hazel's need for solace was greater, his desire to offer it more unassailable, still.

She pressed the cloth to her mouth, her throat, her eyes. "Thanks."

Guy scraped the side of a forefinger across her cheek because it was the kind of thing he did. He didn't mean anything by it and he certainly didn't intend to feel the rush of sensation that lurched through him when her unexpectedly all-too-vulnerable dark eyes settled on his and she accepted the gesture without jerking away. This was neither the time nor place to further the discovery of things like that, but there it was.

He withdrew his hand and they returned uncomfortably to their study of the box's contents.

There were actually three photos underneath the braid. The top one was a picture of Emma Poley standing against a nondescript backdrop obviously crying while she held up the braid and a current newspaper. The hair had clearly and carelessly been shorn from her head.

The second picture was identical to the school photo Guy had picked up in the Poleys' house. The third might also have been Emma except that the picture was more faded around the edges and the time period and clothing were fifteen or sixteen years out of date.

Guy held the photo up to the light beside Hazel's face. "You?" he guessed.

Her face was hard when she nodded. "Me."

"Just because she looks like you at the same age doesn't prove she's yours, Hazel." And if it didn't, he thought, someone was going to an awful lot of trouble to make it seem otherwise. "Somebody could still be yanking your chain tryin' to get something out of you." Did he sound as cynical—or perhaps that was *hopeful*—to her as he did to himself? It would be so much easier to deal with this case if he didn't feel uneasy about her intentions…if he didn't feel she could be blackmailed through the use of a child.

"She's mine." The statement was simple, a declaration of belief—and of war.

She looked again at what had lain inside the box, looked at Guy. Her eyes were frighteningly calm and revealing, her world reduced to everything clear and straightforward. Guy understood, but wasn't sure he'd be able to live with what he saw.

For other children she would willingly die. If anything happened to this one, without compunction, she would kill.

A minute and a half later, when Guy withdrew the torn, note-wrapped photo from the plastic sleeve addressed to him, he quit worrying about preventing Hazel from killing anyone; he understood all too well how she felt.

He also knew beyond doubt exactly which scumbag had to have orchestrated Emma Poley's disappearance. The problem would lie in proving the scumbag's involvement, since Grigor Klimkov, the former KGB agent turned Russian Mafia kingpin, was currently locked in solitary confinement in a maximum-security federal prison.

The small, malnourished child that looked out of the picture was easily as precious to him as any child Hazel had thought dead for eleven years might be to her. He knew this child well. And Sasha Levoie, formerly Klimkov, was as healthy and chubby as any two-year-old should be since Guy's brother Jeth and sister-in-law Allyn had rescued the tot from the clutches of the Colombian drug cartel, who had been using him for leverage in a territorial war with the Russian Mafia. The adoption wasn't quite final, but Sasha's mother, never married to Sasha's father and therefore Sasha's sole custodial parent, had signed off on the child shortly after Klimkov's arrest.

A cocaine addict who'd originally sold Sasha to her dealer in exchange for a cleared debt and a few days' worth of highs, she'd been offered witness protection for her testimony against Sasha's father. Instead, like so many lost people before her, she'd disappeared back into the streets. The brothers Levoie had been told only a few weeks ago that she'd turned up dead of an overdose in a homeless warren in Baltimore not far from where Sasha's involvement with Jeth had begun.

Although unable to corroborate anything at the time, Guy, Jeth and Russ had wondered about the circumstances surrounding Sasha's mother's death. Addicts OD'd; it was a sad truth of their disease, but the timing on this one, her prior association with Klimkov and the purity and uncut quality of the drugs in her system—especially added on top of this—well, it all added up to big-time speculation.

At the moment, however, horrifying as that was, it was neither here nor there. What mattered was that Guy held a picture of Sasha in one hand and a note he didn't want to read in the other. If anything happened to Sasha…

He shut his eyes. It didn't bear thinking about. Ever. Because losing Sasha on top of the guilt Jeth felt over his part—real or imagined—in Marcy's death three years ago would destroy Guy's younger brother and devastate his sister-in-law. Not to mention what would happen in the aftermath when it became a race between Jeth and Allyn to see who got to Klimkov first.

"Investigator Levoie?" Her voice trembled only slightly, was soft but sharp, a command to snap out of it and share what he had.

He opened his eyes and looked at her, suddenly not sure if he could—or should. Something uncomfortable and possibly toxic trickled through him, premonition or instinct, he didn't know. The urge to protect sliced deep, an ax into a log. Her, Sasha, his brother's family, himself, the child who might be Hazel Youvella's biological daughter—all of them needed to be gotten through this without wounds, damage, scars. All at once he couldn't place the order of his priorities. Two kids, two families, and quite possibly two purposes within one already-huge dilemma.

All he had to do was open the piece of paper he held and find out what was wanted of him.

He could guess what was wanted of her: worm Sasha's whereabouts out of the Levoie brothers and return him to a man who had committed unspeakable acts against other children in exchange for the safe return of her allegedly dead daughter to her.

In other words, and among other things, play to the sympathy-empathy factor: someone had taken a child from Hazel the way someone had taken a child from Klimkov.

Only not exactly.

"Guy."

She utilized his familiar name the same way his brothers used his professional title or his mother called him by his full name: to get his attention. And the same way they succeeded so did she. Only not exactly. Only more so. Because his name in her mouth brought him aware differently. All of him, nerve endings to arteries, fingertip to fingertip, spirit soul to foot sole. He looked at her again and, much as he wanted to, couldn't look away.

"May I see?" she asked—and held out a hand.

It was the hand and the gentleness of her "may I" that he couldn't resist.

Without relinquishing the torn photograph, he turned it so she could see Sasha. She eyed him puzzled.

"Who's this?"

"My nephew," Guy said tersely, savagely. "And without reading this note I can tell you, he's what the kidnappers want as ransom for your Emma Poley."

Chapter 5

Sasha was indeed what the kidnappers wanted.

The note wrapped around his picture specified an identifiable point north of Keams Canyon between Oraibi and Polacca Washes and said simply, "3 p.m. You and Youvella. Bring him."

A muscle ticked in Guy's cheek when he read it a second time. Everything inside him receded behind the hunter's instinct that made him the best at what he did.

He'd spent every waking moment of his childhood at the knee of his great-uncle learning the spirit of the earth, the movements and ways of animals, rocks, plants and water. He could follow someone or something anywhere, anytime of day, season or weather. Yes, sure, he needed a place to start, but Emma's kidnappers had just given him more of one than he'd already had.

The desert and surrounding mesa was no small grid to map, but if that was where they wanted a meet, he doubted they'd be hiding far away. Take them too long to set up the kind of surveillance they were using to keep track of every move he and Hazel made otherwise. Also take too long to get from here to there without the noise and notice-ability of some kind of airborne recon. If they were any-where in the Four Corners, he would find them. It was just a matter of time.

He only hoped they had enough of that commodity avail-able when they needed it.

"You all right, Investigator?"

He glanced at her, registering somewhere at the periph-ery of his consciousness that they were back to the for-malities, and regretting it. "They've got my attention."

She nodded. "And mine. Now fill me in." It was a re-quest, quietly made, a "we're in this hole together for sure now" acknowledgment.

Like you did me? He didn't say it out loud, but accusa-tion was clear in the tightening of his mouth and the mud-dark depths of his eyes. Then, as quickly as it had arrived, reproach disappeared, and Guy gave Hazel the briefest and most complete account of Sasha's history he could.

Fury and compassion warred for residence on her face. In the end neither won. Instead she contained them both and asked what she had to know. "What about your broth-ers?"

"He's Jeth's kid," Guy snapped. "He and his wife brought Sasha out of hell. The rest of my family's been hiding him for months. This threatens them all. What do you think?"

"That it's as personal for you as it is for me now."

His laughter was short and humorless. "Y'got that right." He was silent for a moment. "We'll have to get rid of him. Russ, too, maybe. Send them somewhere else. Dis-tract them."

"Someone should interview my family and Klimkov."

Guy's grin was suddenly wide and wolfish. "Jeth'd go for that—especially dealing with Klimkov. Russ might think twice about letting him go, but better Jeth with Klimkov than anywhere near your family. Boy's kinda intense and he's got a temper. He won't play nice on this one, and he won't think twice about anything."

"What about you?"

He snorted. "Oh, baby, you're stuck with me fer sure. We have to take him out there, but Sasha doesn't leave my sight. We get him out, I get a bead on these turkeys and we take 'em down."

Hazel caught his arm, demanding his attention. "After we get Emma back," she said. Her voice held an undercurrent of wildness that verged on fear. She didn't know if she could trust him, either.

Guy squeezed her fingers, grazed her cheek with his thumb and gave her a clipped nod. "You got it," he agreed, hoping he told her the truth, praying that was the way it would go. "After that."

"No," Jeth said when they told him—although what he really said was a good deal less polite and more profane.

"You're out of your minds," was Russ's somewhat-more-restrained response.

Allyn was even less enthusiastic than either her husband or her brother-in-law about sending Sasha into the wilderness. Her maternal instincts had been fully engaged from the moment she'd laid eyes on the tyke a few months previously. She and Jeth had finally just gotten back the child who'd brought them together after months of hiding him among the children of Jeth's family's tribe.

She also, however, took one look at Hazel when the young ASAC's half of the story was told, then explained to Jeth and Russ unhappily but precisely *why* they would not only do exactly what Guy asked, but trust him to do it right. After all, as she reminded Jeth, her own mother had been Hazel once, just a couple of years older at the time. And if anyone had ever scammed Alice Myers Book in order to take away her twins the way Hazel's family had scammed her, not only would there have been hell to pay, but also Allyn's mother would have moved heaven and earth to save her daughters—and get them back.

Which also, as Allyn grumpily mentioned, made her understand Klimkov's apparent motives all too well and not like the fact that she did.

Damn it.

Hazel, Guy noted, watched Allyn with something akin to awe during the other woman's diatribe. She seemed to be seeing for the first time that there were other ways for a strong woman to deal with men than by trying to outdo them or outbe them or outstoic them. Because it was obvious that Allyn simply knew who she was, what she meant and what she was about.

It was also clear that she was perfectly happy with who she was, not to mention that she was both perfectly capable of following through on any threat she made regarding handing a man like Grigor Klimkov his head, as well as willing to do so.

It was that, more than anything, that made even her frighteningly intense and probably dangerous husband and his macho brothers sit up and take notice when she spoke her mind.

If the situation hadn't been so fraught with tension, Guy might have laughed at the look on Hazel's face—then told her that Allyn usually had the same effect on people who'd never met her before. As it was, he couldn't check the slight twitch of his lips when Hazel glanced his way, thoroughly boggled when Jeth and Russ caved without further argument when Allyn finished hers.

The reluctant tug of strained amusement and appreciation around Hazel's mouth when she glanced his way after his brothers' capitulation to Allyn made him shrug and wink at her, offer the intimacy of a moment shared. But it was the slightest incline of her head toward him, the pull of her brow and lips into a silent but heartfelt "thank you for bringing me into this"—the one more hint that she might really want to be human and not merely a hard case after all—that brought a rush to his pulse and a more primitive recognition into his belly.

Bad timing or not, he would fall in love with Hazel Youvella. It wouldn't be just because falling in love was the sort of thing he did. It would be because exploring all of the possibilities of falling in love with this particular "her" had just become a *have-to* of utmost importance.

It took all of the allotted time to bring Sasha covertly out of hiding and to arrange the local deputies into a sort of shell game of rugged, white utilitarian vehicles in which to better mask Sasha's exact location. A shell game Guy hoped to utilize in reverse when it came time to leave the area, so he and Hazel could stay behind undetected and begin their search.

The desert sky was intensely blue, the air hot and arid against the skin. Guy left the engine and the air-conditioning running when he stepped onto the sand at the appointed place and time and shut the Blazer's door behind him. On the other side of the vehicle Hazel did the same with the passenger door.

Inside, behind bulletproof glass, Sasha napped in his car-seat, oblivious.

"See anything?" Russ's voice was a gnat-like buzz in both Guy's and Hazel's ears.

"Not yet." Guy turned slowly, surveying the bumpy but open desert and low-lying scrub that stretched to the striated canyon walls several thousand yards away. "You?"

"Nada."

"Anybody else?" Hazel asked, checking with the rest of the hidden team. The ensuing negative responses set her teeth on edge. "Show, you bastards," she muttered under her breath—then started when the truck's radio sputtered to life as though in direct response to her comment.

Guy got to the mike first. "Levoie. If this isn't police business, get off this frequency."

"Where is the child?" No preliminaries, merely a demand made difficult to understand by the thickness radio-garble lent the already harsh accent.

"With me. Where's Emma Poley?"

"Show the child."

If there was any possibility of locating the place the voice was transmitting from, Guy knew he had to stall, give Russ and Hazel's FBI electronics techies time. "You first."

Impatience was a bark of guttural laughter. "You will lose a chicken contest, Investigator Levoie. We are not stupid. Now show the child and let us be done here."

Guy glanced at Hazel. The color in her cheeks was high, accented by the pinched-white edges of anger around her mouth and the flat darkness of her eyes. She gave him a curt nod: he spoke for them both. He pressed the button on the mike, brought it back to his mouth.

"What assurance have we got—"

"None except the word of my employer," the voice snapped.

"Which is how good, given the—"

"No more debate. Show him. Now. Before I am forced to send Special Agent Youvella a more…personal…gift."

Hazel blanched. Guy's jaw cracked with tension. This was it. Whoever had Emma would do no more negotiating on this point. He was left without choice. The only thing he had to bargain with was Sasha.

God help him.

Deliberately calm, so as not to transmit his fear to the toddler, Guy opened the Blazer's rear door and eased Sasha gently from his car seat, protecting his soon-to-be-nephew with his body as much as possible. By the time he had the baby in his arms, Hazel had rounded the vehicle to stand in front of them both, a tigress's demeanor and high-powered rifle at the ready. In spite of the situation, Guy had to smother a grin against Sasha's nap-'n'-sweat-created curls. Yep, this one was definitely a keeper.

Now if only he could manufacture the time to show her this quality in herself.

Before he had opportunity to speculate further on his options in that direction, however, the voice over the radio issued another demand.

"Walk twenty feet north and turn him so I can see him."

Hazel snorted something unladylike and vehement under her breath and grabbed the mike. "Turn him *where* so you can see him?"

The unholy chuckle that came through the radio was palpable, a thing of substance rolling down Hazel's spine. "Do a…" He paused as though considering a term. "Turn his face outward and do a…three-sixty. I will see."

"Damn." Hating the sense of powerlessness over the situation, Hazel looked at Guy. "I don't like this."

"Me, neither." He grimaced. "Choices. Crumb." They considered each other for five seconds while the silence on the other end of the radio collected. Then Guy hissed out a tight breath. ''Break out the Kevlar. They won't do any-thing.'' Who was he trying to convince? ''But I'll cover him with it. They want to see his face, make sure it's him and not a doll or something.''

Unconvinced, Hazel nonetheless did as Guy suggested. Sweat collected between her shoulderblades—less from heat than from a nerves-on-end hyper alert—when she turned her back on the desert to help Guy with the reluctant-to-be-disturbed toddler.

It was impossible for them not to touch accidentally under the circumstances, impossible for her to ignore even the most impersonal graze of his skin under her palms—the sensation of a heat that did not come from the sun that cursed the flow of blood in her veins. Nor could she disregard his gentleness with the nap-fussy Sasha, the flutter of some maternal awakening and recognition that did not merely stem from her instinctive urge to comfort a crying child. No, what the flutter in her belly said was that Guy Levoie would make some lucky child or children a wonderful parent one day.

That he would have made her own Emily Claire a wonderful father, regardless of who had sired the child now called Emma.

Startled she stepped back from man and child, reached almost reflexively for the rifle she'd set aside to help cover Sasha with the Kevlar. Awareness was a rabid thing from which the only salvation was to stand back, stay back, turn and run. But she couldn't. Not from here, not now. Not when there was so much at stake.

Oh, God.

She drew an unsteady breath and cast a fleeting glance upward. His eyes were bright and dark, devoid of laughter, curious and wary at once.

Frightened by the madness—the timing—of a desire she

didn't want and refused to admit, she let her gaze drop to
where she could almost see the beat of his pulse within his
throat. It was as erratic as her own heartbeat, as heavy as
the breath in her lungs.

Unhealthy, she thought wildly. *Look away.*

But she couldn't.

Neither could he.

Inside the Blazer the radio *shirred* with white noise. In
Guy's arms Sasha kicked and squirmed, forcing his attention; the mood was blessedly broken.

"We'd better get moving." Guy's voice was harsh.

Hazel only nodded, unable to trust hers.

Then, side by side, she with the weapon and he with the
child, they stepped away from the Blazer and moved into
the desert to do a fashion model's turn on the devil's run-
way.

It felt very much as if they posed for pictures, Guy
thought.

Nerves prickling from the urge to duck and cover Sasha
with his body, Guy made the requested revolution while
Hazel scanned the horizon for flashes of sunlight on metal
or anything else that might be out of the ordinary.

The radio in Guy's SUV remained ominously silent.

And all the while the murmur of Russ's voice settled in
their ears, feeding them a frustrating snack of negative information. Nothing out there, nothing out there, nothing—

Then it came, the sharp command from Russ, "There.
Stop. Go back. Hold it," followed immediately by, "Close
it up, Guy, get Sasha out of there. We got a bead on where
they're transmitting from."

Too easy, he'd known it.

In the orange-and-purpling dusk, Guy stood in the canyon the tech team had pinpointed and tried to tell Hazel what wasn't there—no sign, nothing to indicate the recent presence of humans or vehicles except a signaling device that might have been dropped from a low-flying plane.

To show her that they'd been electronically had.

Hazel was dead-set on hope.

"We go out tonight from here," she told him flatly.

"Where to?" He was equally adamant. "There's nothin' here to start from. No, we *don't* go from here. We go back to the bus stop and the path she takes home, cover ground I've already covered, pick up where I left off. Then we go over to where the backpack was dropped. There's sign there, I saw it. We've been dinkin' around long enough— they've got a lead. Just because they had her hold up a Flagstaff paper doesn't mean she's not in another state by now—"

"Tonight, not tomorrow," Hazel repeated tersely. "Get a head start, maybe take them by surprise."

"Oh, that'll happen." The sarcasm was born of frustration and waning light—came from attempting to protect a hardheaded woman from the disappointment and anxiety he was sure lay ahead of her in the next few hours. "They haven't done anything particularly stupid so far, Hazel. What makes you think they've started?"

"Everybody makes mistakes. Besides…" She once-overed him, taking him—as his father might have said— "up the back and down the belly" then, craning her neck so she could be eye to eye. "…I thought you were supposed to be Mr. Bigshot Tracker. You're supposed to be the best. You telling me you can't track these jokers anytime from anywhere, day or night?"

Guy snorted. "Don't," he advised her. "I don't take dares and I don't shame easy."

"What *do* you do easily?"

The minute the question was out of her mouth, she knew she'd made a mistake. The gaze he fixed on her was half-amused, half-challenging, wholly, arrogantly male.

"I already told you, honey." He gestured at the sere and cooling land around them. "One, I track people."

He stepped in close to her and lifted his hand to trail only his fingertips down her arm. Even through the Egyptian cotton of the long sleeves, the almost nontouch was electric, raised gooseflesh in a champagne fizz up her spine. Her breath caught, and without thought she turned her face up to him.

"Two, I seduce women. And three—"

He cupped her cheek for an instant, then curled his hand under her chin, touched the elusive tip of his tongue to the seam of her lips before brushing her mouth lightly with his. The bubbly explosion along her spine fed into her blood-stream, and her body seemed to liquefy, her lips parted to accept him.

Instead he merely traced them with his thumb, stooped to breathe in her ear, "—I fall in love with them."

Then he stepped away, turned and headed for his truck. "Come on," he said—a little shakily, truth be known.

"Wh—" She cleared her throat, rudely awakened from some dream place she'd never been before, knowing she should have smacked him for his outrageousness, but unable to lift a finger, let alone her entire hand. "Where are you going?"

"Back to the beginning like I told you." He opened the passenger door for her and let down the step. "From there we pack up shop and walk."

Chapter 6

As the Northern Arizona desert light faded, the air filled with a multitude of twitterings and scuttle-skitters that made Hazel's skin crawl and her nerves jump. Eyes darting nervously, she pulled on a flannel-lined denim jacket Guy had talked her into buying and placed her feet carefully, glad he'd also made her buy boots. The thought of stepping into the proverbial scorpion's or rattlesnake's nest scared her spitless, but she couldn't let *him* know that. He already had her at a huge disadvantage. Not only was this his turf, but he knew too much about her fears for comfort. She knew nothing at all about his.

"So ask me," he invited out of the blue, apparently reading her mind.

"What?"

"Ask me what I'm afraid of."

She stared at him, startled. "Wha—how did you—what?"

He paused long enough to glance up at her from the track he studied. "Hazard of the profession."

When she looked askance, the grin that ghosted his features in the twilight was crooked and wry.

"It's the way you move," he elaborated. "Signature's in your step. Everybody's got his own, unique, like snowflakes or fingerprints. You're afraid but don't want me to know it, so you're trying to move like I do, but you're stiff when you do it—you take little steps, plant your feet like you're not sure what you might step on, keep jerkin' around whenever something moves, things like that."

"Y-you noticed?"

He gave her matter-of-fact. "It's what I do, Hazel. Ever since I can remember, it's what I've always done. Now go ahead and ask me."

She had little left but the defensive shield she wrapped around herself. And the truth was, she was more than a tad unwilling to relax enough out here to carry on a conversation with anyone, let alone him. Getting comfy with him in any way, shape or form sounded like as bad an idea as stepping into those nests that she didn't want to step into—and probably would be worse for her emotional health. "What on earth makes you think I'd want to know?"

"Because I know what scares you," he said gently. "I figured you'd want at least an equal advantage on me. Not to mention—" she could almost hear him grin "—we talk, you'll calm down, maybe we'll get farther faster."

Hazel rolled her eyes; her mouth formed a lopsided smile in spite of her efforts to contain it. "I knew there was an ulterior motive."

"Yeah, well." He shrugged, charming and full of it at once. "You wanna know?"

She sighed and bit, too tired and stressed out to maintain her guard. "Okay, sure, why not. What scares you?"

"Big cities." Guy angled his flashlight to cast a shadow on the next set of tracks. Not generally noted for their subtlety, the Russian mob members who'd grabbed Emma had nonetheless gone to the trouble of laying false trails and doubling back over their tracks. As well, they'd tried to destroy them by dragging tires behind their vehicle. He'd hoped they'd be less knowledgeable about the desert than they appeared to be. "Not getting to Emma in time."

His voice softened and he eyed Hazel steadily. "You."

Hazel gaped. "Like hell!"

"'S true." A roll of his right shoulder brought a visible wince. He rubbed it and shifted the flashlight he'd begun to use into his left hand. "I am afraid of big cities and not getting to Emma in time." And given the time this search was taking, majorly afraid of the latter.

"Not that part," Hazel said, exasperated. "I believe that part—or at least the part about Emma. It's the rest—" She stopped flat, off to the side of trail he was inspecting when he hunched his shoulder again and grimaced. "What's wrong with your shoulder?" she demanded. "You've been favoring it all day."

"Tension." Another grimace. *Klimkov and company have a lot to answer for.* "Cold. Nothing five or six aspirin, a massage and a whirlpool wouldn't cure."

"Guy." Exasperation was quickly turning to irritation. "What don't I know about you that might jeopardize us out here?"

"You didn't pull my file before you came up here?"

She studied him without answering, waiting. Sure she'd read his file. Didn't mean she didn't need to hear the details from him.

"Fine." His mouth compressed. "Took a broken shovel handle in the shoulder the last time we were messin' with these characters. Only been about three months. Muscles act up sometimes.''

"You going to be any good to Emma when we catch up to these jerks, or not?''

"Yeah." His voice was harsh and unequivocal. "I'll be fine.''

"Good." Hazel said it lightly because what she heard in his tone told her he was dealing with more than just getting Emma back and protecting Sasha. Probably something to do with male ego and physical weakness. Probably something that would only embarrass him if she asked about it—if she could figure out what to ask, that is—so she didn't pursue that selection. Even though she might have preferred to. "Now about that other thing that scares you…''

"You?''

She nodded, afraid to know, needing to know.

"You. Hmm." All the harshness went out of him. He stooped and smudged the edge of his thumb along her cheek. "I'm not sure yet, Hazel. I just know you do. Let's leave it there for now, huh?''

Blood flushed fire through her veins, her breath jitterbugged in her lungs. "If it's going to get in the way, I don't know if I can—or should.''

He straightened to his full height to look down at her. "Try." It was less request than demand. "It'll get in the way less and be safer for both of us, I promise.''

"Do you?" she asked, wanting to believe him, but not sure she could.

"You don't believe me?''

She shook her head. "I don't know.''

A visible shudder went through him. "Then allow me to demonstrate," he said and, without warning, stuck his flashlight in her free hand, cupped her face between his palms and kissed her.

A roaring started in Hazel's ears almost at once. There was nothing "almost" about *this* kiss. It was long and deep, thorough and possessive, as demanding as it was giving. When his tongue touched her parted lips she didn't consider refusing him access—couldn't consider it, truth be known, because her ability to think was demolished. She opened and took him in, reveled in the taste and feel of him. When he slanted his head and slid a hand into her hair to anchor her closer, allowing his tongue to plunge deeper, she accepted him greedily. When his other hand curled around her waist and under her pack to haul her lower body against his, she stood on tiptoe and went, arching and stretching to meet him, not caring that the discrepancy in their height made it awkward. She didn't feel awkward, she felt alive, wanted.

She arched her pelvis to brush his fly. Not only that, but she wanted.

She *wanted*.

Him, now, here, instantly, without thought or caution. Just like that other guy with the rattlesnake tattoo....

Fire became ice in a heartbeat, desire changed to self-loathing and self-distrust, then to a struggle for freedom. She couldn't, she *couldn't*. Not again. Not ever. Not with anyone, and especially not with Guy Levoie.

No matter how his kiss made her feel.

Or maybe that was *because* of how his kiss made her feel.

The minute she pushed, he let her go and backed away from the burn that flushed his body, heated his blood.

"Now do you see?" he asked, breath rough.

Gasping, chest tight from a lack of oxygen, Hazel could

only recoil far enough to regain her balance, then she stepped in and slapped Guy's face hard.

"Don't you ever—"

"Don't ask me to explain things I can only demonstrate again and I won't," he shot back. *At least not until I've got the time to finish it and make it good for both of us,* he amended privately.

"As long as we're clear."

"As glass," Guy agreed tightly.

Then he bent to pick up the trail again and moved out apace.

It was a slow, painful process, one designed to stall Hazel's heart all too readily and frequently.

When she saw up close and personal how Guy performed his calling, she began to both understand and appreciate his reluctance to have her as a tagalong. He touched tracks and signs with delicate fingers that sent her exhausted imagination into overdrive over what else he might use those fingers on, got down beside them, studied them from ground level and measured them. When the last of the sun was gone, he turned entirely to the flashlight, showing her patiently how to get out in front of him, turn around and angle it just *so* while he sought the prints that would take them where they needed to go.

Nothing the army had taught her came close to the thoroughness and ease with which he read, separated and followed tracks. He moved swiftly even in the darkness and would have lost her on any number of occasions if he hadn't deliberately paced himself to let her keep up. That he was frustrated by the need to slow down for her was clear, no matter how hard he tried to hide it. He was good at his job, and she was in the way of him doing it right.

He was focused on the hunt, and she was a distraction to whom everything had to be explained.

A distraction whose nearness he needed to avoid.

In fact, once she saw what tracking with him involved, and if her grandparents and the Poleys hadn't confirmed that Emma was indeed the daughter she thought she'd lost, Hazel might have left Guy to work the trail on his own and in peace.

But Emma was Emily, and Hazel couldn't leave the chase even if it slowed him down. She had to be there. For the first time in Emma's life, she, Hazel, the woman who'd given birth to Emily Claire, had to be there.

Had to. Even if it meant staying near him, watching him, knowing now what he tasted like and how good he felt or could make her feel...

She breathed, forced her attention back to the matter at hand. No matter how bad an idea it might be to be alone with him, and no matter how big or how good he was, Guy would need backup when he caught up with Emma's kidnappers. *She* had to be that backup. Not one of his brothers, even though they had as much at stake in this as Guy did, and certainly not one of the other deputies or special agents who were available. As bad an idea as it was to be this personally involved in a case, she still couldn't bring herself to trust any of them as much as she trusted herself to care as passionately about the outcome of this search.

Hazel told herself those were the only reasons she followed Guy deeper into rattlesnake country with each passing hour. Assured herself that it had nothing to do with the man himself or her own growing, dry-mouthed attraction to him.

She also told herself that her willingness to follow him in spite of her nerves had everything to do with Guy's desire to take out the kidnappers before they named a time and place wherein he was supposed to hand over Sasha. That she only wanted to be there when he did it in order to keep Emma alive.

Tried to convince herself that it wasn't because she was afraid that Guy's top priority would be Sasha's safety over Emma's.

Just as she was afraid she might be willing to jeopardize everything for Emma.

And around, within and through it all, their awareness of each other grew and strained against the darkness, frightened her and made him wary. There were enough conflicting emotions involved in this case without adding some purely adult passions to the mix.

So they watched each other, talked as little as possible about anything except the events before them and let the pot of unwanted emotional madness Hazel thought she'd pulled neatly off the fire simmer and stew....

By false dawn Hazel was more cold, hungry, exhausted and squirrelly feeling than she'd ever felt in her life.

Between the sense of something she didn't want to meet lying unseen in the darkness, the fear of what might be happening to her daughter even now, and the all-too-real bulk of the man who hadn't kissed her nearly the way she'd unaccountably ached for him to and then *had,* every nerve and every nape hair she possessed was on end.

She knew she had to concentrate, but being up for better than twenty-four hours on a case she'd instinctively known better than to accept, old emotions and new desires she wasn't sure how to handle, *concentration* was one commodity she found herself fresh out of.

Helluva first date, she thought tiredly. *No dinner, no movie, no concert, no dessert.*

Something akin to hysterical laughter caught in her lungs

along with the bad pun. *Desert*, yes, but no *dessert*. Not of *any* kind: not to taste, touch, smell or even to lap off Guy's body.

Dumbstruck by the sudden and wholly uninvited urge to try something she'd never considered in her life, Hazel clambered to a halt on the side of a small gorge amid a slide of sand and rock, and scrubbed a hand across her face, horrified by the non sequitur. God, what was she thinking? She was out here looking for her daughter, her *kid*, for pity's sake, not a prelude to a possible one- or two-night stand—or even a month's worth of them. What was wrong with her? She was not a well woman, she was delirious, she had moon-stroke, she—

"Watch it, Youvella, there's cactus in there."

She started when Guy's big hand caught her elbow and held her upright when she would have sagged to the ground. Immediately that *sizzle* crackled between them, that thing like a live wire fallen on wet pavement: powerful, electrifying, deadly if left ungrounded and jumping about out of control. She heard his breath huff roughly from his lungs—or maybe that was hers. His grip on her elbow shifted so he supported her between his thumb and two fingers.

Even that small contact was too much.

Heat flared, wiping out the autumn night's chill. She felt him start to drop her arm and pull away, then stop as though moving away was as impossible as stepping closer had to be. There was something in his face, in his eyes—passion barely contained, desire as potent as lightning, hunger like a distant rumble underneath the surface.

There was also irritation, with himself, with her, it was impossible to tell. He might well be in the habit of falling in love easily, might indeed do so with her, but that didn't mean he wasn't used to choosing his own timing in that department—or that he chose to be all lovesick and can't-keep-his-hands-off about it.

She also instinctively knew he didn't plan to allow whatever falling in love meant to him to get in the way of finding Emma before Klimkov's men tried to contact them about Sasha again.

"You all right, Hazel?"

There was both real concern and a level of fine control in his voice. Textured nuances experience had taught her better than to trust because when it came to men-women-love-sex she couldn't trust herself to read them properly.

"Dandy." She shook her head slightly, trying to rattle her brain back into some semblance of order. "A little groggy. It's been a long day—*night,* I mean."

"You got that." The statement was dry; the hand around her elbow relaxed. The heat in his touch faded to something both less and more intimate that warmed and was warming. He guided her to a patch of ground protected by short scrub on a low bluff. "You gotta drop, drop here. Less thorny. Where's your Thermos?"

"Side pocket, I think." She gestured vaguely, hunching to ease her pack from stiff shoulders.

He squatted on his heels and dragged her backpack over to retrieve the Thermos of sweet black coffee she'd forgotten she carried. "Don't get too comfy. You'll stiffen up."

She draped her arms over her knees and glared at him. "Why in hell not?" Tension made her waspish. "We've been on this trail for hours, and if you ask me, all we're doing is going around in circles. I'd think we'd get farther if we got some rest and went on again by daylight."

"You want to do this or not?" Guy didn't sound too pleasant himself. "We gotta keep movin' if we're going to catch these guys anytime soon." He thrust the Thermos cup at her, careful not to graze her fingers when he did. "But, hey, you want, I'll leave you here and do this alone. Easier than feeling distracted by wanting to kiss or touch or *something* you every other step—especially when I barely know you well enough to understand you let alone like you without reservation yet."

"Like hell you'll go on without me," Hazel snapped, trying not to let her body hear his admission. It was less complicated to fight with him than it was to crave him or his lovemaking—or even just sex or a hot-and-sweaty encounter that might relieve the stress between them.

Might allow her to momentarily forget the simultaneous rediscovery and loss of the daughter she'd borne, her parents' and grandparents' betrayal, of being back on the rez…

Of wanting him to like her and not just understand her.

Of not being sure why she wanted him to understand her when she'd never looked for that commodity from anyone before.

Oh, hell, she didn't know what she craved—or why. Or maybe she didn't *want* to know what she craved.

What she needed.

Or why.

"You like having me around for the aggravation factor— you like to aggravate me." She would have preferred to be sure that her voice was steady; she wasn't. "Not to mention it would offend that damned guardian machismo thing you got goin' on too much, if you leave me here alone. God forbid you should think I can take care of myself."

"Can you?" The tone was a drawl, light and almost teasing over a layer of something taut and contained with effort. "I mean you gotta remember, Hazel, there're rattlesnakes out here, and they sure do like crawlin' in where it's warm. Me, they see my tattoo and know I'm brother to the snake. You, they don't know from Eve. So you wanna lay around out here alone in the cold in your sleeping bag, they'd like that, come along, slither in, snuggle up real close to you—''

"You bastard."

She shoved hard and he tumbled over the edge of the shallow bluff and into the wash beneath in a shower of coffee and sand. And lay there and laughed at her.

"Don't like snakes, huh?" he guessed.

"You absolute bastard," she repeated hotly.

For someone who'd just hiked for hours over rough terrain and bathed in coffee, he was a good deal too cheerful. "Not according to my parents."

"You—" Hazel made a sound of strangled fury. He would never be helpful, and she would never get in the last word; she knew it. "God bless it, if I thought it'd do any good, I'd stick my tongue out at you and bat you a good one 'round the ears, but you'd probably consider something like that foreplay."

Guy rolled to his feet and dusted himself off; his grin showed merciless and white in the beam of Hazel's flashlight. "Probably." He bent to retrieve the sandy Thermos, straightened as a thought struck him. His grin widened. "You'd stick your tongue out at me and bat me 'round the ears?"

"If I thought it would do any good," Hazel reminded him—tartly. Apparently, exhaustion, hours of familiarity and a nagging backache from carrying too much weight for too long had taken their toll on both her common sense and her professional demeanor.

He chuckled. "Drink up, babe, and let's make tracks. We got hours till full light, and they don't know we're night trackin' yet. Let's keep the jump."

She ignored the *babe* for the moment, promising herself he'd pay for it later. Right now there was a more important question to ask. "What do you mean, we've got hours till daylight? My whole body's killing me. We seriously can't rest awhile?"

He eyed her levelly. "I told you before. You know we can't. Right now we've got as much of a lead on 'em as we're going to get—you said it yourself. And the light's not much good when it's straight up. I want it between the tracks and me. Nope. We'll hole up before midmorning. Wait out the sun and the heat." He climbed the bit of hillock, sat beside her and nudged her gently with his mending shoulder. "C'mon, Hazel. It'll be safer for everyone if we keep moving—you, Sasha, Emma *and* me. You know as well as I do there's more out here than snakes want to crawl into your sleeping bag with you to warm up, and it's not the wildlife."

Hazel stared at him, left speechless once more by his frankness, wishing she'd had a course in comebacks for this sort of thing either at the academy or elsewhere in her life. "You, ah, you…"

"Yep." He put on a look of apology that had at its core a trace of sincerity that disarmed Hazel, when she didn't want to be. "That's me, but what are you gonna do? There's no place to run, and your back hurts." He settled his hands on her shoulders, found the top of her spine with his thumbs and leaned over to breathe in her ear. "Let me work the kinks out for you and let's beat feet, hey, darlin'?"

She knew she should move, pull away, be furious with him for taking liberties and calling her "babe" and "darlin'" or whatever other terms of *endearment* entered his head. Instead she sat still, dropped her head forward and groaned with pleasure. He had better hands than the professional masseuse she went to once or twice a week in Phoenix to relieve some of the stress of her job; seemed to know exactly where she hurt and what to do to ease the pain without putting her to sleep.

When he touched her, she didn't want to sleep.

He pushed his thumbs up the back of her neck and into her hair, scraped them down to the knob at the top of her spine and kneaded her shoulders, then made small circling motions down the center of her back with the pads of his thumbs. There was more than mere voltage in the undercurrent of the motion. There was magic, contentment, promise and something that smacked of everyday familiarity, reassurance and rightness—something it seemed she'd lived a lifetime without.

Something she had no right to experience now.

But she couldn't help herself. She let the tension ease and didn't hold back the appreciative ''Mmm'' that sighed out of her.

''Better?'' Guy asked.

''Mmm.'' She should make him stop, but couldn't muster the energy. ''Doesn't it bother your shoulder to do this?''

''Not enough to make me quit.'' His breath was a whisper on her neck, tickling beneath her shirt collar and into her hair. ''Sit forward.''

She did what he asked without question—and had the feeling that if he'd said, ''Now let's follow the garden path to hell,'' she'd have gone there, too, just for the feel of his hands on her.

''Tell me about her, Hazel.''

The request came out of nowhere, caused her to straighten and stiffen, raise her guard. ''What?''

''Emma.'' He worked his fingers over the muscles beneath each of her shoulder blades, stroked them up and down the sides of her back until she felt loose and boneless again. ''I told you about Sasha, it's your turn to tell me.''

"Emily Claire." Her response was fierce and so automatic it surprised her. "I named her Emily Claire."

"Okay." His voice was as soothing and compassionate as his hands. "Emily Claire. Tell me, Hazel."

"You saw the papers." She arched her neck in wordless request for him to turn his attention there. "There's not much more to say. I got pregnant. They couldn't convince me to give her up. They took her from me."

"How old were you?"

She made a sound somewhere between laughter and sorrow. "Sixteen and a bit. Old enough to want, but young enough to be stupid about getting. Mature enough to tell my parents I'd accept responsibility for my baby, but not enough to be able to tell them how I'd care for her or how I'd keep us both going. Immature enough to think love and determination would be enough."

"A scared kid at a vulnerable age," Guy said softly.

Hazel shut her eyes against the burn of unexpected emotion. Nobody that she could remember had ever taken her side so immediately and unequivocally—regardless of her age at the time. "Don't make excuses for me, Levoie. I've made too many for myself over the years."

He nudged her companionably. "Martyr?" he guessed, half laughing, half serious.

She shrugged. "Sometimes." Then, laughing ruefully when realization struck, "Okay, a lot." She grinned suddenly and chuckled. "But I didn't *like* it."

"I can understand that." Teasing. "Martyrdom has always struck me as a fairly painful way to live."

She looked over her shoulder at him. "How would you know? You don't strike me as the martyr type."

"I'm guilty of a lot of things, but not that." He pulled her back to lean against him, spoke into her hair. Too comfortable and warm to protest, Hazel forgot to object. Besides, if he was sidetracked, she could rest longer. "Jeth is. Three years ago our baby sister was kidnapped by some people who wanted him to back off a case he was working on. He didn't. She died before he could get to her."

"Oh, Guy, I'm sorry." Sympathy was quick and genuine, a heartbeat from total understanding. "God, so that's why..." She shuddered.

"Yeah." Guy nodded. "That's why this one's kinda personal to all of us. We didn't see Jeth again until he brought Sasha and Allyn home to protect them from the Russian mob and one of the Colombian cartels. Turned out his worst enemy that time, too, were the same people who took Marcy, and he worked for one of 'em."

"In the state prosecutor's office?"

His smile was wry. "See, I knew you pulled the file."

"I'm anal retentive, not stupid, Guy."

For a moment silence reigned. Then Guy buried his face in her neck and laughed hard.

"It wasn't that funny, Levoie," Hazel snapped, not sure she liked being the butt of her own jokes if this was the reaction she could expect.

"Yes, it was." He could barely speak. "Your file didn't say you had a sense of humor."

She stuck her nose in the air. "I don't."

"Sure," he agreed too readily, still chuckling. "Anything you say."

"Levoie..."

"'Guy,'" he said. "You don't call the guy you make your first joke to by his last name."

"Levoie," she repeated firmly. Then huffily, "And that wasn't my first joke."

"No?"

"No. I'm perfectly as capable of standing around the water cooler and forgetting the punchline as anyone."

He made a strangled sound. "Good. Glad to hear it."

She sighed, half wishing fury or something equally distancing would get her somewhere practical. Like through to him. "You bastard."

"Ah-ah." He pulled up her chin and dropped a quick kiss on her mouth. "We talked about that, remember?"

She viewed him, disgruntled by the heat he elicited from her so easily. She'd known him for one tense and trying *day,* for God's sake. Did he have no decorum, no sense of time—as in too short a—or timing whatever? "Yeah, but it still doesn't change my feelings about whether or not you might be the devil's spawn."

His chuckle was uncomplicated and infectious. He climbed to his feet, pulled her up after him. "Ah, you don't mean that."

"I do," she said flatly—but even she could hear the declaration lacked conviction.

"Nah."

"Yes."

He gave her a maddening grin. "Liar." Then, before she had a chance to even attempt getting the last word in, he picked up her flashlight and handed it to her. "Time's wastin', sweetheart. I'm readin' these signs right, they stopped here and started lookin' for something, a landmark maybe." He turned to head out. "Probably means we're not more'n an hour or so behind 'em."

She grabbed his arm and tried to swing him around. "We—what did you say?"

"We're an hour behind them, maybe a bit more." He glanced skyward, hesitated as though tasting the air. "Rain'll wash out sign in the next couple hours, we don't move now."

"Why didn't you tell me?"

"Had to be sure." He eyed her seriously. "And just because that's what I read here doesn't mean that when we get wherever *there* is Emma'll be there."

Chapter 7

By what should have been sunup they'd picked their way up the cliffs to the top of one of the rocky mesas that comprised the reservation. Here and there fractured and unoccupied stone buildings dotted the landscape, remains of a people from whom Hazel's ancestors were descended. In the distance Hazel saw what she thought might be caves or pueblo dwellings set into cliffs.

"Here." Guy crouched abruptly and held up a hand, fist closed in the signal for silence. When Hazel halted beside him, he pointed to tracks she could barely discern, then placed his mouth to her ear. "Somebody big left the vehicle with a load could be about Emma's weight and walked in. Truck took off west."

"Then we go in." Hazel's reaction was immediate.

Guy shook his head. "Not yet. First we call, see if we can raise backup, then we take turns resting and watching till it comes."

"What about the rain you said's coming?" Hazel felt

every bit as testy as she'd sounded. "We don't go on, we'll lose the trail. You said so yourself."

Guy measured her a look, clearly gauging the benefits of honesty versus something more calculated. Decided to stick with the candor that was his strength. "I planned to do some recon, but I can't do that safe for anybody if you tag. You willing to stay here while I go?"

Hazel's mouth thinned against the oath she didn't utter. How could he ask it of her? It was her baby out there....

She sucked a breath of prerain air that was soaked with the bitterness of history. No, not hers. Not anymore. Her *baby* had been taken from her. This was an eleven-year-old child who didn't know Hazel Youvella from the Hopis' first people, Sotuknang, Spider Woman or the twins—and never mind that Hazel should be shocked that she remembered the names from the creation myth. She didn't have time for memory-shock because this child...this...

Child!

This was a child she had never met, and might not get a chance to meet, if she didn't swallow her pride and trust Guy to do what he'd illustrated he really was the best at: scouting the trail to its conclusion without her.

"Oh, God." She blinked, worked her mouth, swallowed. Looked up at Guy and nodded once. Looked away. "Go."

"Hazel." He caught her chin, forced her face toward him. His eyes were dark and fierce, compassionate and understanding, more revealing than Hazel could bear. "If I find her and there's any way to bring her out with me, know I will."

Hazel pushed his hand away, eyed him with all the ferocity and passion of a nature she'd long denied. "As long as you know that if anything happens to her, the world won't be big enough to hide them—or you."

Guy's mouth tipped in a smile that was unnervingly affectionate and feral at once. His fingertips brushed her cheek. "Trust me," he suggested lightly. "I'm a lot smarter than I look."

Then he turned his back on her, radioed their location to Russ and made preparations to head out.

Waiting was definitely *not* her best thing. There was so little to do during a stakeout. Where boredom didn't lie there were only fearsome or inappropriate things to think about.

For the first time in her life, Hazel truly wished for boredom.

Blanket and arms wrapped tightly around herself to keep her from moving, pacing, prowling, calling attention to herself, Hazel crouched in the makeshift shelter-cum-cover they'd swiftly erected before Guy left and watched the rain drive in like a traveler from out of town. It announced itself in a roll of thunder, then, in the most stunning lightning display she'd ever seen, it crossed the land outstretched in front of her in a sheet of clouds she could literally see coming.

The fearsome things she had to think about were automatic, built from gruesome pictures she'd seen as the result of botched negotiation attempts in other kidnappings. The images were doubly horrifying when her brain refused to let the wound heal by continuously superimposing Emma's photo features over the faces of other victims, children or adults who didn't make it.

God, she couldn't think about that.

She *wouldn't*.

Scrabbling desperately for other places to send her thoughts, she tried to itemize her grocery list by what was in the aisles at her local market.

Efficiency, that was the key to mind control and distraction at this stage of the game.

Okay, so the store manager put things like milk, eggs and produce directly across from the cleaning supplies. In soups she'd pick up, well, soup. Across the aisle from the clam chowder she'd grab shampoo, conditioner, moisturizer, spermicide and condoms...

For some reason her mind stuck on the word, and something like anticipation pooled in her belly, jellied her limbs. It had been a long time since she'd had any use for spermicide and condoms. A long time since she'd allowed herself to make any warm, human connections at all, let alone one that would require forethought in order to bring about fore-*play*....

Her breath caught and moved shallowly in her lungs. She shut her eyes, unintentionally touched her tongue to her lips. Something liquid pooled through her belly to her lower body, settled heavily and with unmistakable hunger in that cleft below her mound.

And that, of course, was when her thoughts became completely inappropriate, but engrossing, strayed thoroughly out of the realm of practicality and shoved out the ruminations that terrified her.

That was when she realized she was suddenly itching and fidgeting, trying to pull her bra around to a more comfortable position.

That was when she noticed that every move she made abraded the seamless satiny thing over her nipples causing them to stiffen the way Guy's callused fingertips would do if he touched them—or came anywhere near them.

Guiltily she forced herself to quit yanking on the offending underwires and started to wish she could go without the restrictive harness altogether but didn't dare, because women who were as well endowed as she was tended to flop about at the most inopportune times and in the most uncomfortable ways. And that was not to mention the open invitation to early stretch marks doing so would issue.

Fuming, she tucked a hand into her shirt to hike each breast more firmly into its D-cup. A picture of Guy sizing her up appreciatively the previous morning came to mind, and the same unwelcome burn that had flared then flashed through her now. A mewl of frustrated appreciation escaped her. His hands were big enough to support her weight, to contain it without restricting her at all.

On a sigh she surrendered the battle and gave in to temptation, shut her eyes and let imagination touch all those places she knew she could not let Guy himself physically touch. As she knew from experience, fantasy was not only the safest, but also—sometimes—the best sex of all. No pregnancy resulted from it, no disappointments, no disastrous breakups, and no distractions on the job due to a relationship that was going either too well or too badly.

Shutting her eyes to block out everything but sensation, she arched into the daydream and *felt* Guy kneeling at her back, reaching around to unbutton her blouse.

Sliding her bra straps down her arms with the lightest of touches, tracing the same path, neck to elbow and back with his lips, his mouth.

His tongue.

She caught her breath at the very real sensation fantasy caused when her nipples tightened again. The desire to lose herself, to cast away care allowed her to let herself feel his kiss on her neck in a dry, shiver-inducing tickle; memory gave her the taste of his mouth on hers, the heat of his arousal—and her undeniable belly-tumbled, take-me-now response to it.

Her lower body quickened.

Oh, sweet mother...

Breathing hard, Hazel ran her tongue around her mouth and opened her eyes. Gad, she shouldn't do this. Fantasy was for home alone in her bathtub with scented candles and no case to pay attention to, nobody's life on the line. It was not for here in the desert—even if she did need to keep her mind occupied so fear wouldn't get the best of—

"Hazel."

Caught off guard and too close to the edge, Hazel gasped and reached for the shotgun lying beside her. Guy stayed her hand before she came anywhere near it.

"It's me." He touched the hand still caught in her blouse. "What are you doing?"

She flushed. He mustn't know the truth. Ever.

Which of course meant that she said the first ill-advised thing that came into her head. "I've been alone in the rain for hours. I got bored."

"Got—" For an instant he stared at her in amazement, then he threw back his head and laughed. Hard. "This is what you do when you're bored?" he asked when he could speak. "By all means don't let me interrupt, but I wouldn't mind watching if you're not finished."

Brow creased she stared blankly at him. "What do you— what are you—" Comprehension dawned suddenly. Her face and neck turned crimson. He thought she.... "You unbelievable, unmitigated..." Words failed—a not uncommon occurrence around him she'd found. "I can't believe you. You...auugh! You have the filthiest mind—"

"Nothing filthy about it far as I'm concerned," Guy assured her, grinning. "Healthy is more like it. And distracting. You, that is, and the pictures I can form."

"Don't you *dare*."

"Mm-mm-mm," he muttered, nodding. "Yep, ve-ery nice. Only thing better would be if that were *my* hand..."

"Oh, for heaven's sake." Hazel yanked her hand out of

her bra and considered slapping him with it. Decided against the physical contact that was sure to harm her more than him. "If you must know, I'm just arranging myself more comfortably. Not that it's any of your business. Forty hours in the same harness is about twenty-two hours too long."

"Don't wear it on my account."

She glared at him. "Yeah, right. Under these conditions, going without is worse than wearing one too long."

"Ah." He nodded in apparent understanding. "So, can I help fix it?"

Yes. "No."

He sighed regretfully. "Too bad. I'm really good at fitting bras, you know."

"I'm sure you are, Investigator Levoie." The recognition that he was probably even more adept than he said because he'd had a great deal of practice dressing—or rather *undressing*—a whole lot of willing women stung. "But you're not here to fit my lingerie—or even discuss it. You're here to tell me what you found." She tried to keep her voice prim and businesslike, distant. But anxiety beat out the sudden spurt of unaccustomed—and untoward—jealousy. "Was she there? Where did they take her? How—"

Guy let the more interesting discussion go with regret. *Later,* he promised himself. *When Emma and Sasha are safe.* "I traced them to a…well, it's a home ruin in one of the old pueblos. She's not there, no one is, but I found where they stopped. Come on." He slicked rain out of his hair, and for the first time Hazel noticed he was soaked. The rain looked good on him, would lend images to her fantasy if she ever had time to indulge in one again— which, of course, she did not intend to do. "We've got to get out of here, make higher ground. Wash's flooding."

"Flooding?" A sense of panic flitted through her. She'd

grown up in Los Angeles, she knew how to swim, but the thought of water closing over her head petrified her. Something to do with getting stuck headfirst near a swimming pool suction cleaner when she was five and being unable to right herself. She batted panic away. "What about Emma? We can't leave her now, we've got to keep going. If it's flooding, we have to find—"

"Not now, Hazel. We can't." He ignored the desire to comfort her physically, instead pulled her out from beneath the tarp shelter and handed her backpack to her, reached back for the shotgun.

"Guy—"

He looked at her through the downpour. Lifted a hand to wipe rain out of her face. Smiled slightly at her. "Don't worry, darlin'. We can't do anything in this stuff means they can't, either. Radios'll likely be out because of the weather and so will the cells. Phones and electric go out around here all the time. Means they got an agenda they can't follow until they can make contact again. Won't do 'em any good to hurt her, they won't have anything to bargain with if they do. Besides, it's not what they're bein' paid for."

She wanted to believe him. Badly. "You sure?"

No. Uncertainty didn't touch his voice. For reasons he preferred not to pursue, it meant a lot to him to offer this woman reassurance, to ease the fearsome burden she would have carried alone if he'd let her. He was big enough to shoulder it for both of them, and it was about time his size was good for something—besides, he reflected with rolled-eye self-awareness, doing the tall, dark, handsome and charming bit.

"Trust me." He caught Hazel's hand and headed uphill. "Now come on, shorty, before I gotta play Saint Christopher and put you on my shoulders and carry you."

* * *

Emma had not been held in one of the ancient Pueblo homes the way Hazel had assumed. Instead Guy hauled her through the rain to climb down into an ancient kiva, or large, underground chamber used by Pueblo men for secret ceremonies. It had a fire pit and an opening in the floor to represent the entrance to the lower world, the place through which life emerged into this world.

Hazel recognized the place instantly, though she'd never been inside a kiva before. On her single visit to the reservation, her grandfather had refused to allow her to even peek into one of the more modern, above-ground structures that had to be entered by means of a ladder and a hole in the roof. Men and women, he'd insisted, played separate roles in Hopi culture and he could not, would not, subsume that even to satisfy her white-man curiosity.

She remembered wanting to tell him defiantly that if he really wanted her to become more Hopi in her ways and her beliefs, he would satisfy her inquisitiveness, show her *why* men and women must be different. That he would let her look and discover for herself that she was missing nothing, at least on the surface; women didn't need to be constantly reminded of how man's birth came about by emulating the ritual. By virtue of their gender they were able to live what men could not.

As she had lived through the pain and the euphoria of birth with Emma.

Firmly she yanked her unruly mind back to the moment and looked around. The ruined cavern was situated high atop the mesa where floodwaters wouldn't reach; the firepit in its center showed signs of recent use. An empty can with relatively fresh spaghetti residue and some crumpled candy wrappers only served to confirm that evidence. Hazel even thought she recognized the wall against which Emma had been placed for the picture they'd received.

She touched the wall with her fingertips, trying to feel the child's presence, succeeded only in terrifying herself when the beam of her flashlight picked out a tiny patch of dried blood and some long black hairs that might have come from Emma's braid.

Side of her hand to her mouth to hold in the keening whimper that threatened, she shrank away from the wall. Guy assessed the situation with a glance, reached out to gather her close, press her face into his shoulder. She fought him wildly, determined not to need him or anyone regardless of the circumstances, determined to take care of herself—before she twisted her fingers hard into his shirtfront and sank into the cradle of security he created for her.

"I don't think it's hers," he reassured her as gently as his own desire to believe it allowed. "Whoever cut her hair used a knife and probably nicked himself in the process."

"Or her."

Trembling, Hazel pushed away from him, morbidly fascinated by the tiny blood-scrape on the wall. If they'd hurt Emily—*Emma*—with an effort she made herself call her daughter by the name someone else had given her, hoping it might help her maintain a more professional distance—it didn't matter how little, how insignificant the injury, payback would be unrelenting. She, who'd only ever found herself able to identify with the Warrior Woman kachina, would see to it personally.

The moment Emily Claire was safe.

Taking strength from the vow, she scrubbed the back of one wrist beneath her nose and collected her wits, deliberately ignoring the ignominious tear tracks staining her cheeks. If she pretended they weren't there, perhaps in this dim light Guy wouldn't see them—or maybe he'd only mistake them for rain.

But of course Guy saw them. He couldn't help it—didn't want to. He may have already been soaked to the skin, but he knew Hazel now—better than either of them might have wished. Where the rain had been cold, her tears were warm against his skin, made her eyes shimmer and swim in the lantern light. He reached out to cup her cheek, scraped away the evidence of rain and emotion with the pad of his thumb. Touched her mouth gently when he felt her jaw stiffen to hold the renewed quiver of her chin at bay.

Withdrew his hand and turned his back to give her a moment's privacy when she blinked and swallowed hard, determined not to give way again.

"I'll start a fire," he said, and stooped to the task.

She wrapped her arms about herself, accepting comfort from the only source she could bring herself to allow. "That would be good." The tremor in her voice had nothing to do with the chilled chatter of her teeth.

"You should strip, get into something dry."

"What about you?"

"I won't look, I promise." Humor tinged his tone.

She gave him an exasperated if slightly snuffle-dampened snort. "I meant you're wet, too."

Laughing, he tilted his head and glanced up at her from underneath his eyelashes. "Is that your way of telling me you care?"

There was nothing either snuffly or ladylike about her snort this time. "That means you'd be of absolutely no use to me if you caught your death of pneumonia because you didn't put on dry clothes."

He grinned and placed a hand to his heart. "Ah, I do love a practical woman."

"If your reputation is to be believed, you love *all* women," she retorted.

"Wrong," he corrected. "I do love women, and yes, I fall in love with them easily. But I only love them one at a time, and that one I love completely until she decides it's time to move on. That's the only way it's fair to either of us."

"It's fair to *you* when *she* decides it's time to move on?" She was curious in spite of herself.

"Yeah." He shrugged one shoulder and nodded. "I believe in monogamy, but I don't believe I'll die if I lose the object of my affections. I know I'll live no matter how much it hurts at the time. I know it's possible to give your heart more than once. And I don't believe it's healthy to pin your entire life on one person. Love is like life. If you're going to have one, you grieve when it's time to and move on."

"You're a reckless man, Guy Levoie." There was both awe and wariness in the statement. "Didn't anyone ever teach you gambling's the devil's pathway?"

"Horse races, games, love, the Pai like to gamble. And I only risk what I've learned is worth losing," he said. Then he turned and cupped his hands, blew gently to ignite the spark he'd lit in the firepit.

For reasons she didn't care to examine, Hazel felt that same spark come alight and curl inside her. She watched his back, studied the play of muscles molded to his wet shirt. His back was wide at the shoulders, tapered only enough through the waist and hips that he didn't appear too lean—decidedly man rather than boy. She recognized the power in those bands of steel as well as the strength that lay deep beneath them that was his core. She could lose everything she valued if she spent much more time around this man. Lord, all she had to do was look at how he'd already managed to trample her defenses.

She swallowed and tried to shift her gaze elsewhere, tried to pretend that she was really in charge here—and wished she were as strong as she pretended to be.

When the fire was going to Guy's satisfaction, he looked up at her again. His eyes were so somber and soft with promise that Hazel's breath caught.

"One man, one woman for eternity and beyond can be a very lonely place, Hazel. I don't know who hurt you so badly you think you can't have something I can see in your eyes you want, but you let me in and I won't hurt you. Ever. You can trust me with anything you care to share with me. Your worries, your body, your heart, your love. You call the shots. All of them. And if it comes to the point you need to run away, I won't like it, I won't want you to go, but I'm hardy stock. I'll survive. I'll bloom again."

"But I might not." The admission surprised her; she hadn't intended to say anything. What was it about him that made her not only want to spill her cares all over him but capable of it? "If I let you—let any man—in, I might forget who I am, might lose myself in...in— God, I don't even *know* what in. I just know that whatever *it* is, it happened once. I stopped trusting myself then. I barely trust myself with...you, with *them*...now. I can't—I *won't*—destroy my self-respect again."

She looked him in the eye. "No matter who I might want or what promises he makes or how much I think I can believe him."

"Fair enough." The corner of Guy's mouth tipped in that lazy grin Hazel found both charming and alarming. "Just so you know, though, I'm going to take that last as both a compliment and an admission. I'm going to do everything I can to weaken your defenses while I shore up your ability to trust not only yourself but me.''

Hazel gaped at him dumbfounded. What did one say to a man—to *anyone*—who made such a bold statement, and *meant* it?

Oh, probably nothing. That had to be best. After all, if she didn't give him another opening, perhaps he wouldn't create one for himself.

Yeah, right. And heat didn't rise, either.

Especially the way it was rising through her belly, chest, throat and cheeks right now. All he'd need to do was look at her to see...

A rustling from the direction of the hole in the floor made her start and drop her flashlight. A long slender shape slid through the arc of light created on the floor and disappeared into the hole. Before she could stop herself, Hazel shrieked and leaped at Guy, doing her best to climb him. Instinctively he wrapped his left arm about her waist and held her up off her feet when she would have slipped. His right hand went unthinkingly to the knife on his belt and he whipped around in a quick circle looking for the threat.

''What is it?''

Dignity destroyed but beyond caring, Hazel wrapped viselike arms about his neck and hung on, pressing herself as close to Guy and his brother-to-the-snake tattoo as she could get.

''In the hole.'' She barely got the words out, her throat was so tight with panic. ''Snakes.'' She clutched him tighter. ''*Snakes.*''

Though all the tension went out of Guy on the word, he didn't loosen his grip on her. ''Is that all.'' He returned his knife to its sheath and picked up the torch she'd dropped, flashed the beam into the hole. Sure enough, the light picked up the disappearing tails of several reptiles—none of which, so far as he could tell, bore rattles.

At least, that's what he planned to tell Hazel. She was strung-out enough without him adding fuel to her panic.

He moved them away from the hole and attempted to set her on her feet. She simply hitched herself higher against him and wrapped her legs around his waist—which might have been gratifying under other circumstances. Now all it did was to make his nether regions tighten and put his brain on overtime trying to ignore the possibilities of the situation and the advantages a lesser man might take due to Hazel's fear.

He assured himself that regardless of how much he might want to take advantage of the situation, he was definitely *not* a lesser man.

Blast it.

He tucked the flashlight into a hip pocket and ran his right hand up and down Hazel's back in soothing circles. "Shh. It's all right, it's all right. Nothin' down there worth gettin' all het up over. They don't want to get any nearer to you than you want to get to them."

"I hate snakes," Hazel said unnecessarily.

"I know."

She clutched him tighter. "People who aren't afraid of them fascinate me."

"Yes." Guy traced her back, reassuringly.

"That's how I got pregnant with Emily." Her trembling increased instead of lessening. "That damned snake dancer and his tattoo."

He'd known the tattoo meant something hard and unforgiving to her. "It's okay, Hazel. I'm here. They can't hurt you, not the snakes and not the dancer. I've got you."

"You won't put me down?"

"No."

"Because I really hate snakes."

"Shh." If she hadn't been so terrified, Guy might have found the situation funny. According to her she didn't like him much, either, but he was, apparently, at least preferable to his skin-shedding brothers. He suppressed a smile. Darn good thing he didn't have ego problems or he might have been maimed for life. He stroked Hazel's hair. "Still, they've got to live somewhere and they keep down the rodent population, and as long as you don't tease 'em or step on 'em, they're not going to mess with you."

He knelt carefully, then eased down so he could sit with Hazel in his lap. Her breathing quickened with distress; clearly she wasn't happy about being moved closer to the source of her terror, but he'd held her off the ground long enough now that it was either sit down or fall down. She might be short, but her luscious little body packed muscle weight underneath its curves, and his shoulder ached beneath the strain of her immediate fears—and his own wide-ranging ones.

He could get lost here in the feel of her, could forget himself and everything he was out here to do in his need to distract her, to hold her—

She wriggled in his lap, and without warning his body went tight with demand.

—in the sudden and blazing desire to shift her underneath him, strip her of her wet things, bury himself within her and warm her from the inside out.

He clamped a tight and furious fist down on his craving for her. If she was frightened now, only think what would happen if he did what he wanted to.

"Hazel," he warned hoarsely, "quit wiggling."

"I—" He felt her give her head a negative shake against his shoulder and tighten her grip on him. "I can't. I need…'' Her muscles trembled, and she attempted to flatten herself more snugly to him. "Closer, Guy. Please."

"Hazel." The ache in his heart and in his loins was excruciating. He tried to put both emotional and physical distance between them. "No. You don't—"

"Yes, I do." She lifted her head, pulled back far enough to look at him in the firelight. Her features were stark, her eyes so wide they were mostly whites. "I *do*."

"No. You're just afraid of—" Her breath feathered across his neck, murmured over his ear and he groaned. "You're just less afraid of me than—" He swallowed hard when she pressed her breasts to his chest and rubbed. Her nipples were peaked, tempting. He tried to thrust her away. "I won't take advantage." He was desperate to take advantage. "You can't know what you're do—"

"But I do, Guy, I *know*. I want—I *need*…please. Please." She hooked her ankles behind his back and undulated against his erection. "Make me forget. Just for a minute. Please. Take this place away."

"Hazel." The protest was weak, his resolve nearly destroyed. "You're exhausted. You don't—not here, not like this."

"Shut up, Guy, I'm not a little girl anymore," Hazel whispered—and settled her mouth on his.

Chapter 8

Reaction was intense and abrupt. Her tongue chafed his lips, and he opened for her, drew it in; groaned when it danced lightly over his teeth, teased the roof of his mouth, the inside of his upper lip.

Went wild when she sucked the sensitive divot created by the center of his upper lip into her mouth, worrying it and mimicking the action she might take on another portion of his anatomy.

Even then he tried to hold back, to push her away—to tell her in so many words, "Hazel, I don't think—"

She only twisted her hands in his hair, pressed against him and ordered between kisses designed to drag him to perdition under the guise of taking him to heaven, *"Don't think."*

Then she slid her hand down between their bodies and tugged his shirt up far enough for her to flatten her hand on his belly and work it into his waistband.

Rational thought abandoned Guy, replaced by the

vaguely uneasy knowledge that something about this was wrong, that regret and not closeness or intimacy would be the result of this liaison. That he did not indulge in quick, loose sexual relationships with any woman, but particularly not with this one—ever.

Then Hazel slipped down his lap and undid his fly, freed him and palmed his manhood, circled it with her fingers, bent and licked the tip.

Uneasiness fled in the face of instant carnal shock and hunger.

"No."

He gasped and his body bowed upward, hands grasped her head, fingers flexed with the strain of forcing himself to pull her upward rather than allowing her to follow her own ends the way his body wanted to let her. Later regrets or no, he would not let this become an impersonal sexual encounter designed to momentarily alleviate her fears. If this would happen here and now—happen anywhere at all and thoughtless or not—it would be lovemaking not sex.

He'd make sure of that.

"No," he repeated savagely, and hauled her up to seal her rapacious mouth with his.

She'd begun this business, but he took Hazel by surprise nevertheless. On the rare occasions when she allowed herself to seek physical release with a man, she controlled the choice, selected the recipient, managed the course of the encounter and the outcome. But not this time. The moment Guy's hand wrapped the back of her neck and his tongue surged into her mouth, she knew she'd somehow miscalculated something—but couldn't for the life of her think what.

His heat melted her bones, destroyed her control, shook her to the core even as she heard herself whimpering and mewling encouragement to him, found herself arching into the palm he scraped first across one uncomfortably bound breast then the other. She would pay hell in guilt later, but not now.

Not now.

"Please," she moaned into his mouth, trying to lift herself high enough to get his hand underneath her shirt at the same time that she squirmed and twisted trying to reach around to release the catch on her bra. "Please."

In response he slid his hand from her neck down her back, shoved her fingers out of the way and with a quick bunching of his fist gathered up the fabric of her shirt and her bra clasp; when he released his fist a second later, her bra was undone.

Freedom. Hazel caught her breath with the taste of it, with the feel of Guy's tongue licking fire along her throat to her ear then down into the valley between her breasts and her bra. Her thighs spread across his lap, and she pushed him back so he was angled against the kiva's wall. She arched and rotated her belly against his while she wrenched free her shirt buttons.

Or tried to.

Quit when Guy dragged her up tight against him and fastened his mouth to a breast and suckled hard before he abraded its nipple with his tongue. His free hand made short work of the fastenings of her jeans.

"Is this what you want, Hazel?"

There was something in his voice, something ugly and furious with self-loathing that some part of her knew she should heed. But the part of her that was engaged here now was stronger, more demanding, bent on heeding nothing but this urgent, primal need her body had to join with his.

"Yes." Breath was a rash sob catching in her throat. She laced her fingers in his hair to bring his mouth back to her. "*Yes.*"

He was damned. Guy understood that, understood the consequences and couldn't stop, anyway. Couldn't tear his Billy-be-damned, passion-engorged body from hers.

Couldn't shove her away.

Couldn't deny and therefore embarrass her.

Couldn't *not* take what she was bent on thrusting on him.

The pleasure, the pain.

The gut-wrenching torture that came from knowing Hazel Youvella was far more willing and *able* to give him—perhaps any man—her body than she was to relinquish her heart.

Anger burned at the back of his mind, a few hot coals that would make tinder of his emotions later after…he and Hazel took each other. But that would be then. Now was now and her cravings were his. Her needs, her desires throbbed within his own pulse, pooled with ever more stunning and painful alacrity in his groin. There was only one route through the ravening haze that threatened to engulf and destroy them both.

Wiping out any last vestiges of thought, Guy wrapped one arm under Hazel's bottom, planted his other hand on the hard-pack and surged to his feet. The ladder they'd used to climb down into the kiva beckoned, a means to keep her back off the floor and away from things that slithered and scared her. He crossed to it, planted her firmly against it.

"Hold on."

Hazel cast one glazed glance over her shoulder, then did as he instructed, reaching up to grasp an overhead rung. Her body arched, lifting and straining upward, outward, offering him a wholly erotic presentation of her breasts and belly that he could not ignore. Before she realized what he was doing, he'd hooked her feet around the ladder and shoved her blouse and bra out of his way. For a moment he didn't move, only gazed at her, his breath hot, moist and quick on her skin.

Hazel moved restlessly, hating the weight of his stare at the same time that she found herself almost unbearably aroused by it. Never in her life had she been so physically exposed to a man—to anyone. Her chest rose and fell, breath as serrated as the staccato beat of her pulse. Her underwear grew wet in a sudden flood of readiness. She saw Guy's nostrils flare, watched him touch his tongue to his lips as though tasting her scent.

Anticipation was excruciating, unnerving, a spring tightening low in her belly, awaiting only a single touch to set it loose. An unbidden plea, really only a soft mewl of sound, found its way out of her throat. She tightened her grip on the ladder rung and raised herself a bit, offering, begging.

He took her then with a low growl and no other warning. His mouth claimed a breast and she cried out with pleasure and relief, pushing her belly into his hands when he undid the fastenings of her jeans and jerked them and her underwear over her hips and down her legs to her ankles. She tried to kick off her boots so she could completely rid herself of the pants, but he was too impatient for that. Instead he gripped her behind her knees and raised her so that her feet were once again caught in a ladder rung, but high enough now so that he could spread her knees and thighs wide and step between them. And then he speared himself high and hard and fast inside her.

Sensation was immediate, electric. Hazel screamed and bowed into him, her body jerking and spasming with a pleasure that was different from anything she'd ever known. Even as she felt him draw back to reenter her, her insides clutched for him. Heat spread. She tried to hold on to it, to prolong the moment, the oblivion, by closing her eyes and tensing all of her muscles.

By concentrating all of her will on the slick motion of their bodies together, on the rain that splattered through the hole in the ceiling and only added to the titillation, the exquisite sensory torture.

But Guy wouldn't have it. "Open your eyes," he ordered. When she didn't comply immediately, he caught her chin between his thumb and forefinger, forcing her heavy-lidded attention. "We're going to do this, you're going to look at me while it happens, Hazel."

"No, Guy, I can't. You don't understand. I don't—I never—"

That was as far as she got before he reached between their bodies and touched her. Hazel's eyes widened and she gasped when that smallest but most intimate of caresses brought her catapulting to the most shattering climax of her life. The entire time she pulsed around him, Guy didn't take his eyes off her face. And when he felt her go slack, he continued to stare up at her and hold her gaze while he withdrew and settled himself swiftly into the sweat-slick crease between her left hip and her thigh. Then he pumped two, three, four times before draining his seed into the subterranean ceremonial room's baked earth.

Only when he'd finished did he finally allow himself to look away from her. Then he dropped his head to her chest and stood for a long moment holding on to her and breathing raggedly. Drawn by something more than the moment, Hazel let go of the ladder rung and let her hand drift down through his hair to graze the side of his face.

Just that fast, things went wrong.

Giving vent to a profanity he never used, Guy jerked away from her hand. "Don't."

"What?" Stunned and off balanced, Hazel tried to right

herself against his shoulder. This was not the sort of reaction she'd expected after making love with Guy. "What?"

"Don't," he repeated angrily, and lifted her quickly off the ladder to set her on her feet well away from him. "Don't touch me. I'll care about you, but I won't whore for you, so don't *ever* try to use me like this again." He raised a hand as though he'd use a gesture to make a point, then fisted the thought and shook his head sadly. "Just…don't."

Then, before she could react, he righted his clothing and hauled himself up the ladder and out into the rain.

For long minutes Hazel stared after him stunned—flustered—and finally angry. Who the hell did he think he was, God's gift? And, what did he think, that she'd *used* him? For sex? Where had he come up with that? How could he possibly imagine that she would ever…? Because no matter how long a time between lovers, nor how lonely and restless she became, she didn't do that. She wouldn't. She hadn't. Not ever. Not just for throwaway and certainly never lightly.

Had she?

With misgiving and the first smattering of doubt, she looked down at herself, at the jeans and underwear still riding her ankles, the shirt and bra crushed above her breasts…

And knew she had. Knew she did. Understood for the first time in her life that short and sweet was the only way she ever engaged in a sexual relationship. Use them and run before they ran from her because she wasn't worth hanging around for.

Because she didn't trust them to find anything in her worth hanging around for.

So she met men on their own terms, competed with them

in the boudoir the same way she did on the job. Made sure she was the one who made the rules, the one who left first.

Oh, God.

She caught sight of the ladder and covered her face with her hands, letting all the shame she'd tried so long to keep buried rise up and nearly drown her. Dear God, she was no better than the shallow, hypocritical men she despised.

Who had she let herself become?

Thirty feet from the kiva, Guy sat on a rock and let himself brood. He felt dirty and he didn't like it.

He did not do casual sex, had never done casual sex, was furious with himself for getting caught up in it here. Sex, as he'd learned at twenty-one when he'd finally decided to lose his cherry with a woman he'd wanted to marry, changed everything. His situation with Hazel was difficult enough without the awkwardness that was sure to follow what had just occurred between them.

He'd wanted her, that was a given. He just hadn't wanted things to happen this way, before they at least had some sort of friendship to hang a physical relationship on. And he definitely hadn't wanted anything physical between them to jeopardize this investigation. Which it was sure to do, if his observation of other casual law enforcement relationships could be trusted.

He was pretty sure it could. There was a reason law enforcement relationships suffered almost as high a mortality rate as relationships between hospital personnel. Job stress was only a portion of the equation. The other issue had to be one of trust. A new relationship of any sort just didn't have that at the beginning. Heck, she wasn't even sure she could trust him to try to protect Emma equally with Sasha. He didn't know the reverse about her. To add the insecurity of ''just sex'' on top of it after they'd known each other for forty-eight hours…well, that was just stupid. He and Hazel had to be able to trust each other to do their respective jobs, not go around worrying about each other's feelings of the moment.

Or trying to figure out the next available opportunity to get into each other's pants.

He sighed and squeezed his forehead between thumb and forefinger, trying to pressure out a sudden headache. Not for the first time he wondered if maybe there was some Comanche mixed in somewhere with his mother's Pai, Kaibab and Southern Ute ancestries.

Though the Havasupai themselves had been wont to practice a sort of serial monogamy where divorces were as easy to come by as marriages, the Comanche, he'd once been told, sometimes had this *thing* where women were concerned. Before the government and the tribe's changing needs had put a stop to the practice, the men often took wives, plural, and managed to fight with and love every single one.

Well, he certainly had his own *thing* for women, that was sure, had managed to find more than one in the past eight years with whom he'd been certain he could happily settle down.

But, as he'd told Hazel, he'd been wrong every time— or at least that's the way the women saw it. He'd never been sure before—at least, not the way he was sure now. Being inside Hazel had been a heaven he'd never imagined.

It had also been on a par with the deepest pits of hell, from which he doubted he'd soon be able to extricate himself.

Even as he'd reviled himself for taking advantage of the situation, he'd found himself desperate for Hazel. He'd lost control of himself when he'd had no intention of doing so. That had never happened before. And the hell of it was he wasn't sure he could prevent it from happening again. Not when so much of him screamed that this time, this woman and her scarred soul was right for him.

Would always be right for him, belong with him, no matter how short a time he'd known her or how often he knew she'd make denials to the contrary.

And no matter that he also knew it could never be his responsibility to help her reclaim the soul she thought she'd lost, the trust she wouldn't place in herself.

Acknowledged with only a minor amount of resignation that he intended to do his level best to make sure she reclaimed the lost pieces of herself, anyway. That she learned to trust herself and, with luck, maybe him, too.

Regardless of what the journey might do to him or where it might take him.

As he'd told her, he would recover, he always did. Because he was fortunate enough to understand something she had never learned: you couldn't hate yourself and be happy, couldn't distrust yourself and grow as a person. If you tried, if you didn't learn from your history and then let it go, you were doomed to an eternity of failure and loneliness. And that was something he knew he couldn't bear to see happen to Hazel.

But he still shouldn't have let his libido run away with him just because she'd needed a moment of escape that they would both regret.

That he already regretted.

He tilted his face skyward, wishing the rain could cleanse him while it made mud of his surroundings. Hazel had to know she was worth more than a single sexual encounter with a man—any man, but especially him—she barely knew.

But maybe she didn't. Maybe she couldn't or maybe she

didn't want to. And now he'd just gone and perpetuated all the male stereotypes he hated—

"Guy?"

He grimaced at the sound of his name, but forced himself to look at her. She stood before him in a shapeless dark poncho that would have been a blessing if his merciless imagination didn't know exactly what lay beneath it—

And sought at once to torture him with the knowledge.

He looked away, willing his body not to feel the renewed sting of desire.

Not to remember what it felt like to be inside her.

"You always rush the gate like that when you're scared, Youvella?"

It wasn't a kind question, but it was the best he could do to help maintain his distance and equilibrium under the circumstances.

"Not quite like that, no." It surprised Hazel to discover she could speak about what had happened calmly, let alone that she could dredge up some sort of wry humor about it. "But then, I don't usually work where there's anything other than human snakes, either." The quip was feeble and she knew it. When he didn't respond, she made an awkward gesture toward the kiva. "Come in out of the rain, Guy. You won't do Emily or Sasha any good if you catch pneumonia."

He snorted. "Sitting in the rain won't give me the sniffles, let along pneumonia. Abrupt changes in temperature might do the trick, but not this rain."

"Fine, blockhead," Hazel retorted, "then at least come in out of the lightning. You're too tall to be out here. With my luck a bolt'll hit your zipper and I'll be stuck with the snakes on my own."

He turned his head, stared at her a long moment before

emitting a snort of dark, incredulous laughter. "Does anything affect you, lady?"

"You already know damned good and well that a lot of things affect me."

Hazel knew this was not the time to bandy words or wallow in her embarrassment. This was the time to face down who she'd allowed herself to become—and get over it or, at the bare minimum, bull her way through it as best she could.

At least for the moment.

"Being on the reservation affects me. That tattoo on your arm affects me. Seeing my grandparents, the details of this case, finding out about Emma—*Emily,* damn it! This whole thing freaking *affects* me."

She drew a steadying breath, tried to continue more calmly. "Knowing that we've been set up to get us on this thing together, that we're both being blackmailed with someone else's life for reasons I can't fathom, that the ransom for my daughter is to somehow bring myself to exchange her for a two-year-old baby… God, all of it gets to me. You've seen how much—how badly I've handled it. You *know* it. You have to."

She stopped, made an inadequate gesture. Crossed to stand squarely in front of him, capture his face between her palms. "But what's gotten to me most on this case is you."

"Yeah, I know, you're fascinated by my tattoo because you had your virginity stolen by some immature fool with one like it and you haven't trusted yourself with men since." Guy tried to jerk away from her, found he couldn't. Found himself trapped in her eyes, held fast by the depth of an emotion she wasn't accustomed to showing—or was even aware she had. "Well, that happened what, at least eleven years and nine months ago now, Hazel. Get over it."

"Damn you." She took her hands off his face, held them in front of her as fists for an instant as though she'd gladly hit him, then dropped them and stepped back. Repulsed. By her or him, it was impossible to say. "Finding out Emma is the baby I thought died happened, geez—when was it?—yesterday, the day before," she snapped. "Give me a minute, okay, Guy?"

Self-loathing filled him. She'd dealt with a lot in the past couple of days and he *did* know it. Maybe better than she did. And she'd done it maybe better than he would've if the circumstances were reversed. He shut his eyes and grimaced. Timing was a trick he really had to learn to master.

"I'm sorry, Hazel." He sighed. He rubbed a hand over his eyes, reached out to run the back of his forefinger down her cheek. "You're right. I'm an idiot. It's just—I just—I don't…" His mouth twisted. "I've never—"

"You don't go whoring," Hazel stated baldly for him.

He nodded.

"Neither do I." He canted his head and looked her in the eye. She found herself squirming to look away. "That is I never…I never thought of it that way before."

His jaw tightened. "I…don't like lovemaking to mean nothing."

"You've never…" She hesitated, not quite sure how to phrase what she wanted to ask.

"No." He shook his head. "I've been with five women in my life, Hazel, and not once was it a casual relationship."

"Oh." She didn't know what to say. Clearly he was not like the other men she'd known, guys who were looking for a little fun and no ties. "What happened?"

He shrugged. "Not all men are commitment-shy, and not all women want one." Another shrug, one-shouldered this time. "And, uh, I might come across like the class clown, but, uh, I've been told I can be a little…intense…when it comes to falling in love. I'm a little too ready for it. You know, wife, kids, my own place on the rancheria, peach orchard. I want it. All of it. Soon."

"Ah." Hazel's grin bore a semblance of alarm. "I see. And your ladies—"

His lips twisted. "Generally broke it off because my goals were too simple to fit in with their five-, ten- or twenty-year plans."

"Because you wanted them barefoot and pregnant nine months out of every year?"

"Hell, no." The statement was fierce, vehement. "If that's what they'd have wanted, fine, but it's not what I want or need from any woman—then or now."

"Then what?" For some reason she wanted to know. Needed to.

His smile was lopsided, self-deprecating, wry. "Mostly they thought I'm not ambitious enough. I like who I am, what I do and where I live. I've turned down promotions because I don't like the baggage that comes with that territory. You gotta play too much politics when you wear a suit, and I've got politics and jurisdictions up the wazoo out here as it is. Fibbies got this, locals got that, Highway Patrol takes somethin' else, county's got that line, BIA does this, and then on top of that you got the tribal cops… Nah. I don't need more of it. I also don't want to end my career as some bureaucratic Washington redskin. I want more from my life than that." He eyed her sideways. "No offense, if that's what you want. It's just not me."

Until yesterday Hazel had known for certain that to take her career all the way to D.C. was precisely what she wanted to do. Today she knew Emily was alive. Today she knew she was capable of emotions she'd forgotten even existed moons and eons before she'd turned seventeen.

Today everything had changed, even if she wasn't sure yet how.

And today, for the first time since she'd joined the Bureau fresh out of college, she wasn't certain of anything at all.

"Hence the regrets." Not a question, a statement.

"Yeah." Guy nodded. "Hence the regrets."

Swallowing, Hazel turned away from him. The rain had all but stopped, the roll of thunder and violet bursts of lightning were distant audio and visual reminders of the thud of her pulse, the flashes of electric heat that had seared through her with Guy's touch.

The warmth and gentleness with which he'd treated her before he'd known her at all. And she knew, more clearly than she'd ever known anything, that she didn't want him regretting anything that happened between them.

Ever.

She pushed back her poncho hood. Tipped her face skyward for a moment to study the clouds. Moistened her mouth trying to get her tongue around the language she needed to find to get through this.

To reach him.

To let him off the hook.

She did apologies but not easily. Admitting to emotions that were still raw, unexplored, deeply personal and which had to do with *him* was even harder.

"I'm sorry," she offered finally, simply. "What happened…complicates…things between us. I realize that. And you're right, I do usually tend to keep my personal life pretty impersonal. I learned young that it's too easy for me to get tangled up in things that are beyond my control so I…set up alarms and gates and put bars on the windows around my private side. Nobody gets in without an invitation, and even when I issue one there's a time limit on it that I control. If I'm not involved, I don't get hurt, and I don't hurt anyone else because I establish the rules from the get-go.''

She flipped a hand. ''I've never had a serious relationship. I wouldn't know *how* to have one—and now's not the time to start one even if I did. But what happened wasn't 'nothing' to me, Guy. It meant something. It *felt* different. Right. Safe.'' She eyed him earnestly. ''I never feel safe, Guy, especially not…'' She hesitated, embarrassed. ''Especially not *during*. Definitely not before. And God forbid that after I should ever have the nerve to talk about it like this.''

He quirked a brow, gave her his self-deprecating humor. ''You tryin' to salve my ego or somethin', Hazel? Because it's healthy as all get-out, if you haven't noticed, and that's not what this is about for me.''

''I know. And no. It's—'' She swallowed and worked her tongue around her teeth a long moment looking for a way to articulate what had to be said. ''I don't…dally…real often. Hardly ever. Once or twice a year, if that. An-and never without a lot of…of thought beforehand. Without precautions. A *lot* of precautions.''

Guy slid off the rock and reached for her. Turned her around and caught her chin on the edge of his hand. Tilted her face upward. The corners of his mouth kicked up. ''You tryin' to tell me you let me put you up against a ladder without thought or precautions because I'm special and you trust me?''

She shrugged her chin. ''Yeah.''

''Ah, Hazel.'' With a laugh that was mostly sigh he dropped his forehead to hers. ''Even to someone who can fall in love as fast as I can that's…I don't know, idiotic. And dangerous.''

She bristled. ''You want my medical history, it's in Phoenix, I'll fax it to you.''

''Hazel, I didn't mean to suggest—''

''Look, you great oaf.'' She poked him in the chest, practically yelling now. ''I'm trying to save you face by tellin' you things I've never even considered saying to *anyone* else, especially not a man. I'm tryin' to tell you that quick or slow, too soon or never, you gave me somethin' I needed when nothing else would have helped. Where another guy might have taken advantage of the moment and used me, you held me.''

She tangled her fingers in his shirtfront, trying to jerk hold of his understanding with his attention. ''You *touched* me. Physically, emotionally. You took me out of myself. You, Guy. Not just some *partner* I'd want to leave immediately after and probably never want to see again. You, damn it.'' She buried her face in his chest and repeated softly, ''Only you.''

Chapter 9

The revelation was not what he'd expected, but then there was so little about Hazel Youvella he might have anticipated.

Stunned and trying to get his bearings in a muddy world suddenly turned upside down and sideways, Guy stood staring down at the crown of Hazel's head. She was so short the top of it barely reached the center of his chest. Such a small woman to be able to unman him in the space of a breath—to be able to make him feel like the smallest gnat on the backside of the universe one moment, like a T-Rex of a man in the next. Good grief, she was so petite that Heaven alone knew how she'd met the Bureau's or the Army's height requirements. Full and luscious little body aside, the key word there was still *little*.

For the first time he recognized just how gigantic her presence was.

He brought an arm up and slipped it around her shoulders, gathered her close, noting with fascination that he could span the width of her shoulders with the length of his forearm, between the crook of his elbow and his wrist. Their bed would require two quilts, he decided, one for each of them else she'd be constantly freezing; the width of *his* shoulders when he slept on his side would tent the covers over her and let in a draft.

She would have to stand on a chair or some steps, or he would have to sit if he was to kiss her frequently—which he definitely planned to do—otherwise he'd wind up with a sore back and a constant crick in his neck. And even if he did it wouldn't matter. If she wanted him on his knees, it wouldn't matter. He'd spend the rest of his life with calluses on them and his shins if that's what it took.

Of course, none of this made a blessed bit of difference just now. Right now they had a working relationship to deal with—one that was in sore need of repair. One that was probably going to get worse now that he truly realized how small she physically was in this big bad world of Russian mobster kidnappers they had to cruise. Because the one thing he hadn't told her that tended to go part and parcel with his intimacies with a woman was his somewhat over-developed sense of protectiveness. And he could predict with some certainty that she wasn't going to react well to him pulling whatever strings were necessary to keep her far from harm's way as soon as he got her back to some semblance of civilization. But so help him, he would put her under lock and key and sit Russ in front of the door in order to keep her safe while he went gallivanting off in search of Emma by himself if he had to.

She was his responsibility now; his heart told him that, even as his head told him she would hate him for thinking of her in such a nineteenth-century fashion.

For thinking of her the same way he thought of the children they were out here in the name of, just because she was short.

Oh, yeah, he thought wryly. He was in for a lot of trouble now. But knowing that didn't change the way he felt.

Or how he intended to act.

Awash in tenderness, he wrapped his other arm around her, too, pulled her in as close as possible. "Hazel," he murmured, a breath of air, a sigh, before he bent his head to drop a kiss on the crown of hers then let his mouth slide to one temple, the other. "Hazel. What am I going to do with you?"

"Help me find Emily." Her response was muffled in his shirt but automatic. "Help me not let Allyn and Jeth and the rest of your family lose Sasha. Anything else till then will only get in the way."

"'Anything else' is already in the way," Guy pointed out. "It got in the way the minute I laid eyes on you. Now that I know you better and we—" His grip on her tightened almost unbearably. "Well, let's just say it's a lot more so. A *lot*."

"Squash it," Hazel advised, rubbing her forehead against his chest and looking up at him. "Because I won't let your macho, I-am-more-than-a-foot-taller-than-you-and-outweigh-you-by-at-least-a-hundred-pounds overprotective baloney stop me from doing what I need to do. I can't let you stop me. Do you understand, Guy? I *have* to do this. Whether your pigheaded mentality can swallow and digest that or not."

Guy chuckled hoarsely, charmed and dismayed by her recognition of his thoughts. "Pigs can digest more than you might realize, sweetheart," he said. "I'm not sure you want to give me that much credit."

"Help me find Emily, Guy," Hazel repeated fiercely. "And don't even think of attempting to shut me out—"

The sudden sputter of the Handie-Talkie attached to Guy's belt startled them both. Hazel sprang away from Guy as though caught in a compromising position by one of her subordinates. Guy unhooked it from his belt with one hand and with the other caught Hazel and hauled her back.

"Levoie."

"Where the devil you been, bro?" Jeth's voice. "I've been tryin' to raise you for hours."

"Picked up a trail into one of the old Hopi pueblos. Looks like they had Emma here not more 'n a couple hours before we got here. Couldn't raise you in the storm."

"Yeah, well, you got me now. Gimme your loc. All friggin' hell's broken loose here, and you needa be in on it ASAP."

"Klimkov?"

"Oh, I spoke with him," Jeth agreed sardonically. "Then he went back to the yard and took a blade between the ribs before I had a chance to leave the prison."

As he explained to Guy, Hazel and Russ, the thing that hadn't made sense to Jeth from the outset was Grigor Klimkov's apparently keen desire to retrieve Sasha while he was incarcerated in the U.S. Penitentiary in Atlanta.

Oh, Jeth understood that the man might have had a desire to control his own blood, to keep and raise Sasha within his Russian family's "business"—to groom him, as it were, to take over one day. But Russian mob "families" differed from other Mafia and cartel families in a crude and very basic way: they vowed to maintain no ties outside the world in which they did business, made sure to have no sentimental attachments that could in any way be used to weaken them individually and therefore threaten them as a group.

Jeth had lived and breathed the world these men lived in

for months before Sasha had come into the picture. It had struck him as unusual then that Klimkov might allow himself to be manipulated by the Colombians through his son. And truth be told, Klimkov had not precisely allowed himself to be pressured into doing anything the Colombians wanted because of Sasha. He'd allowed the Colombians to *think* they had him over a barrel when what he'd really done was manipulate and maneuver to get Jeth into place to take care of Sasha for him.

That had been Klimkov's somewhat startling revelation to Jeth during their interview the previous day—the fact that he, Klimkov, had been the one to "choose" Jeth for the Baltimore case that had brought both Sasha and, inadvertently, Allyn into the latter's life. Jeth had known his former boss was working for someone mobbed up, but the fact that she'd not only been responsible for his baby sister's death but had sold his deepest guilt to Klimkov for the crime baron's use... It was too much.

It had been by no means the last of the shocks Sasha's biological father had to offer. No, the greater shock had come when Klimkov offered to sign off on Sasha, commended the boy into Jeth's and Allyn's keeping for life, allowing them to adopt the youngster without a battle. He'd also suggested somewhat cryptically that the couple keep Sasha and anyone else they cared about away from certain groups that might have an interest in putting casinos on Indian lands.

Then he'd left Jeth reeling with suspicion and returned to the yard. Grigor Klimkov never offered anything without exacting a price in return; that was simply the way of things. Guy's younger brother was halfway out the gate when the guard flagged him down. A sharpened spoon had been shoved neatly and silently upward between Klimkov's ribs and nicked his aorta. The crime boss had nearly bled out by the time he was discovered lying in the center of the yard and was not expected to recover.

A search of Klimkov's cell turned up nothing that might be considered remarkable—except for several inexpert attempts at modeling kachinas from clay and a few simple, but exquisite kachina-like dolls fashioned from toothpicks, glue and embroidery floss. Among the latter there was also a small tableau embedded in clay. The plastic-coated card with it suggested that the scene depicted Warrior Woman fighting off her clan's enemies until help arrived. The print on the card was painstakingly neat, clearly the work of a child.

The signature was Emma Poley's.

Hazel's throat closed when she looked at the tableau and read the card Jeth handed her. She couldn't breathe.

She tried, but the air wouldn't come in. Something as big as hell and twice as fiery lodged in her chest. The edges of her vision blurred, caught in a fine red haze. Her fists clenched and her body went rigid. Fury closed in, as hot and alkaline as the borax flats on one of the rancherias some distance to the west of them.

And still she couldn't breathe.

"Hazel."

Guy's voice. She heard it from a distance, as though she'd dropped from a great height and he was calling out to her, frantically trying to reach her.

"Come on, honey." Jeth, Russ, some other male she couldn't identify. It didn't matter. She'd have his badge for calling her that, whoever he was. "Take a breath before you pass out."

"Hazel." Guy again, sharp, urgent, demanding and stooped so he could be in her face. He caught her chin roughly between thumb and forefinger. "Breathe, blast it. So he had some of Emily's dolls. Deal with it."

Air returned to her lungs in a gulp and a gasp. Anger, red-hot, blind and lethal came with it.

"*Deal* with it?"

She was shaking so badly she could barely make a fist. Even so, when she did, when she gathered all the rage of a lifetime's worth of family betrayal and two-day's worth of unacceptable conditions, then drew back and let fly, punching Guy solidly in the jaw, he staggered.

"*Deal* with it?" she repeated.

Furious, she shook out her hand while Guy offered her a crooked grin and worked his jaw as if trying to put it back in place. He'd needled her into this reaction on purpose she knew. Now her knuckles stung like a son of a gun, but damn it had felt good to hit him. Empowering somehow. Like taking some of her own back—even though Guy wasn't really the one she needed to take it back from.

She bit back a sigh in favor of holding on to her rage. Ah, hell, she'd apologize to him later. When this was over and she could see straight again.

"You deal with it," she advised him acidly. "Nobody's using your daughter—your *baby,* blast it—as a pawn in a…a *game* somebody wants you to play but nobody's given you the rules to."

"They've involved Sasha," Guy said quietly but with an equal amount of acid in his tone. "That's close enough."

"Fine," Hazel snapped.

"You got that right," Guy agreed.

"What went on between you two out there?" Russ asked. He might as well have been talking to himself.

Guy eyed Hazel. "So, you ready to blow this pop stand, find out what's really goin' on?"

"Oh, yeah." Hazel nodded.

In tandem they headed for the door to Russ's office. Jeth started after them.

"Hold up, I'll come with you."

Russ called him back. "Better not. If they don't kill each other first they might kill you by mistake."

Hazel cast a baleful glance over her shoulder at the eldest Levoie brother. "Charming." Then she shot Jeth a look full of pure maternal anxiety. "Stay close to Sasha," she said. "Keep him and Allyn safe. There's no telling how much more complicated this thing'll get before it's done."

Then she stepped through the doorway, turned abruptly, causing Guy to run into her. Again.

"What?" he asked.

"Whatever happens out there," she said, "whatever we find, don't even think about trying to protect me from it or keep me out of it."

"Who, me?" There was more guilt than innocence in the query.

She gave him exasperated. "Yeah, you." Then quieter, more serious. More insistent. "Promise me, Guy. No overprotective stunts. We've both got a stake in this. We go in as equals. Think of it as a life lesson you need to learn if you're ever going to find that permanent relationship you want so badly."

Guy studied her a moment before giving her a single clipped nod. "I'll do my best, long's you do yours to keep the chip off your shoulder and get behind me if size matters."

Her smile was faint but real. "And if we're in a situation where less is more, you'll do the same, right?"

He made a face. "Fine. I won't be happy about it, but you got it."

She stuck out a hand. "Then we've got a deal."

"Good." He took her hand, used it to draw her forward.

Bent and dropped a kiss on the bridge of her nose. "Now let's beat feet, Youvella, daylight's wastin'."

When they'd gone, Jeth turned to Russ.

"He's deep in it this time."

"Heels over heart," Russ agreed. "Course he's been there before."

Jeth shook his head. "Not the same. And not with her. What do you think of her?"

"Not fighting it as hard as she was when she came in."

"Yeah, but will she let him catch her, you think?"

"Oh, hell," Russ said. "She's already caught. She's just going to make him pay for catchin' her. And then she's going to keep him."

"Hmm." Jeth peered through the window at the parking lot where Hazel and his brother swung up into Guy's truck and peeled out. He looked back at Russ. "I didn't wear a tux to my own wedding, they'd damned well better not think I'll wear one to theirs."

"I doubt they've even realized they're having a wedding yet, let alone thought about what they'll make you wear to it," Russ said dryly.

"True." Jeth grinned abruptly. "Guess that means we'll just have to make sure that when they figure it out they can get to the altar in one piece."

"The way things are starting to look, that might be easier said than done." The observation was grim. Russ shoved back his chair and rose with sudden purpose. "Why don't you try talking Allyn into taking Sasha and going to visit her mother and that overprotective former Fibbie stepdad of hers until we get this figured out?"

"Why not?" Jeth agreed. "She'll bust my chops over it, but when she's done with that…" He smiled to himself in anticipation. "Lord, I do like making up with her."

Without another word to Russ, Jeth went whistling out of the office.

The eldest Levoie brother scowled after him. He envied his brother's new happiness, but not the route Jeth had taken to find it. After Marcy was killed, Russ wasn't sure he'd ever see Jeth smile again, let alone happy. But in the end, through serendipity and Klimkov's unwitting matchmaking, happiness had found Jeth, plucked him up into the midwestern tornado that was Allyn, spun him silly and dumped him out whole.

And now here was Guy maybe headed in a similar direction.

Russ sighed. Only one woman—really little more than a girl at the time to his little more than a boy—had ever made him feel the way Jeth felt about Allyn and the way Guy was acting with Hazel. Protective, possessive and like his blood was boiling in his veins all the time.

He stifled unproductive reminiscence with an effort. But that had been an eon ago, twelve, thirteen years easy, high school and a moment or two after. Time beyond comprehension and control at the moment.

Resolved not to let thoughts of Maddie interfere with either of his brothers' present, Russ picked up his phone to call a friend with ties to the National Indian Gaming Commission and the Bureau of Land Management. If Klimkov hadn't merely been jerking Jeth around when he'd all but suggested that someone with an interest in building a casino on Indian lands might be involved in Emma's kidnapping, then there'd have to be a paper trail that backtracked to it from somewhere.

Tongue locked firmly behind her teeth to prevent her aching jaw from quivering with fury, Hazel stared through the windshield of Guy's truck at the arid short-blue-corn farmland adjacent to Hopiland's flat-topped baked-brick reservation homes.

Hard as she'd tried to leave it well behind her, it seemed all the roads of her life wound continually and unforgivably back through the bowels of her history. The only thing that differed on this trip from the one two days ago was the fact that she understood Guy was here *with* her this time. That she no longer saw him as a burr under the saddle of her authority, but as a partner proven.

Of course, her confused head and heart still viewed him as a complication, but she didn't have time to think about that now.

And neither would he, if she could help it.

At that moment, however, the complication in question reminded her of his proximity by reaching across the seat to squeeze her thigh. Even through her anger, Hazel experienced the warm tingle of possibility and awareness.

"You gonna be able to do this without ripping someone to shreds?"

Hazel grinned in spite of herself. The man did have a way with words. "I don't know," she admitted. "Are you?"

Guy shrugged, smiled grimly. "We won't know till we go in, will we?"

Her chuckle was small and tight. "Don't make me have to try 'n' pull you off of anyone, Guy."

"Why, don't you think you could?"

"Mmm. That and I don't know if I'd want to."

Guy laughed outright at that, caught up her hand and planted a damp kiss in her palm. "I'll bear that in mind."

"Do," Hazel murmured, a little astonished that the intimacy didn't bother her—despite the fact that it was a little late to worry about things like that now. If he'd felt perfectly comfortable touching her before the kiva, he wasn't going to be less so now.

Regardless, she reminded herself, this wasn't the time. So she pulled her hand out of Guy's and folded the kiss into her fist for future reference. Then, heart full of savage purpose and stomach in knots, she waited for Guy to park the truck outside the Poleys' house.

Guy went in first, whether to shield Hazel from her grandparents and the Poleys as long as possible, or them from her, he wasn't sure. Everything was as it had been before, but less welcoming, more…fearful and perhaps surprised—though not pleasantly, he thought.

There was the same shadowed interior, the same guarded inhabitants—plus, Guy surmised, a few added council members—within. Over on the stove a pot of fresh coffee, and there, ready on the table, a fresh plate of blue-corn pancakes.

But this time he carried with him fresh information, and fresh eyes through which to study the place, which meant new things to see.

And see he did.

Saw the collection of rough-carved cottonwoodroot kachina dolls he'd only absently noted before. They were the sort of dolls, he decided, that might have been created by a beginner or a student—or a child—in the art, who'd used a small pocket knife instead of a craftsman's sculpting tools. He glanced over his shoulder and signaled Hazel who arched a brow and nodded imperceptibly at him. *Go ahead, take the lead.*

This time.

Lips twitching over small concessions to their agreed-upon efforts at teamwork, Guy carried a few of the dolls to the table and spread them out. Hazel stepped into the room and shoulder-leaned against the wall, silent and implacable.

"Did Emily make these?" he asked, deliberately using the name Hazel had given her daughter rather than the bastardized version of it supplied by the people who'd stolen her from Hazel.

Dextra Poley flinched but nodded. Hazel's grandfather cleared his throat and said, "She asked to learn. I was—I *am*—teaching her. She is a good student."

There was an undercurrent of pride in his voice that didn't go unnoticed by either Hazel or Guy.

Neither did the heartbreaking sense of hopelessness wanting to be hope, nor the past tense "was." But it wasn't enough to diminish their ire.

"What about the clay kachinas and the toothpick-and-floss dolls my brother found in Grigor Klimkov's prison cell? You teach her to make those, too?"

The old man paled considerably. "She learned to do those in school."

"Who gave them to Klimkov?"

"She did." This hesitantly from Hazel's grandmother. "He came here many times. She liked—*likes* him."

"You let her *near* him? You let her speak to him?" Hazel came away from the wall in a rush of palpable fury. Guy grabbed her by the shoulders and yanked her back.

"How many times did he come here?" he snapped. Grief, he wanted to hit someone, hurt someone, anyone—preferably one of these adults who'd wronged Hazel and her child. He wanted to do it bad. And soon.

So much for being the laid-back lover of his youth who might have been a little intense in his relationships but who still mostly took them as they came, he thought sardonically. But he didn't regret the change—or what he already knew it meant.

"Starting when?" When no one answered immediately, he took a menacing half step forward and enunciated forcefully, "Starting. When."

"A year ago," Dextra's husband said finally. "Maybe more."

"A year?" Guy asked, rocked. A year ago, give or take, would have been about the time Jeth started the deep-cover operation that had eventually brought Sasha into their lives. An operation he'd been specifically requested for because no one knew him in Baltimore, but also because the drug trafficking he'd been investigating for the Tucson state prosecutor's office seemed to be related to the turf war in Baltimore. A year during which the corruption Jeth had managed to expose only three months ago at the state level did not seem to have been corrected. Or perhaps had been expanded. "A whole freaking *year?*"

"A *year?*" Hazel echoed. Why had nobody known, *seen?* How could the ultra-visible Klimkov's visits to reservations considering casinos have gone unnoticed to the FBI, the IRS, or even the state, local or tribal police agencies, gone unseen by *anyone* who might have done something about it sooner? It wasn't possible he'd managed to pay off everyone—was it?

For a man like Klimkov, maybe it was. After all, mobsters went freely about their business everywhere else in the world, why not here as well? It was, after all, dangerous or not, only business.

Built on greed.

She charged recklessly forward again bent, no doubt, on mayhem. This time Guy didn't bother to stop her. He couldn't. In fact, if she started anything, he planned to help her finish it.

Instead she halted in front of her grandfather, planted her fists on her hips. "What the hell were you thinking bringing a man like that onto the reservation, letting him near her? Do you know who he is, what he's done? Did you know what he was capable of?''

"Yes," Joseph Youvella admitted. "But we had no choice. His was the lesser—" he hunted for the word "—evil."

"Lesser *evil?*" Hazel spat, aghast. "Do you want to know where your 'lesser evil' is now? Dying, maybe dead, because somebody knifed him in his prison yard. That's what you invited into Emma's—into *Emily's,* damn it—life. Now look where it's gotten her. Kidnapped by someone who works for a dead man. Disappeared, damn you. Maybe irretrievable. Maybe—" She gulped back something close to a sob. She would not give them the satisfaction. She would not. "Maybe dead."

She made a throwaway gesture as though tossing everything she felt, everything she was, everything she had to do into her grandfather's face. "And you say you did this for her own good. For mine. Because I was too young. Because she's three-quarters Hopi and you wanted her raised with your beliefs, your culture, your ways the way you couldn't get my mother to let you raise me. And now you've lost us both. God."

She spun away, unable to look at him any longer. Exhaustion from more than forty-eight hours without sleep did nothing to aid her mood. "You lied to me." It seemed she'd said that so often in the last two days it had become a mantra. "How could you? She's your great-granddaughter and you let her learn to trust someone who's killed people, who's responsible for the deaths of other *children.* You told me once that to be Hopi meant to revere and protect children above all, but you sold her out, gave her up to a man who let his own son be used as barter in a damned drug war. You *lost* her."

Abruptly she turned her back on the room and brushed by Guy on her way to the door. "Ah, hell," she muttered, spent. "You talk to them—*make* them talk. I can't bear the sight of them anymore." Then she stomped out into the sunlight and headed for the truck.

Guy watched her retreat for a moment, considered going after her and discarded the notion as quickly as it rose. Hazel would not appreciate him intruding on her privacy just now. She needed time. And by telling him to go ahead without her and get the answers they'd been denied too long, she'd offered him a trust he couldn't refuse.

Pleased with their progress in spite of the circumstances, he returned his attention to the Indians in the room, swept each a cool, probing glance, gauging weak links and searching for the "tells" that would give him an idea of who would break first. Settled on the oldest man present, swung a chair away from the table, straddled it and began.

Chapter 10

She hated them, despised them all, but her grandfather most, because she'd loved him best, had always, somehow, yearned for his approval.

Too heartsick and tired to do anything else, Hazel put her back against the truck grill and knew things about herself she could no longer deny.

While she'd visited her grandparents that fateful summer, her grandfather had wanted to teach her to make the kachina dolls the way the reservation youngsters learned to, but Hazel had refused to be taught. Kachinas and the myths and culture surrounding them didn't fit the world she lived in, so she'd denied them—no matter how much the mythical beings had attracted her. To her they'd been cute or ugly or picturesque, but that was all. Even when she'd liked the stories about them—though she'd never have admitted it to her backworld grandparents. She was from Los Angeles and far too modern and sophisticated to have anything to do with them.

Either her grandparents *or* their beliefs.

The vague niggle of envy that her grandfather had found another family member to share his art with astonished her. That the child he taught was her unknown daughter…

She passed a hand across her eyes. Judas, Emily. If Klimkov was now out of the picture—had perhaps never really been in the picture other than through Sasha—how would they ever find her? Who else was there? Out there in the world beyond…inside Hopiland—somehow the two worlds worked together on this one, she could feel it. But she was too close to the source to figure out how.

How, damn it, *how?*

Talk to me, Emily, she whispered to herself. *Help me find you. Tell me where you are.*

Oh, geez, she thought nonsensically from nowhere, she put this case down, and her reputation as the Ice Maiden would be in shreds.

Who was it had once told her to quit being such a hard-ass?

She crossed her arms over her chest and allowed herself a sad lip twitch. Besides Guy that is. The whoever had continued: because, in the long run cold and hardass would buy her squat and she might as well get that into her head right up-front. Understand that sooner or later, at some point in her career and ambitions be damned, *The Case* would find her, the one that would either sever or severely mangle her Achilles tendon, leave her completely maimed, lame or at the very least limping—perhaps for the rest of her life.

Probably one of her academy instructors. One of the ones with more than his or her own share of demons to deal with. And there were certainly enough of those to go around.

Almost as many of them as there were bureaucrats.

The deliberate scuff of a foot across dirt caused her to look up. Halfway between her and the only home Emily had ever known, Guy stood waiting for her to notice him. Respecting her privacy. Impatient, nevertheless.

Appreciating his circumspection, she pooched her lips into a sign of okay-so-tell-me. He closed the distance between them, opening his arms to her when he drew near.

She eyed him with misgiving. "I'm going to need those?"

He shrugged unhappily. "Maybe. Does it matter if you will or not? They're here regardless."

"Guy…"

"Don't be such a hardcase, Hazel."

The echo of her recent thoughts locked her gaze with his. The man really did read minds.

Or perhaps he only read hers.

"This one's gonna get to you no matter what. It already has. And maybe this is for my benefit. Maybe I don't want to have to see your face when I tell you."

Hazel felt her mouth curve. "You'd be able to look Saint Peter in the face if God sent you to tell him to turn over guardianship of heaven's gates to Saint Paul."

"Mmm." Guy dropped his arms, joined her against the truck bumper. The vehicle sagged beneath his weight. "Doesn't mean I'd be happy about it. Or that I don't just want to hold you."

"Give you that inch, you'd take the mile," Hazel said lightly. But her insides ached to reach out and let him hold her.

To give in and give up and give over.

To let him take square feet and hectares and entire interstates worth of miles.

She wondered if he ever felt that way with a woman.

Wanted to let someone else handle things for a while. If he ever had or ever would.

Let *her*.

One half of the team's crises at a time, she reminded herself. That's how her parents handled things. Couldn't have them both sick at once, else who'd take care of the children then? And no, she didn't intend to consider that she'd thought of Guy in the same context of marriage—and children—regardless of whose marriage it was.

"Quit stalling, Guy. I can stand here imagining nightmares, but it won't get worse until it's *worse*. Tell me."

He glanced at her, made a quick assessment, nodded. "Don't know if it's somethin' you keep up on, but a few years ago the Hopi voted against building a casino on a tribal-owned industrial park near Winslow. Close vote, mostly old-school, older traditionals versus let's-bring-in-the-dough progressives, sixty miles off the rez, far enough to avoid if you wanted to, close enough to create jobs and revenue for the tribe otherwise."

What he didn't say, of course, was that regardless of the distance, the reservation would feel the influence of the casino in the sheer modern pressures, mores and wants the newly employed or disenfranchised Indians would bring back with them.

"I know about it." Hazel drummed her fingertips along the nearest fender, impatient to get to the crux. "My father came here for the vote when grandfather asked. Grandfather thought Dad agreed with him that religious and cultural mores were more important than cash and jobs. He didn't. Strongly."

Guy nodded. Much the same discussions and disagreements occasionally occurred within his own family—and over much the same things. Except that the Havasupai elders had nothing in particular against games, and the Hopi elders did.

"Okay. Well, take that, resurrect it, bring it closer to home and multiply it. Then add Klimkov and organized crime into the mix."

Hazel paled. "Internal strife and roulette wheels when the Hopi way is pretty much antigaming. So it's not really about kid for kid. It's not about Sasha."

"I think it was to start with," Guy said. He hunched a shoulder. "Sort of, anyway. Something Jeth said made me wonder. Without giving him overly noble motives, I think Klimkov wanted some clandestine way to make sure Sasha was safe before he got involved with this gaming thing on tribal lands."

He paused to shift a quick look in Hazel's direction, see how she was taking this. Her expression was carefully schooled, her eyes vigilantly blank and emotionless. Her hands betrayed her. They were stiff, white-knuckled, bound in brittle claws about her elbows. The sight made him want to drag her forcibly into his embrace and build a solid-walled, protective cocoon around her that nothing could breach.

He knew she wouldn't let him. Not now, and maybe not ever.

He was also pretty certain that if he touched her now she would shatter. And for her that would be unacceptable.

Especially now.

"But that's not all you think," Hazel prompted, though she didn't want to hear more.

Knowing she had to.

Guy sighed unhappily. "No." He settled himself a little closer to her on the fender, making sure that if she needed warmth his would be available. "You're right. I don't think getting hold of Sasha is the original reason Emily was snatched.''

He looked at her until she glanced up at him. Then he told her what he'd worked out straight-up and bluntly. ''I think Emily was kidnapped because someone among the Hopi progressives—probably someone she knows—is working with the Russians and saw a way to bring the unwilling Hopi leaders to heel. Then when Klimkov's partners wanted something from him and showed him the trump card they had to play on the tribal leaders, he saw his chance to check on Jeth's kid and make it look like part of the deal.''

It was too much to take in at once.

''Oh.'' Air whooshed out of Hazel with the word. She couldn't feel anything. Her lungs tightened, squeezing her heart. ''You think Klimkov's stabbing is coincidence or a hit?''

''I dunno.'' *Let me hold you, Hazel,* he thought in anguish. *Let me try to make a difference. For you if no one else.* ''I think his mother overdosed herself, but this…'' He shrugged. ''Depends on how convenient it turns out to be for someone.''

''And until we know or they contact me again, we're a long way from Emily.'' The threads of her control were fraying into nonexistence.

''Not necessarily.'' Guy's mouth formed a grim smile. ''We can talk to the council members who want gambling brought in, look into who gains, where the money's coming from, who's backing the new venture for them.''

''And who's drumming up support for it on the reservation.'' Hazel's color and determination returned with the prospect of positive action. She smacked a palm against the fender and straightened. ''Let's go,'' she said.

''Where to?''

"Grandfather didn't tell you who the opposition is?"

"I've got a list of council members who want the casino, yeah. Figured I'd give it to Jeth. He's good at intimidating people into giving him information without having to bang heads." He grinned and amended, "Well, at least not too hard."

If anyone had to do any head banging, Hazel would have preferred to be the one doing it.

Unless, that is, her hunky partner had something better tucked up his biceps-hugging sleeves.

She gazed at him hard. This was her case, her kid, but if he had a clue she was deferring to him on it and no longer cared. "Which leaves us doing…?"

Guy sucked a breath. This was the hard part. "We may need to take a trip to Los Angeles, possibly one to Albuquerque."

Hazel's eyes widened, puzzled.

And instantly suspicious.

And downright leerily, throat-convulsingly, eyes-shut-against-the-unthinkable afraid.

He nodded. "You heard right. Sam Poley saw me to the door. He gave me two names that weren't on anyone else's lists. He didn't seem to want your grandparents to know he'd given them to me."

"Why?" Hazel asked first, then said suddenly, hoarsely, as an almost-thought occurred to her, "Who?"

Guy's jaw tightened. Judas, he wished…

"Spill it, Levoie. Break my damned heart. Get it over with."

He gestured at the bumper. "Why don't you sit?"

"God bless it, Guy," she snapped. "I'm not made of sand. A good wind won't scatter me up and blow me away. Make it worse and get it done. Give me the names. Maybe they're friends of my grandfather's, but I doubt I've ever been involved with them let alone know—''

"Hazel."

She looked up at him and her heart constricted at the knowledge she saw in his eyes. He was about to bring her more pain than she could imagine and there was nothing he could do to stop it.

Staggering back a step, she braced herself against the truck and waited.

"Who?" she whispered.

"Your father," Guy told her quietly, "and Emily's sire."

It seemed like forever before the pulse in her head stopped pounding too loudly to hear herself think, forever and a day before the heart in her chest began to beat again.

"M-my *father?*" Her voice was little more than a thick squeak. "And…" She could barely bring herself to think it, let alone say it. She could hardly even remember his name.

She'd seen him three times one week that summer. He was gone after their single…time together. She'd never seen or heard from him again. And she'd made damn sure that her family knew she didn't ever want him hearing about Emily. What had been the point, after all? Emily was hers alone. She'd accepted the responsibility, taken the blame for her looseness—done the work, carrying Emily for nine months, making sure to eat the right foods, take her vitamins—even during those awful weeks and months when she'd tried so hard to be naive.

To deny Emily's existence in her womb.

Even then she'd done her best to stay healthy.

Just in case.

But her parents and grandparents had lied to her once

already, so what were the chances they'd kept their word not to tell *him* about Emily?

Slim to none, Hazel realized bleakly. Emily might have become Emma Poley, but there was no doubt in her mind that her grandfather and her father would have seen to it that *he* knew about his daughter, too.

"Oh, God." She slumped onto the bumper and wrapped her arms about her stomach, rocking. "Oh, God."

"It might not mean anything, Hazel." Guy squatted in front of her, chafing her arms, stroking her cheek. Solid enough to carry the weight for her, wanting to take it, but helpless to do so. "We have to look at them, take apart every lead to find her, but it could be nothing."

"Grandfather and Grandmother, Mrs. Poley, none of them gave you their names."

"No."

Hazel swallowed bile. "It's something."

Guy shook his head. "Maybe it's not. How well do you know Sam? He's the only one who said anything about them. He might say he's against the casino when he's for it. We have to look into them all now. Dextra, your grand-parents and Sam, too."

"I know." She nodded, not looking at him. "But we won't find anything except what Grandfather's been hiding. I feel it, Guy. It's something."

"Hazel…"

"No." The word was ragged but firm. "Time for me to grow all the way up. No more lies. No more hiding. No more pretending. My father's in Los Angeles, but *he's* in Albuquerque, isn't he?"

A nod. "Supposedly."

"Okay." She dipped her chin, an affirmation to herself. "Would Russ be willing to go to L.A. personally and bring my father back here do you think?"

"Oh…" Guy's grin wasn't nice. "I think I can pretty much guarantee it."

"Good, good." A little distracted, but gaining momentum. Not quite so helpless feeling and pale.

She was not only the ASAC out here, but also the case agent, the coordinating agent. She might have had to follow the Bureau's rule book to achieve her promotion, but now that she was out here on her own, so to speak, there was no reason she couldn't make—and break—a few rules, too.

And her recent promotion and all future ones be damned.

Decisions made, she glanced up at Guy, nodded firmly and repeated, "Good. Then he takes care of my father and we go to New Mexico."

Guy bit back a grin. When she made up her mind to a thing she'd be hell on wheels, and pity the Joe Schmoe who got in her way. "I'll radio Russ, ask him to request Albuquerque PD to pick up our guy and put him under lock and key till we can question him. Then we can get a couple hours rest—"

"No, Guy, now. We have to leave *now*. We've lost too much time already."

"Hazel, you're—we're both—practically runnin' on empty. If we don't catch up a little bit—"

"Now, Guy." She planted herself in front of him, tilted her head back to look all the way up so she could capture his eyes. Gave him a look that was damn-the-torpedoes forceful and, though she didn't know it, pleading. "Now."

Guy grimaced. "Crimeny Pete, woman, you're going to be the death of me."

Then he strode around to the driver's door of his truck and climbed in.

Not quite caving, but definitely not quite getting it all his own way, either.

Chapter 11

In the end, of necessity, they compromised.

A local pilot friend of Guy's, who was willing to stick her—yes, Hazel noted the fact that it was a *her* somewhat sourly much to her chagrin—neck out when the need arose agreed to fly them to Albuquerque. The "but" was that she couldn't do it until after her husband—yes, Hazel's heart cha-cha'd when she heard that—returned home from Phoenix to take care of their children, about three hours out.

Though they could probably drive the distance between the Hopi Reservation's Second Mesa and Albuquerque nearly as quickly if Guy floored it all the way, they'd both been without rest for too long for him to deem it a safe choice. Besides, as he pointed out, not only could they go to his trailer on the way, but they could meet his pilot friend in Holbrook where she lived and kept her chopper.

What he didn't say, and what he wouldn't say—at least not to her—was that he was afraid for Hazel. Afraid to watch her walk into this situation where she would meet the man who'd deflowered her and who held the cards and might possibly also hold the keys to Emily's safety.

Afraid because even longtime grown-ups sometimes forgot who they were when suddenly faced with who and what they'd been in a situation they'd prefer not to remember.

That they sometimes reverted to who and what they'd been when the "thing," whatever it was, had happened.

Which made him a trifle more than concerned that Hazel might unwittingly and unwillingly give that other "guy" with the rattlesnake tattoo some sort of power over her again.

Made him worry—for her—that she'd lose it, blow the opportunity and wind up finding her daughter the way Jeth had found Marcy: way too late to make a difference for the child.

Because he knew that "way too late" could only bring her nightmares for the rest of her life.

Understood, too, that he couldn't let that happen—for any of their sakes. Because losing Emily would affect more people than the mother who'd never gotten the chance to know her. It would affect Jeth, Allyn, Russ and all the Levoies, and it would kill him. Because he *never* wanted to see Hazel in that much pain and know he couldn't fix it.

Know he wouldn't be able to do much, if anything to help heal such a deep and terrible wound.

He didn't say it, but it was there in everything he did, in the persuasiveness with which he spoke and cajoled and irritated Hazel even as they rattled, banged and bumped back out to the highway that would take them through Winslow on the way to his trailer.

Since it was still the most expedient course of action, Hazel acquiesced to it, albeit somewhat crankily.

Her spirits improved a degree when Russ informed them

that the Albuquerque PD already had Emily's sperm donor—his term for the errant pater—in custody. He himself was on his way out the door, headed for a visit with Hazel's father, who, Hazel's mother had informed him, was en route to the reservation via a flight through Phoenix. Russ figured to take two men with him and intercept Clint Youvella before he had an opportunity to enter any Hopi-owned lands.

Meanwhile Jeth had marshaled his own team and set out to whittle down Guy's list, one person at a time. He'd been unable to convince Allyn to fly to Michigan with Sasha for a visit with her family—because she'd no intention of once again involving her family and their kids in another dangerous game.

On the other hand, she'd promised to dye Sasha's hair with vegetable dye the way Jeth's family had done during their original frantic dash to make sure the toddler stayed safe. She also reminded Jeth that he had her securely tucked away in Supai on the Havasupai Reservation. It had worked for them before; he could only pray it would work again now.

All in all, with the bases covered as well as they could be for the time being, Hazel was offered little choice but to let Guy take her home to his trailer—situated between Winslow and Holbrook, it was another fair drive—with him and temporarily give in to her exhaustion. In fact, by the time he pulled up under his carport, she'd already been drifting in and out of sleep for miles.

"Hazel." Guy shook her.

She curled more comfortably into the seat and shut her eyes more tightly. "Umm?"

"Come on. We're here. Shower. Bed. Sleep in one."

She grumbled. "I'm not sleepin' in your shower, Guy."

"Sleep in the bed, get rid of the grit in the shower. Come

on, sweetheart, don't make me cart you in. Tired as I am, I'd probably drop you.''

"Not very chivalrous of you," Hazel pointed out, but she woke up enough to stagger into the trailer after Guy.

The interior of Guy's home was small but neat, spare but warm and homey at the same time. As comfortable and unapologetic, Hazel reflected, as the man himself. She watched him toss his keys onto the counter to the left of the doorway, bull's-eyeing the small basket that had obviously been placed there to catch them and his mail.

"Shower's down there—" He pointed to a short hallway beyond the kitchen area. "Clean towels 're over the sink. Bed's here.'' He gestured right. "I'll change the sheets while you get clean." He was all at once more than exhausted, and he sounded it. "You want coffee or something to eat? My insides are gnawin' their way out. Made a crock of soup last time I was home, froze half of it. I can thaw some and make corn bread to go with it."

Hazel shook her head, feeling suddenly ill at ease and aware of exactly how close were the quarters they intended to share. The bed took up most of the living space when it was unfolded, leaving little room to move around or for the booth table. They'd hardly be able to sidle about without brushing up against each other—not something that should concern her after the kiva, but somehow it did.

The kiva had been neutral territory; this place was Guy's, which gave him the advantage, and her BMW was still parked at the Winslow station. She had no means to leave here if things got hairy between them. That was why she always named the places she met anyone: if they were on her turf, they played by her rules. She liked—no, she *needed*—to be able to control the situation, and she needed to be able to leave when she wanted.

As though he read her thoughts—again, but this time it

didn't surprise her as much—Guy said, "Nothing's going to happen, Hazel. We're here to shower, sleep and fuel up, that's it."

She hugged her elbows across her chest. "I know. And it's stupid to even think about it after…but—"

"That wasn't my place. I know." He moved to pull a plastic zipper bag from the small freezer and busied himself breaking the contents into quarters in order to fit them into a microwave dish. "Trust me, though. You're safe. I'm too tired to get fresh even if I thought now was the time." He looked at her, his eyes dark and fathomless, burning and brimful with passion—and fatigue. "Make no mistake, I want you. The way I feel I'd want you if I were half-dead. But I couldn't do you justice then and I doubt that I could the way I'd like to now."

She grimaced. "I trust you, but you only have one bed." She said it baldly, astounded that she said it at all. "I've never…never actually *slept* with anyone else before."

His eyes lit; he grinned. Hazel's stomach flipped. What was it about that arrogant, devil-lying-in-wait-in-the-tall-grass grin that made him so…so…*Guy?* So…so…

Right?

"In other words, I'd be your first, then."

He watched appreciatively as the flush climbed her neck. Even with dark circles under her eyes and ripe from too long without a bath, she was darn cute when she was flustered.

"Y-yes." She hugged herself tighter, made herself as small as possible. "Unless there's someplace else…?"

He pretended to think about it a moment—a long and devilishly well-considered moment—then took pity on her. "I could sleep in the truck bed if that'd make you feel safer."

It didn't. She wanted him nearer than that. Just not too

near. Not within touching range. She didn't trust herself with him. Couldn't, clearly—at least not judging by her actions around him thus far, and she'd be damned if she made the same mistake with the same man twice.

She'd already made the same impatient, jump-the-gun mistake in Hopiland twice.

"Isn't there someplace in here?"

He shrugged. "Take out the table, the booth turns into a bed, but it's cramped. And no—" He held up a hand to forestall her offer to take it. "Don't even think about you using it. The truck's more comfortable, I guarantee. And I'm used to sleeping in it. Or on the ground."

"Oh." Small voice. Silly, really, but she felt like such a city girl all at once, used to far more comfortable, more accommodating quarters.

Used to having people nearby in surrounding apartments, but not in hers.

Ever.

Not even her parents had been invited to visit since she'd first gotten a place of her own right out of the army. When she wanted to see them, she went to theirs.

Where she still had her own undisturbed and very private room.

In a flash of insight, she understood fully why her city-bred mother hadn't been able to make it in the one-room homes on the reservation: no privacy. No chance for modesty.

No chance to keep anything to herself.

Especially when she was a private enough person to want to keep most things to herself and away from her daughter—and oftentimes her husband.

"I guess we should just share the bed then," she said finally. "It's yours after all."

He put the soup in the microwave and bit back another

smile. "True." Then he turned to her, moved to her, linked his hands around her shoulders and let his thumbs fiddle with the back of her neck. Said gently, "Sleeping together can be the best and the hardest part of a relationship, Hazel. Better than sex because it's more intimate. No threats, just safety. Sex is easy, physical. Sleeping together takes trust."

Guy grinned suddenly, wryly, unlinked his hands and stepped back when the desire to kiss the wary expression out of her eyes and off her face started to get the better of him. God help him, there was so much he wanted to do for her and with her. Teach her.

Learn from her.

"Especially if you're going to get any rest. And you need that more than anything right now because who knows when we'll get another chance at it. So you take the bed, I'll take the truck—"

"No." She flipped a hesitant hand. Took the biggest leap of faith she'd ever taken in her life. "Please. Don't. I'd rather you stay."

"Sure? Because—"

"No. Yes." She gulped. "Both. I'd just…prefer to have you in than out, that's all." Hazel shut her eyes and hesitated. Made the admission she'd never intended to make to any man. "If they call…if anyone…if Emily…"

Her throat worked and she looked at her feet. "It's hard for me to need anyone, Guy. I don't like feeling dependent. But you…just stay." She looked up at him, eyes dark and pleading, needing. "Okay?"

"Okay." He nodded. Then deliberately, carefully, so as not to spook her, he stepped across to her and cupped her cheek in one large hand. Turned her head, bent down and breathed the lightest of kisses into the hair beside her ear. "Thank you," he whispered.

The most pleasant warmth she'd ever experienced skirled down Hazel's spine. "For what?"

"For the gift." He unfolded, caressed her cheek, her jaw. Ran such a gentle thumb across her lips that they parted slightly, readily and tried to follow when he drew his hand away. "For being willing to take the risk. For having the courage to want to trust. Me."

"Oh, that." Absurdly thrilled by his praise when she didn't remember ever being even the slightest bit elated by any other man's flattery, she smiled shyly.

Girlishly.

Good grief, she thought, dazed. Smiling *girlishly?* She'd never smiled girlishly. Well, maybe once or twice when she was fourteen or fifteen, but certainly not *since* then. What had he done to her? And why didn't she care more that whatever it was, she was succumbing to it?

Guy offered her a purely male, purely wicked grin. "Yeah, that."

"Well, I guess you're welcome, then."

His leer was teasing, designed to lighten the mood. "Am I?"

She missed it at first. "Are you what—oh!" She shoved by him and headed for the shower. "You!"

"Would I be welcome in the shower, Hazel?" he called after her, laughing.

"No, you would not. Besides, I thought you were too tired to get fresh."

"I believe I could be persuaded to wake up."

"Go to hell, Levoie," she called back without rancor and closed the bathroom door behind her.

Chuckling, Guy stared after her. She was a piece of work, all right. Insecure and tough, feisty and afraid, fierce and full of bluff, altogether amazing and astounding, breathtaking and absolutely beautiful.

All at once laughter faded. Because in a little more than two full days he'd discovered something astonishing about himself, and if he'd been smart it would have scared him.

For better or worse, though, all it did was make him feel more human and more powerful, more...*himself* than he'd ever felt in his life.

Her shower was short, ten minutes, no more, something she knew desert conditions warranted. Nevertheless Guy was asleep by the time she surfaced, bare-footed, shirtless and sprawled easily and accommodatingly on only one side of the bed.

As though he'd shared the limited space before.

Which of course, Hazel thought dourly, he no doubt had. Because he was good at sharing, generous not only with his space but his life and himself. And she was all of a sudden and quite terrifyingly having to fight the hadn't-known-him-long-enough realization that she was starting to not want him to share himself with anyone but her.

Drawn in spite of her fears, she traipsed to the foot of the bed and gazed down at him.

He'd shoved his hair behind his ear; a length of it trailed over his right shoulder while the rest of it lay thick and finger-inviting between his shoulderblades. Without warning a fire lit deep within her while she looked at that dark and infinitely silky stuff. She inhaled sharply, burned. The mental picture that tempted her imagination was too much to resist. She wanted his hair swinging above her, tickling her breasts while he moved, raising gooseflesh, playing along her nipples like a million extra-fine fingertips, heightening the madness.

She wanted it wrapped around her hands while she held him to her, wanted it in a curtain sheltering her face, blinding her vision, blocking out the world and everything except his eyes, his face.

His incredible, enticing, comforting, bring-it-on-babe, killer of a smile.

She wanted *him*.

All of him.

She wanted to absorb him into her, let him fill up and build up all those places where she lacked. Good and bad, physical and emotional, soul and heart, stripped-to-the-bone bluntness and rip-your-heart-out-and-put-it-back-healed-at-the-same-instant circumspection, she wanted every bit of him.

And knew with trepidation that she probably always had. That he was the man her heart had no doubt been day-dreaming of when she'd let adolescence and rebellion and the desire to explore get away from her some eleven years and nine months or more ago.

That he was the man that both her youthful and adult spirits had longed to find.

As fascinated by the realization as she was shy of it, she moved closer to the bed to get a better view of the man every part of her, girl and woman, had hungered to find.

The sight of the massive patch of still-angry-looking scarring in his right shoulder made her clench her fists until her nails scored her palms, bite her lip until she tasted blood. She'd never imagined. When she'd read his file and discovered he'd taken a shovel handle through the shoulder she'd practically laughed, the idea seemed so ludicrous. I mean, a shovel handle, for pity's sake, how did that happen? And how bad could it be?

Judging from the location, near to deadly. If it had been, where would she be now?

Farther from Emily, she admitted—and that despite the

fact they hadn't located her yet. And she herself would be alone out here to deal with...

Everything.

She'd known him less than three days, and he irritated her to death, but she couldn't imagine having to go through this nightmare without him.

Didn't want to imagine it.

She needed him.

And that made him dangerous.

She waited for the irrational fear, the customary scuttle, to put distance between her and the thought. It didn't. Oh, she felt anxious about it all right, but mere anxiety didn't debilitate her the way terror might.

The way she'd always thought that needing someone else might.

Behind her the timer on the microwave dinged and she started. In the bed Guy stirred but didn't wake, flinging an arm over his head as though to block out the intrusion. For a moment a pucker of something like trying to place the sound put a crease between his brows, which Hazel wanted to smooth away, but then he sighed in his sleep and relaxed once more.

Envying Guy his ability to find a moment's peace amidst the chaos around them, Hazel went to open the appliance door. Scent-filled steam enveloped her, making her stomach rumble suddenly and her mouth water. How long since she'd eaten? Forever, now that she thought of it.

Grabbing hot pads from the magnetic hooks on the refrigerator door, she removed the nuked dish from the oven, set it on the counter and lifted the lid. Inside was some sort of meatless stew made with black beans and corn, sweet and spicy peppers and rice. She closed her eyes and breathed deeply. Whatever it was it smelled like heaven.

Quickly and quietly she opened cupboards and drawers

searching for bowls, cups, spoons. Ladled stew into a bowl
for herself and set the rest aside for Guy. Opened the refrigerator in search of something to drink, discovered not
only an unopened bottle of juice but what appeared to be
homemade fry bread.

She sent a wry glance in the direction of Guy's recum-
bent form. Trust him to be able to cook not only a decent
meal but also a good, nutritious one when she could barely
bring herself to fuss with instant oatmeal in the morning.

On the other hand, she reminded herself, placing stew,
fry bread and juice on the table, Guy's domestic talent was
her good fortune. She scooped up a spoonful of stew, blew
on it, tasted it. Waved her hand in front of her mouth trying
to cool it off when the stew proved to still be too hot.
Closed her eyes on a smile and savored. Yeah. Definitely
hers and her stomach's good fortune.

"Glad you like it." Guy's voice was rough with sleep.

"Mmm-hmm." Nodding enthusiastically, Hazel swallowed, trying not to choke herself in the process when she
glanced at Guy. Damn, he looked good. Rumpled and very,
very sexy. She should look half so good when she woke
up from a nap.

"It's wonderful." He'd put the husky rasp in her voice
down to the food in her mouth, right? "Where did you
learn to cook?"

He covered a yawn and offered her a self-deprecating,
one-shoulder shrug. "My mother made us all learn. Said
the way we behaved we were bound to spend a fair amount
of time on our own before we found anyone who'd have
us, so we'd better learn."

Hazel laughed. The sound was light and genuine in the
small confines of the trailer, and Guy liked it; it fitted her
immensely.

Fitted him right down to the ground. The way he wanted to fit her. Now, here.

In his bed.

He forced himself to think of something else before she noticed the erection even his jeans couldn't hide.

"Sounds like the perfect woman to raise boys," he heard her say. "I think I'd like her."

"Probably." Even to him his voice sounded strained, deeper than normal, ragged and husky. Ah, the heck with it. He'd told her often enough how she affected him, now was *not* the time to go all shy over the violently physical and revealingly visual aspects of it. "Most people do unless they cross her. Then it's 'Whoa, Sally, what was that and how fast can we get away from it?'"

He rolled off the bed and padded over to the table. The button of his jeans was open and the fly was partially undone. Hazel couldn't help but notice he was also quite obviously aroused and apparently not embarrassed by it in the least. She blushed and looked away.

He grinned and shrugged, slid into the booth opposite her. "I'd apologize if it was something I could help," he said. "But I was dreaming about you, and now that I'm awake you smell too good and you look mmm-mmm-mmm..." Both murmur and head shake were appreciative. "Even better in person, so I can't help it and no apologies."

"Oh." Hazel swallowed. How did he always find just exactly the words that would worm under her defenses and charm her? How did he make her feel so good, so desirable, when she was often fairly certain she was not? "Thank you?"

Guy picked up a piece of fry bread and tore it in half, gave her that killer half grin. "Is that a question?"

"No?"

"Well, it was a compliment, so take it that way."

"Umm…" Uncomfortable, Hazel cast about for something that would turn the talk in another direction. Her eyes lit on the stew she'd set aside for him. "Would you like some soup? I'll get it for you."

She started to rise. He caught her wrist with one hand to hold her still, used the other to scoop up some of her stew with his fry bread.

"Don't bother," he said around a mouthful. "I'll share yours."

"But I should."

She couldn't seem to take her eyes off his mouth. There was something blatantly sensual in the way he appreciated the food, a none-too-subtle suggestion that he would take even greater pleasure in satisfying other oral appetites as well.

Hers, for example.

Her lungs tightened and her belly coiled; her womb quickened.

"It's not sanitary for us to share." She was spewing nonsense and couldn't stop herself.

"You're kidding, right?" He heard the breathiness in her voice, felt it gut deep, groin hard in the throb of the erection trying to lower his zipper even more, but he momentarily kept the knowledge to himself in favor of eyeing her incredulously. "Hazel, don't even try to get all priggish on me now."

"I'm not being priggish," she snapped. "I'm being prudent. You told me where you stand on fast-and-furious relationships and now you're crossing my comfort zones too blasted fast and I'm trying not to lose my head."

His thumb traced unbearably light, sensual circles on her wrist. He might not whore, but he *did* seduce, and he did it incredibly well. Whatever defenses she'd assured herself she needed to keep between them in order to concentrate on what was important were melting at speeds she couldn't begin to comprehend.

"So 'it's not sanitary' was the best excuse you could come up with?"

"It's what popped into my head."

"Ah." Amusement attempting to masquerade as gravity.

She huffed. "Not everyone can say whatever comes into her head as easily as you do."

His lips twitched. "Probably just as well." He scooped up more of her stew. "Candor gets me into plenty of trouble, but at least I always know where I stand. Here—" he pulled her closer across the table, held the loaded bread to her mouth "—bite. Try it."

"Guy—"

His name opened her mouth just wide enough for him to stuff a bit of the bread inside. She sputtered. He grinned.

"See?" he said. "Good that way, isn't it?"

"You—" She had to chew and swallow in order to speak. Furiously. "You are the most obnoxious, contemptible, onerous—"

"Don't forget charming," Guy supplied. "Or that you said you'd let me sleep with you anyway," he reminded her smugly.

"You—" Words failed. She wrested her wrist from him and flung a piece of the flat bread at his head. He caught it, laughing, and slipped out of the booth.

"Lighten up, Hazel. Play a little." He leaned over and dropped a scorching kiss on her mouth before heading toward the shower. "Have fun when you can."

She cast him a scathing glance. "I'll *fun* you," she muttered.

"I look forward to it," he called, and ducked into the bathroom before she could quit fuming and find anything resembling the last word.

Chapter 12

For the few minutes he was in the shower, Hazel's existence was quiet and almost peaceful.

She hated it.

First she checked her cell phone to make sure the battery was fully charged in case the kidnappers called about Emily. Then she thought about Emily and the Russian mob and casinos on Hopi lands. Then about her grandfather. And her father and Emily's—as Russ put it—sperm donor.

And about her grandmother and Sam and Dextra Poley and wondered what element tied them all together, which now, apparently, had to do as much with gambling as with the Russian mob.

Wondered what piece of string or bit of glue she and Guy were missing that would bring them to Emily and close this godforsaken case, take her and her daughter far and away from all things Hopi once and for all.

Which of course brought her around to thinking about Guy.

Again.

Constantly.

And when she managed to stop her brain from *thinking* about him in so many words, it pictured him.

Imagined him.

Heard his laughter, his fury on behalf of her and her daughter and at her family.

Remembered him siding with her against the world as she'd known it, in a way no one else ever had.

Felt him deep inside her—not only physically but emotionally—and wanted him there again.

Often.

As frequently as possible.

And maybe even more regularly than that.

Doomed, she decided morosely. Doomed, doomed, doomed, damned. Might as well just get someone to shoot her now and get it over with. Her heart was engaged whether she wanted it to be or not.

He was more than she'd ever thought—heck, ever *wanted*—to find in a…companion. She couldn't bring herself to seek out a more appropriate word at the moment, although there were undoubtedly many.

Like *lover*.

Friend.

Love.

She shuddered and shied physically, refusing the word, the implication and the possibility. She didn't want the complications a man of his sort was bound to bring into her simple-and-ordered existence.

Her usually lonely and always-one-dimensional and vacant life.

Damn him.

She was thus preoccupied when Guy reappeared sleek

and wet from the shower, scooped her out of her seat and let his wet hair drip in her face.

She shrieked. "God bless America, Guy. Who taught you how to dry your hair?"

He nodded at the towel hanging about his shoulders. "Since you're not already asleep, do it for me?"

She was tempted in spite of her better judgment. "I don't know if...touching...you too much is wise."

He nuzzled the side of her face; little trickles of water drifted tantalizingly inside her shirt and down her neck, across her chest. "Do it and find out."

"Gu-uy." The protest she made of his name was weak at best. "You said it yourself when I—when we—*if* we..." The water-heavy weight of a lock of his hair made contact with one bra-freed breast. She hissed in air and arched unconsciously into the contact. When her breast swelled higher and her nipple puckered, betraying, hard and insistent, she was sure no one had heard her. "It's too soon."

Hungrily aware of what it was doing to her, Guy turned his head in order to drag his hair back and forth across her breasts. "That was hours ago," he said blithely. "We didn't know each other as well then."

Hazel clutched his forearm and tried not to stiffen and push herself into greater contact with the too-delicious torture. What was he doing to her, what was she letting him do?

Since she'd learned her lesson at fifteen, her body had ever since always been hers to control. But not this time. This time she could barely think, let alone breathe.

This time she was his.

She tried anyway. "Oh, and we do now?"

"Yeah." His voice was low and gravelly, knowing. "We do. We've learned more about each other in a couple of days than I learned about the last woman I dated for months before inviting her to my bed.''

Jealousy rose unbidden. Without wanting to know why, she gave it air. ''I hate it when you bring up other women.''

''Good.'' A trace of his tongue along the ridge of her ear. ''Consider them history. Oh, and by the way, I hate it when you bring up other men.''

''You can't be serious.'' She pulled the towel from his shoulders, blotted at her soaking front. ''I work with other men.''

''Me, too.'' He nudged his face against the towel in her hands. ''Now dry my hair for me.''

''Guy…''

''Fine.'' Exasperated, he took the two steps to the bed, dumped her on it and followed her down, spooning around her and putting an arm over her, throwing a leg across hers to anchor her in place so they shared the same—and quickly soaking—pillow. ''I'll go to sleep with it wet.''

Hazel tried to wriggle away from him, but naturally only succeeded in wiggling closer. ''Guy!''

He clamped his arm more firmly about her. ''Quit squirming, Hazel, or I won't be able to ignore you. We can play later. Right now you're tired and need your sleep.''

She growled.

He chuckled. ''Gotcha.''

''All right, fine.'' She kicked him in the shin—well, actually, more in the knee since her legs weren't long enough in this position to reach his shin—with her heel. ''You want me to dry your hair, sit up and I'll dry your blessed hair.''

''Promise?''

''Guy, for pity's sake. You're driving me mad.''

He swung away from her and sat on the edge of the bed. ''Turn-about's only fair. I headed there the minute I laid eyes on you.''

She shouldn't be pleased to hear that, she told herself, she really shouldn't.

But she was.

Smiling ruefully, she knelt on the bed behind him, covered his head with the towel and began to pat his hair between the folds. "Why don't you shut up and rest your mouth awhile," she suggested.

Fondly.

She'd told him to shut up *fondly*. "I've never dried anyone's hair but my own. Don't distract me. It might prove disastrous."

"Okay." He pressed his back against her breasts, chafed deliberately back and forth across them a few times before he settled down and made himself utterly and emphatically at home.

The contact felt incredible, right, so she let him.

The towel drifted between them, a presence, a tease. Hazel worked it gently down the heavy length of his hair, patting and rubbing, brought it up to cover his head again so she could massage his scalp.

He groaned.

And dropped his head back into the hollow of her neck.

She *mmm*'d.

And fitted herself more tightly along his back.

Warmth turned to heat in a heartbeat. Heat turned hot and then fiery on a breath.

He drew a shallow draft of air into parched lungs and shifted slightly around toward her. "Hazel?"

"Yes?"

"I have to kiss you now. I'll go mad if I don't."

The woman inside Hazel woke and reveled in her power, recognized her victory, commanded precedence, insisted that this was her man.

Demanded that she give him herself and anything else he needed.

She dropped the towel over the side of the bed, leaned over his shoulder and put a gentle but claiming palm to his face. "Don't go mad."

"No." He twisted farther about, snaked his tattooed arm hard around her waist. "I won't." Then, laughingly, as he cupped the back of her neck and brought her mouth down to his, "Unless I can take you with me."

The kiss was everything a kiss should be and, though she hadn't realized it, never had been for Hazel.

Before Guy.

Soft and sensual, dark and erotic, it asked permission and quested; made promises it already fulfilled. Hazel tumbled into it headlong, for once forgetting to check how deep or shallow the waters might be, or worrying that she might be injured.

Guy angled into her and trapped her face between his palms, and the waters closed over her head. On a hungry, inarticulate murmur she abandoned her lifeline and sank into them recklessly and instinctively, certain that Guy would not let her drown.

That he would feed her on his own breath, buoy her on his own unquestioned ability to stay afloat.

Or sink with her.

She discovered she didn't mind the thought of falling into storm-ravaged seas as long as he came with her.

With the discovery came a sudden, intense clarity and freedom, a liberation. With this man—with *Guy* and Guy alone—she could lose herself and not worry about going unfound. Because he would always be able to find her. It was what he did, after all. Found what or whoever might be lost. The way he'd found her, ferreted out her secrets, confronted her fears, met the darkest part of her without flinching or leaving her to the wolves of her sins.

Found her and released her from the prison in which she'd caged herself for the better part of twelve years.

Found her the way she understood she could trust him to find Emily while he somehow kept Sasha safe at the same time.

The way she could trust him to keep *her* safe, her heart protected and her soul intact no matter where things went between them from this moment on.

She felt the sudden telltale sting and burn behind her eyelids, the spill of tears down her cheeks and welcomed them by snaking her arms around Guy's neck and holding on for dear life.

Committing herself wholly to whatever paradise or devils might come.

"Hazel?" Guy pulled his head back, stroked his thumbs through the dampness on her cheeks, rubbing it back along the sides of her face and into her hair. It was a comforting caress for all its simplicity, made the tears flow even more freely. "Hazel?" Alarmed. "Are you all right?"

"Fine." She sniffed, sobbed out a watery laugh and nodded. "Good. Better than. Really. A little scared. A little anxious. Worried to death about Emily. A lot afraid I don't deserve this and can never live up to what you deserve, but really, really good otherwise."

When he eyed her, nonplussed by her for the first time, wanting, she understood, to comprehend her needs fully, she drew in a snuffly breath and brushed his damp hair back behind one ear, stroked his face with the backs of her fingers. "You're one special person, Guy Levoie. Those women who walked away from you are idiots if they didn't recognize that."

Reassured, he smiled. "Doubtful."

His breath rasped heat across her lips; his tongue flicked along the corners of her mouth, darted and teased and stroked. The hand cupped at her nape squeezed and kneaded, easing down into the muscles and ridges that shaped her spine. "Their lives had different needs and directions than mine, that's all."

He rolled the base of his thumb into the small of her back, and she shivered in response, crowding closer. "They didn't make me want to take on all comers or make compromises to keep them with me. They weren't the kindling that makes me go up in flames. Hot, yeah, but not explosive. Not flaming."

His hands drifted to her waist, slid down over her hips to slip underneath the edges of her shirt and ease upward. "I thought they were, but I was wrong."

His fingertips found skin, softer, smoother and warmer than silk. Grazed tantalizing butterfly circles up and down her sides, across her stomach and back. His breath tickled her ear, caressed it when he placed his mouth there. "They weren't you."

Heart in her throat, afraid to believe him, afraid not to, Hazel threaded her fingers into Guy's hair, wrapped it around her fists the way she'd imagined doing. Tried to pull him back a little to make sure she had his attention.

The way he was gaining all of hers.

"Guy?"

He ignored the tug on his hair in favor of running his tongue up the column of her throat, along the delicate underside of her chin. Licked up the teary wetness first on her left cheek and eyelid, then her right. "Mmm." His breath teased and caressed, shivered across her ear. "You taste good. Sweet and salty. Potato chips and ice cream."

"What?" Hazel gasped, thrilling to the frissons of anticipation coiling in her veins, pooling in her belly even as she choked on startled laughter. "I taste like potato chips and ice cream? You are the *strangest* man I've ever met, and that has to be the most unromantic come-on I've ever heard."

Guy pulled back to grin at her. "You're an expert at romantic come-ons now?"

"Yeah, right." She snorted. "But I think I know what's *not* one when I hear it."

He leaned back into her and ran his lips lightly over her chin. "But you're going to let me use it to seduce you anyway."

Not a question. Damned smug man.

"Guy?" She leaned in to nip at his lower lip and drag it between her teeth.

He groaned and his mouth followed hers, begging for more of the same attention. "Yeah?"

"I'm seduced, so shut up, okay?"

His breath was hot, his answering kiss deep, clinging and bone melting. The stroke of his hands up underneath her arms and over her shoulders then down her back, over her rump, skimming the backs of her thighs was light as cloud mist, enticing as a cool rain in the desert. Hazel rose into it, prickled alive under it, shuddered and gave herself up to it and Guy's whispered, "Okay."

Led the way when he tipped her backward onto the bed and swung himself in to lean over her.

And turned every fantasy she'd had about him and then some into reality.

His fingers were slow, inexorable and thorough, opening a single button of her shirt at a time and flitting up and down the path between while his mouth plundered hers, took it, made it his. Hazel had never experienced the pure sensuality of a lover's patience before. The phenomenon was novel, left her arching and gasping, aching for a fulfillment ever just beyond her reach, striving to hang on to each new sensation just a little longer than Guy made it last.

He seemed to recognize every quiver of her body before she felt it, every limit of her endurance before she reached it.

When he undid the bottom button of her shirt, he simply stopped there, his fingers hovering almost within reach of her straining flesh. For what seemed too long, and to the increasingly impatient thud of her pulse, he laved her throat and her lips with his tongue before leaning more deeply over her to whisper a breath across the sensitive pulse below her ear. Then at the same time that he finally spread his hand beneath her shirt and over the flesh of her belly, he captured her earlobe between his teeth and worried it a moment before treating it to a full suckle.

Hazel went mad.

With a strangled moan she came up off the bed; her hands clutched hard in his hair, her body writhed beneath his—*writhed,* for pity's sake! Writhing was the overwrought stuff of romance novels.

Or so she'd always thought.

But apparently she'd been wrong, because no way could she remain still—or silent—against what Guy was doing to her.

"Guy, please." She sounded so frantic she barely recognized her own voice. She only knew it was hers because she could feel the strain of forcing the air out of her lungs and into her mouth, felt the vibrations of the words in her throat. "Please. *Please!*"

"Shh." His mouth against the pulse in her throat was gentle, soothing. "Don't rush, just feel. Ride it."

God help her, she whimpered. "I can't. Please, Guy. I *can't.*"

"You can." His voice was a whisper feathering a hot mistral against her skin between the open edges of her shirt. "Trust me. You can."

"No." Her body was surging recklessly toward somewhere she'd never been before, someplace where, even as she fought to reach it, she wasn't sure she wanted to go. "Just *pleeeeaase*." Begging. Trying to squirm her shirt all the way off. Trying to get at the zipper of her jeans while he shoved her hands away and pinned them. She couldn't bear this. *Couldn't*. She didn't beg, darn it. Demanded, yes, but never begged. "I want you inside me. Do it *now*."

"No." Her shirt was wider open now, pushed back so that only her breasts were still caught in it, covered by it. His hair lay heavy and damp, cool against her fevered flesh. "This time you wait. This time you learn what loving can be. What it is."

"But—"

She gasped and bucked against his mouth, whatever protest or argument she'd been about to make dying in the burning, building delight of the nibbled kisses he used to crisscross her rib cage, to paint her belly, to brush the very outside edges of her breasts. When he traced his tongue delicately through the valley between her heavy, wide-splayed breasts she stopped fighting burgeoning sensation and surrendered to the consuming conflagration.

He savored her.

There was no other word for it. Every taste he took was lingering, as though he filled his mouth with all of her various flavors and found them each ripe, beyond-groaning rich. Discovered within each mouthful an individual sample of heaven, which had to be held on the tongue and against the palate to be fully appreciated before he moved on to the next minute morsel and claimed the quintessence of that, too.

By the time he eased the zipper of her jeans down and flattened his hand low on her belly but still too high to satisfy, she was molten. When he added a flirty dab of his tongue across one nipple but through the fine cotton of her shirt, she was undone.

And when he finally edged the shirt off her other breast and let his hair drag across its tip then blanket the whole of it in a constantly moving, silk-feather mass, she was ready to come apart.

But still he held her, touched her, drove her, merciless but observant, tormenting but gratifying, playful but caught in his own sorcerer's web. Every bit of tension, then puddling, he elicited from her made his breath against her skin harsher, hotter, more deliberate, carved granite through the fingers, hands and muscles that played her to perfection. He controlled himself for her. Because he wanted something for her, needed to give her everything he had inside him to offer and infinitely more. Even in her wildness, Hazel recognized it, knew it, cherished it.

By the time he finally pushed her shirt off of both breasts and clamped his hot mouth over the exposed nipple at the same time that he eased a hand inside her panties and sent his fingers to tryst with her most intimate secrets, she was moaning, keening, sobbing, twisting...

And unbelievably wet.

Slick wet, honey wet, scorchingly, sizzlingly, blisteringly wet. Like rain in the desert, snow melt from the mountains, lava along the slopes of a volcano.

The scent of her was his undoing.

"Hazel."

He rasped her name against her lips just before his tongue surged into her mouth, lay claim, delved in and out while his body covered hers and his jeans-clad loins rubbed against her and made promises he was about to keep. Then he pulled back and turned her over to rid her of her shirt, to tug her jeans off her hips and over her rump. When the denim was gone, Hazel tried to turn onto her back to watch him get rid of what remained of his clothing. Eyes hot, he shook his head and held her still, sent his hands flaring appreciatively over her buttocks, stroking up to the point of the inverted heart they formed at her waist, down and over her hips to linger on the backs of her thighs.

And she blossomed.

"Don't move."

It was a command, a request, a plea.

Hungry for him, but full of the knowledge of the power she wielded over him at this point, Hazel simply turned her head to send a searing look over her shoulder at him. When he groaned and made short work of his jeans, grabbed for the drawer in the small table beside the bed, she smiled.

Lazily.

With smug satisfaction.

That was quickly replaced by a huff of excitement when he fitted the condom he'd sought to himself, then lifted her on her knees to stuff a pair of pillows under her hips, spread her thighs, splayed a hand low on her belly and fitted himself to her.

Slowly.

Exquisitely.

An increment at a time.

Until she'd taken every fully engorged inch of him.

Then he began to move. In and out, deep and deeper, filling her, stretching her, giving as he took, learning as he taught.

Touching her and lifting her. Bringing her to the peak and holding her back. Again and again.

Stoking her fires, then banking them.

Bringing pleasure sobbing from her.

Meeting every movement of her body with his until she could bear it no longer and he leaned over her, wrapped his arms around her, buried himself as deeply inside her as he could and sent her spinning into that place where darkness and stars meld and ecstasy lives.

Her climax was long and convulsive, draining and glorious. She laughed and sobbed into it, reached back to hold him to her until her body went slack and limp around him.

He was still hard.

When she could move, she turned her head to look over her shoulder at him. "Guy?"

He grinned and rocked into her gently. "Don't worry, we're not finished yet."

"No?"

"No." He withdrew from her and turned her over, reached up to kiss her deeply. "Not by a long shot." He lifted her knees, wrapped them about his hips and entered her in a rush. "But this time we'll go together."

Then he propped himself on his arms, leaned down to take her mouth and began to rock her cradle again.

And made sweet slow love to her until they were both limp and wrung out and deliriously sated.

And ready for more.

After which they fell asleep tangled together with Guy still embedded inside her.

Chapter 13

Guy woke in predawn darkness to find his body aching hard and already deep inside Hazel. The delicate, involuntary contraction of her inner muscles around him was what had wakened him. They pulled at him, courted him, tightened and released in exquisite torture, beckoned him to move.

He hiked himself gently forward and held very still, savoring the moment, the total capitulation of her body to his and of his to hers.

Making love with Hazel had turned out to be even more awesome and perilous than he'd anticipated. He'd kissed more tears off her face than he guessed she'd ever wept in her life—more than he'd known how to comfort. She'd tried to tell him she cried *because* he comforted, because he made her feel comfortable in a way she'd never thought to find.

Didn't deserve to find.

He'd tried to assure her that was so much hogwash, that

every person deserved comfort, respite, happiness—but that comfort, respite and happiness weren't things that just dropped into one's lap at will. When you found them you had to reach out and grab them with both hands, hold on tight and be willing to work to strengthen your grip. To toughen tender hands because comfort, respite and happiness were slippery commodities always eeling through the waters of life and bent on escape.

Then he'd tried to tell her, to show her, and she'd cried harder, wrapped her arms around him and clung, whispering fierce dark promises in his ear. Telling him by word and action that she hadn't really understood what he was talking about after they'd had sex in the kiva.

She'd thought that was the equivalent of lovemaking because in her experience that's what lovemaking was, how it was. Quick, momentary, uncomplicated. Pleasure but not joy, escape but not serenity, a measure of physical comfort but not contentment that lasted beyond the moment, that sated but did not satisfy.

That did not fill or fulfill.

Explained to him in word and action that she'd never made love before, never been made love to.

Never made love *with*.

That despite her body's experience he was her first, her only.

He'd shattered inside her then, stunned by the magnitude of her trust, the awesome responsibility, the power of his reaction.

Lost control and come apart vowing not to let her down.

He had never in his life made a vow to anyone. Promises, yes, but never vows. Vows were heavier commitments, cut across the barriers of common sense, and Guy had always before prided himself on his common sense.

Hazel made him forget he had any.

He watched her face, took in the REM movements of her eyes beneath her lids and couldn't remember ever finding another woman so beautiful. Her body fitted his as naturally as though she'd been born the yin to his yang. His tattooed arm was wrapped protectively, possessively, around her—chasing away her snake demons, he decided with a wry grin. She seemed partial to having that arm around her, unconsciously drew it back about her even now and draped her own arm snugly over it when he tried to ease it away so he could stroke her face.

Smiling, he buried his mouth in the warm hollow between her shoulder and her neck making tentative forays along the tender skin with lips, teeth and tongue without remembering giving himself permission. Her throat arched in her sleep and she sighed, seeking contact with his lips.

Growing more heavily aroused by the instant, he nuzzled her neck, planted a long, lazy, open-mouthed kiss over her pulse. Its beat quickened to his ministrations; she moaned and pressed her hips up into him, tipping her pelvis and opening her thighs to take him deeper. Moving restlessly, sliding her knee up his flank to fold her leg around his back while she rocked and undulated against him.

He cupped her bottom and angled her breasts away from him even as he embedded himself more firmly inside her. Leaned forward and laved the tang of sweet salt and sweat from the basin of her throat with his tongue. Grazed down to nip at her breasts until her back arched eagerly and her nipples lifted and went taut begging for him. He opened his mouth over one, intending only to tickle, but the taste of her was indescribable. His mouth closed hotly on her, tongue rolled the nipple against the roof of his mouth and he sucked.

Hard.

Deep.

Greedily.

She went rigid. Her lips parted, breath went shallow and sharp with excitement. Her body shifted against him, lifting high to bring him as hard and deep as she could take him in this position. Her hands fluttered up, glided along his arms, fingers speared eagerly into his hair to hold him to her, then finally to drag him up and bring her mouth to his.

Air caught, slammed down into Guy's lungs, hammered against his rib cage with the thunder of his heart. He had never felt so awake or alive in his life.

So aroused.

His entire body stiffened and stilled, senses unbearably roused, body needing to slam into hers, to claim and possess, to brand immediately.

He tried to calm his racing heart. Remind himself that she wasn't even awake yet and that he couldn't just take a sleeping woman no matter how many times she'd willingly given herself to him in the preceding hours.

No matter that he'd woken up to find himself still buried inside her.

No matter what kind of requests and promises her internal muscles were making, or how demanding their contractions, or needy and rapacious her mouth was on his. He simply couldn't presume so much on her fragile trust yet. His conscience wouldn't allow it.

But then her hand framed his face. Her tongue traced the seam of his lips, slipped between to sketch the sharp edges of his teeth, touched his tongue at the same time as she arched tight into his arms. The decision was made for him.

He was damned to find heaven again.

With a groan he opened his mouth and gave himself up to her: to her questing, restless, reckless mouth and body.

To his own hunger for her—to the raw, overpowering

need to explore every secret she still possessed and make it part of him.

He rolled onto his back, bringing her astride. She rewarded him by opening her eyes and offering him a sleepy cat-in-the-cream smile, bending over him so her heavy breasts would tease his lips before she claimed them again.

Her mouth and tongue stroked his, devoured his; from her throat issued an impatient song of encouragement. She slipped a hand down between their bodies, stroking where they joined, then trailing lower to cup and squeeze the pouch below his sex. He grunted and surged upward, impaling her more forcefully upon him. She gasped, murmuring something inarticulate, and levered herself upward, downward, rocking with him, rubbing, tantalizing until the throb in his loins was excruciating.

Until he knew he had to either take control of the moment or lose control completely.

He didn't mind losing his control as long as she lost hers with him.

His turn to reach between their bodies, to find the slick, glistening center of her sensation. When he touched her, she folded mindlessly over him, her fingers dug into his hair and she moved wildly, her breathing fast and frantic. He held her to him, found one distended nipple with his tongue and teased it until she pressed it deep into his mouth and begged him to take it; stroked his thumb over her until he knew she was at the edge of her own release...

Then gripped her about the waist and lifted her off of him and flipped her onto her back.

"Guy, no, wait, please. Please." A frantic, insensible entreaty, a high, keening whimper of pure need.

He slipped two fingers inside her and stroked, kept his thumb on the swollen nubbin of her sex.

"On my way, darlin'," he muttered, barely able to marshal his own thoughts and contain his own need long enough to scrabble among the plastic-foil packages beside the bed, rip one open and slide it over the tip of his sex. Then he turned and blanketed her with his body, thrusting into her in a motion that made her bow upward and scream.

"Yes...yes...*Guy*..."

"Hang on to it, darlin'," he rasped. "Wait for me." Then he cupped the smooth brown globes of her rump and hoisted her high against him.

Pounded into her until he couldn't tell where his body stopped and hers began, until he was heavier and more engorged than he'd ever felt.

Until she lifted her arms above her head and grabbed the rails of his headboard, locked her ankles around his back and tilted her body as high as she could to take him.

And looked at him, her eyes all dark fire and passion— and trust.

For a heartbeat he paused, awed and shaken, humbled by what he read in her face. Impossible though it seemed, everything written there was more than she'd given him already.

More than he'd thought she might ever find it possible to share.

And more, certainly, than he was sure he deserved, but no more than he intended to take and keep safe, hold against his heart.

No more than he intended to give back.

He would give her everything he had to offer, return everything she offered in kind and more. And she would see. She would learn that it was safer for her to love him than it might ever be for him to love her.

But he would love her, anyway.

However she allowed him to.

Always.

Reeling from and awed by the realization but not stunned by it, Guy touched his fingertips to her face. Hazel turned her head to kiss them. Then she smiled, beautiful, beatific and rolled her hips and he was the one who threw back his head and shouted. The one who was lost, found, pulsing, pouring himself into her at the same moment that she convulsed and cried out and surrounded him with her own release.

The aftermath was equally as intense as the coupling.

When he could move, Guy rolled onto his side and gathered Hazel tightly into trembling arms, kissed her temple with trembling lips, stroked her face, her hair, with trembling fingers. She locked her hands behind him and kissed his throat, his chin, and rubbed her forehead into his shoulder.

And trembled not at all.

"Thank you," she whispered into the side of his neck. "I didn't know."

She didn't know? Like he had?

He tried to say as much, but he couldn't speak past the emotion that closed his throat. His shaking increased.

"Guy?" Worried, she tried to pull her head back to see his face. "Are you all right?"

Wordless, he shook his head and pressed her face back into his shoulder. He couldn't let her see him like this.

She was having none of it. "You're not all right?"

"Fine." The word came out on a watery croak. Oh, swell. First she cried because of what they'd shared, now he did.

Fine buck he made, he thought with disgust, but the tears running down the sides of his face and catching in his hair didn't stop.

"You're not fine." Trust a woman to state the obvious.

"You're shaking." Hazel shoved away from him, jacked up to touch his face. "Are you crying?"

He rolled his eyes. "No."

"You are." Consternation shadowed her eyes. "What— no, *why?* It was wonderful…" Hesitation and insecurity came rushing back. "Wasn't it?"

He touched shuddering, wondering fingers to her face, trying to ease her anxiety. "Yes. It was incredible. It was more." How could he tell her what he had no words to express? "You said you didn't realize. Neither did I. You gave me…you…Hazel…you need to know…I have to tell you—"

Across the room Hazel's cell phone trilled. As one they turned to face the sound.

Hazel blanched. "Emily," she whispered.

Guy swung his feet over the side of the bed, wiping his eyes with the heel of his hand. Whatever he'd been about to tell her would have to keep. "I'll get it."

Crossing the room, he caught up the instrument the way he might a live grenade, and flipped it open. "Levoie."

"Guy?"

Guy swallowed, shook his head and mouthed *Russ* at Hazel. Cleared his throat to work out the last of the emotion that belonged to him and Hazel alone before he said, "Yeah."

"You okay, bro?"

Apparently Guy hadn't cleared away enough of the hoarseness if his brother had picked up on it.

"Better than," Guy admitted, sending Hazel a private smile. "Terrific."

"That mean you got some sleep or that you and Hazel came to some sort of understanding?"

Guy ignored the question. "Did you call Hazel's phone for a reason or do you just not have anything better to do?

Because if that's what this is, you're goin' down the minute I see you.''

"An understanding then." Russ sounded satisfied. "Hope it works out for you, bud."

"Me, too," Guy muttered profoundly. "Now would you get to it? If this is nothin' I have better things to do than talk to you."

"Yeah, well." Russ hemmed uncomfortably. "Put 'em on hold. Albuquerque called. They got an order to turn our guy loose that supposedly came from Hazel. Desk sergeant had a funny feeling about it, called me right after they let him go. When I told him whoever called it wasn't us, he said he'd figured. Didn't see where it could hurt to see who's taking your lady's name in vain so I asked Albuquerque to put a loose tail on him. Looks like he's headed here."

Guy muttered the word he almost never used and watched Hazel through guarded eyes. She'd been right when she'd told him they should keep going no matter how tired they were, should start driving immediately when they'd learned they'd have to wait to fly.

Of course that didn't guarantee that Albuquerque wouldn't have turned Emily's sire loose before they'd arrived, anyway. And Russ didn't seem to know for sure how long the man had been on the loose.

On the other hand, try as he might, he couldn't—wouldn't—regret the interlude or finally and really having the chance to make proper love with Hazel.

Even if it had somehow made him woman enough to shed tears that weren't made of grief.

"Somebody still got him?" he asked—and instantly wished there'd been some other way to get the information out of Russ when Hazel tensed and her features grew shuttered. All the headway Guy thought he'd made with her seemed to fade into some distant memory.

He started toward her; she withdrew, backing up, closing her eyes and turning away. Ah, hell and Judas-be-damned. If he could somehow spare her the grief, he would. If he could find Emily, wrap her in swaddling and put her in Hazel's arms he'd walk through fire to do it.

If he could even just take her history and punch its lights out, he'd do that, too.

He considered that a moment. Well, maybe he could punch out at least a portion of her past for her. As soon as they ran the snake-dancing bastard to ground, he could do that and his conscience would consider it a pleasure.

"Yeah," Russ was saying in his ear. "He's taken a couple of side trips, made a couple of stops—"

"Where?" Impatience got the better of Guy.

Understanding Guy's edginess, Russ responded without remarking on it. "Couple of the smaller reservations. Spent fifteen minutes at the Jemez Pueblo, another fifteen or twenty down on the Isleta Rez, then hit I-40 West. Took another detour down to the Zuñi Pueblo, then spent some time on the Fort Wingate Military Rez. Hit Gallup maybe ten minutes ago."

Guy's jaw clenched. For the first time since he'd risen, he glanced at the clock. He hadn't even considered what "predawn" meant in terms of hours spent in Hazel's arms when he'd noted the color of the sky, he'd just known he was grateful for the time. Now however...

Gallup was maybe halfway between Albuquerque and Winslow. Give or take. Which meant that Hazel's snake dancer had been on the loose and on the road for too long.

"And you waited till now to reach me?" He didn't hide the anger.

"Guy." Russ's patience was infuriating. Guy wanted to

strangle him. "You needed some sleep. I don't care how bad you want to put down Hazel's demons for her, you're not in this alone—either of you. We got him, remember?"

"You personally? Jeth *personally?*"

Russ's silence answered the question for him.

"Right," Guy snapped. "Outsiders. Guys without a stake in it. Maybe Highway Patrol or county mounties, maybe even tribals—good people, good cops maybe—but how many jurisdictions we talkin' here? Nine, twelve, fifteen? And that doesn't include the Federal Bureau of Ineptitude. Geez, Russ. What the devil were you thinking?"

"That while we may resemble the Three Musketeers in attitude, we aren't them. We are not the only ones competent enough to trail one damned Indian who doesn't know he's being watched."

"Damn good thing we're not the Musketeers," Guy muttered under his breath, "because that'd make Jonah D'Artagnan—" Their youngest brother was a hotheaded twenty-three and tended to prefer shooting first over ever asking questions. Which was why they were *all* glad the most recent addition to the LLET—Levoie Law Enforcement Team—was currently almost as far across the country from them as he could be, doing a stint studying up on how to pursue cold cases at Quantico. "…and God help us then."

"Mmm." The concurrence was heartfelt.

Guy watched Hazel gather up her clothing. He put out an arm to catch her and collect her against him when she would have eased by on her way to the bathroom, shook his head at her immediate inclination to struggle. Bent close and pulled the receiver far enough from his mouth to say softly, "You're not in this alone anymore," he reminded her, "so don't run now."

Then, when she'd eyed him a moment, subsided into him

and drawn his tattooed arm as tightly and securely about herself as she could, he brushed a gentle kiss on her temple and whispered a simple, "Thanks," in her ear.

She swallowed and nodded, then dropped her clothing, wrapped her arms about his waist and held on with all her strength. Stretched up as far as she could on tiptoe so she could place her ear near the phone and hear as much of the conversation as possible.

Mouth curving with satisfaction, Guy hugged her and met her efforts halfway, returned his attention to his brother. "What's he doin' when he stops?"

Russ's shrug was in his voice. "Hard to say. He picked up a couple of small packages at Isleta and Fort Wingate. Didn't appear to take anything in with him at any of his stops. Met somebody didn't look Indian at Jemez and again at Zuñi."

"What's he doin' in Gallup?"

"Fast food at a drive-through," Russ said succinctly. "You want to know what he ordered?"

"Somethin' to clog his arteries and slow him down if it doesn't give him a heart attack, I hope," Guy shot back. Then reluctantly, sheepishly, "Why, they know?"

Russ barked a laugh. "Yeah, they know." Then quietly, "These are good cops out there, Guy. They know this is family, and they know what they're doing. Soon's he crosses our lines, we'll take him. For questioning," he added, as though some sort of clarification was needed.

Perhaps it was.

For all three of them.

"And then we'll find her."

"No." Hazel startled not only Guy and Russ but also herself with the violence of her outburst. When Guy looked askance, she flipped a hand, unable to verbalize what in-

stinct suddenly told her to do. "*Don't* pick him up," she said finally.

Guy eyed her for a tick, then his mouth thinned into a grim smile. "Better plan," he agreed. And into the phone, "Let him lead us."

"If he knows where she is and is headed to her," Russ said tightly. "Otherwise time's wastin'."

By the time the *if* was out of his brother's mouth, Guy had straightened and twisted slightly, putting as much distance between the receiver and Hazel's ear as possible. His fingertips idly stroked the soft skin over Hazel's rib cage, distracting her from his intent to protect her from the conversation.

"Keep it to yourself, hey, bro?" he said for Russ's ear alone. Only it wasn't a request, really, it was advice. The kind that promised problems for the person who didn't follow it. "This one's Hazel's call—"

He pulled the phone away from his mouth and sucked a hard breath, turning back and gritting his teeth against the abrupt, intense ache in his loins when Hazel made her own deliberately provocative and distracting maneuver and yanked him back down into her hearing range. He wanted her. Immediately. Several times. As many times, in fact, as she could take him.

And fugitives and work be damned.

He hoisted her high against his erection, let it prod and rub her belly, torturing them both. "*Quit,*" he rasped against her ear, "or I won't have a choice except to put you on the counter and take you right here, right now. Whether Russ is on the line or not."

Hazel's stomach flipped, her nipples went taut, moisture pooled between her thighs. *Do it,* her body screamed, instinctively, reflexively seeking to fit itself to Guy's. To take him into her wetness, to melt around him, to feel his hardness spearing high and hard and fast...

She moaned and felt her body buck against him, knees start to sag, the heels of her hands itch to find the edge of the counter so she could lift herself onto it. *Do it,* her body whimpered. Begged. *Right here, right now. Do it, do it, do it!*

She caught her own breath, leaned away from him and steeled herself against the wonderfully uninhibited but time-imprudent urge.

"You told me not to run, now quit trying to distract and protect me from whatever he said," she murmured hoarsely back.

He groaned and nodded, tipped his head down to bite her lower lip then lick away the bite's sting. "As long's you promise I can chase the fantasy I'm havin' right now when this is done."

Her turn to clutch his arm and shiver, to dissolve into him and dare to make a promise she badly wanted to keep. "If I can...if..." She lifted a hesitant finger to trace his mouth. "If there's any possibility...we'll chase it together."

He kissed her. Hard. "Good enough," he whispered.

Then he reluctantly returned his attention to Russ, who was hollering his name impatiently.

"Guy, damn it, get your mind off the body parts, put it on business and keep it there. Geez-oh-Pete-to-hell. This is why we don't fraternize on the job, too blasted much interference—"

"Like you wouldn't give you eyeteeth for a similar situation of your own—" Guy began mildly only to have Russ cut in. There was the sound of some sort of ruckus in the background.

"What I'd give my eyeteeth for at this moment is your

undivided attention," Russ snapped. "We brought in Hazel's father. Claims he doesn't know anything about Emma, but Jeth just manhandled a couple of Hopi youngbloods in here who say different. That and one of my men says your guy just detoured out of Gallup up US-666."

Guy came alert. The mention of the "devil numbers" seemed to him, somehow, full of portent. "He'll stay on him?"

"Damn straight or I'll take his badge."

"Long's he doesn't lose him," Guy muttered. Then, more clearly, "Keep us posted on his travel pattern, hey, but I think we might want to talk to Hazel's dad and the guys Jeth brought in first—"

He glanced at Hazel for confirmation. Her jaw tightened and her eyes darkened with something deeper than anger, but she offered him a stiff shrug and a clipped nod. *Your call. This time.* Only partial quarter given. Whichever course would bring them to Emily faster was the only one she wanted to take.

And since her own instincts in the matter were overgrown and muddied, the only thing she could do at the moment was hope that his were intact.

The only thing she could do was trust him.

Chapter 14

Hazel's father looked much like Hazel but with all Hopi features instead of Hazel's unmistakably mixed ones.

He was on the short side, brown-skinned and muscular with a broad, flat nose and hair worn the same way it must have been cut at whatever boarding school he'd attended during his youth: short and with buzzed scalp showing for an inch or so just above his ears. It identified him at once as a white-man-taught indigenous person and one who, perhaps, continued to embrace something other than the Hopi Way, the beliefs and morals inherent to his native culture. He was seated at a standard-issue interview table in an interrogation room borrowed from the Navajo County sheriff in Holbrook. He shifted restlessly in his seat when Guy and Hazel entered the room, but not once did he raise his head to meet his daughter's carefully expressionless eyes.

"Mr. Youvella." Guy pulled out a chair for Hazel, turned one around to straddle for himself. "May I call you Clint? I'm Investigator Levoie from the BIA Criminal Investigations Division. Lieutenant Levoie or one of the deps explained why you're here?''

''She's safe,'' Hazel's father blurted suddenly, turning lowered but beseeching eyes in her direction. ''They told me she's safe. I wouldn't let anything happen to her, you have to know that. There wasn't any other way…''

Pain. Betrayal.

Truth she could no longer even attempt to deny.

Nearly gasping from the shock of it, the unexpected bluntness of her father's all-but-confession, Hazel stared at him and felt grief fill her, sharper, deeper, more jagged and more unbearable than anything she'd ever experienced in her life. It squeezed the breath from her lungs, tore holes in her heart that she was sure not even time would be able to mend.

Why?

She wanted to leap across the table and shout it in his face. Instead she temporarily checked her grief with the rest of her historical baggage, locked it in the same cage that housed her anger. Pushed aside the red haze of fury at the periphery of her eyesight. Asked calmly, flatly, ''Where is she?''

Clint's gaze darted nervously to the lower half of her face, to the relaxed but none-too-subtle fists Guy used to prop his chin on the back of his chair. His Adam's apple bobbed in his throat. ''I—I'm not sure,'' he said.

Guy recognized it as admission. Hazel understood it as evasion. Her father was not a stupid man—or so she'd always believed. If he didn't literally know where Emily was, she was fairly certain he could offer an educated guess.

''Who's holding her?'' she prodded, changing directions slightly.

Again Clint's eyes did the uneasy dance in his face. He'd been out in the world too long, Hazel decided; he'd forgotten how to maintain the legendary impassivity of their native peoples.

Not that she remembered him ever being particularly impassive in the first place, she realized. Blankness had never really impressed her as part of his character. His face and body language now told her a lot about the lies he was trying hard to keep from speaking to her.

"I don't know," he said finally.

An nth of Hazel's self-control snapped. She shoved her chair back, stopped herself from leaning over the table to grab her father's shirtfront with an effort, even before Guy drifted a hand across the space between them to prevent the action.

"Don't," she told her father softly between her teeth. "You've lied to me about her for eleven years. It stops here. Who's holding her? Tell me."

For the first time Clint raised his head to look at her directly—or as directly as it was possible for a man who'd deluded her for eleven-plus years to look at his daughter.

"I'm not...sure," he said haltingly.

Hazel bit down impatience and waited for the rest.

There had to be a "rest."

"But you've got an idea?" This quietly from Guy.

Clint glanced at him, nodded hesitantly. "Russians, I think. Men who want to—" he paused, pulling words together "—front us the money to put a casino on the highway through Hopi. Or on lands outside the reservation that the tribe owns. Either place would mean jobs, revenue, growth, civilization, perhaps...more." He paused, drew an unsteady breath and shrugged. Hopefully. "Enough maybe I could get your mother to come back here with me, be near to watch our granddaughter become a woman..."

Hazel's jaw went lax. She was gaping and she couldn't seem to do anything about it. Of all the things she might have predicted he'd say...the Russians, yes. That his not-quite-confessed "reason" behind his involvement was to get her mother to return...no. This she could not have anticipated. Not dreamed in her worst nightmare.

Not thought of him, ever.

And if he'd seriously thought it would work, she knew better than she'd ever known anything that he'd deluded himself far more than he'd ever mislead her about Emily.

But that knowledge was for later. Now was the time for disbelief and rage.

"You knew they would take her." She was shaking so badly she could barely speak. He appalled her. "You let them take her, use her as leverage to blackmail the council and get the tribe to vote yes on gambling so you could maybe, eventually, possibly talk Mom into moving back here when you know she won't, she can't, she never will? And you did this because you want to be near enough to see Emily grow up...as *Emma?*"

Her fists clenched lethally tight. Her voice was rising by the word; she couldn't stop it. "You *bastard!* Did you see what they sent me? They sent me her hair. They kept her in a snake-infested kiva. I have a picture of her. She was *crying,* damn you. She's afraid. And you *let* them because you hope to someday live *nearer* to her? How could you? God."

She ducked her chin and shut her eyes, rose to turn her back on him. "I can't look at you. You disgust me."

"Hazel." Heartbroken. Beseeching. Half rising to stretch a hand across the table.

"I didn't *let* them," Clint pleaded. "I *didn't.* It was done before I knew. It's my fault they learned about her, but I didn't..." He stopped, worked his mouth around something that looked as if it tasted bad. Protestations of innocence were neither accurate nor dignified at this point. "When your grandfather told me she was gone, that he suspected...I told him to bring you in, that you were her best chance.''

"Who took her?" Dispassion born of numbness filled her. "Give me a name—names. How is—was Grigor Klimkov involved? Did the Russians come and take her on her way home themselves or did someone she knew pick her up for them?''

Clint shook his head. "Klimkov's powerful. If he says 'make it so' it happens. We heard his son was with the Pai. Maybe with a new tribal cop who used to work some undercover for the Arizona state prosecutor.''

News traveled fast even in country where phone service was often primitive at best. Watching her father, a kind of hatred she hadn't even experienced when she'd found out about her parents' earlier betrayal of her burned through Hazel. He'd have taken Sasha, too, sacrificed him at the altar of let's-modernize-the-world-at-all-cost no matter who it hurt.

Or maybe killed.

"The information was..." Hesitation and a sidling glance at Guy. Clint Youvella was clearly aware of who the BIA investigator across from him was related to. "...valuable to them. It was—" another searching pause "—traded. I believe they...found...someone Emma would trust to bring her to them.''

"Her father?''

Clint nodded. "That's what I believe, yes.''

Her soul ached to hear the answer. Needing to be certain she asked carefully, "It was all right for her to know Thomas Dawavendewa but not me?" She spoke his name aloud for the first time in twelve years. Her tongue did not fit gently around it.

"No." Her father looked away, back. "I don't think so.

Maybe. Only because he lives on the reservation. But he's not who I meant.''

"Then who—''

Breath caught, heart stopped a beat, then slammed into her throat. Dropped in dead weight to her stomach. Righted itself and began to pound like Apache war drums in her chest, her temples, her ears. She stared at her father unable to speak.

Guy flattened his palms on the table and spoke the name without inflection for her. "Sam Poley,'' he said.

Clint Youvella nodded.

Judas-be-damned. Thirty-six months give or take, and here was another pretty little preteen no one was sure they could get to in time. He wanted to choke someone. It hit too close to home, felt too much like Marcy all over again.

What had it been now, three days? At most four? A lifetime and more. And all that time the person who purportedly had the most to lose was the one Clint Youvella believed knew the most about his adopted daughter's disappearance. And Guy hadn't once suspected. Not since the opening gambit when the parents were, of course, at the top of the list of suspects in the disappearance of a child. Because they'd been checked out and dismissed almost at once, especially at the point when the concentration was still less on the "whodunit'' than on the "where is she?''

Than on finding the girl.

And then Hazel had been called in and, despite the fact that he'd known his attraction to her should wait, he'd let himself get distracted.

Had set out to do his best to distract and attract her.

His knuckles white-tight about the steering wheel, Guy drove north as though all the demons he'd only ever half-believed in were on his tail. Fighting the bile that made his throat raw and his gut knot. Rushing against time, not knowing where they were going, who or what they were combating.

Besides the unacceptable thought of failure.

This had been Jeth's private hell for three years—the guilt-sickness that Guy and the rest of his family had tried to convince Jeth wasn't his to bear alone, if at all. Now he understood it. Empathized with it.

Knew that if the worst came about, Jeth's hell would be his, doubled. Because not only would he have failed Emily, but Hazel and the tenuous faith she'd placed in him.

Keeping his eyes on the jouncing and occasionally mud-slogged road ahead of him, he nevertheless let Hazel into his peripheral vision. The ruts he couldn't avoid sent her banging forward into her seat belt with bruising force; she held it down across her chest and away from her throat to prevent its throttling her or crushing her windpipe with each jerk. He'd have to make sure to get one of those custom kits that would allow her to adjust the belt not only across her lap but across her shoulder as well. It was the least a considerate lover could do.

The least the man who wanted badly to simply love her could do to make her short self comfortable in his truck.

Keep your mind on the task, he ordered himself savagely. Time enough to be a considerate lover later. If they weren't too late. If he hadn't managed to waste enough time to destroy her heart again. And if she let him be any kind of lover to her after this.

If she let him love her.

From overhead, growing louder by the moment, came the pounding *whoop-whoop-whoop* of an approaching heli-copter. At about the same time that Hazel rolled down her window, stuck her head out to look, ducked back in and shouted "Mine" over the noise, meaning it belonged to the FBI, Guy's radio *shurred* to life.

"Youvella, that you and Levoie?"

Hazel grabbed the mike with a deceptively calm hand. Inside she was quaking a Richter scale ten. "Yes. Who'm I talking to?"

"Agent Danny Greene. We met in the office your first day out here."

"I remember you, Greene. You got something?"

"You all're headed back out to the Poley's, right?"

Hazel made an affirmative.

"Yeah, well, a rattletrap took on off away from there headed northeast 'bout fifteen minutes ago. Couldn't tell who's drivin' but they're goin' like Indy."

"Thanks for the tip, Greene. You see a shortcut we can use to ground intercept?"

"Map, door," Guy shouted over the noise.

Hazel nodded, reached into the pocket on her door and retrieved a detailed BIA issue map of the Four Corners area. "Got it." Into the mike, "Tell me where, Greene."

"Peel off 87 to Indian 60 to 15 at Dilkon. Head up 6. From there it's all rough, but keep north. Looks like that'll put you on 'im direct."

"Copy. Thanks, Greene."

"No sweat. We'll hang around, make sure he doesn't swing back."

The helicopter beat away. For the tick of seconds, for six or ten almost audible thumps of their hearts, the relative silence spread out in waves, circumspect yet determined to be heard. The same way they couldn't quite ignore each other, they couldn't disregard the silence between them, either. Still neither broke it until Guy took the turn onto Indian 60 without slowing. The rear of the truck sashayed back and forth across the road. Watching him, Hazel grabbed the strap above her door and braced herself against the dash.

He blamed himself for slowing them down. She read it in the tension in his body, his jaw. He thought he should have known sooner, that those infamous instincts of his should have kicked in and laid it out before him the way her mother laid out a deck of tarot cards and read celebrity lives and futures with seemingly uncanny accuracy. The thing about her mother was, though, that she prepared for her clients, utilized resources like the Internet, gossip columnists, movie buzz, trade papers to do her research, to help her be more specific.

There was no denying Zoe had a gift, but she was smart enough not to rely solely upon it, wise enough to realize that outside knowledge could only enhance her abilities—and that sometimes her readings could only be as good as her information. The thing Hazel would have to make Guy understand at some point, when they were done with this, was that he couldn't possibly have known more—instinctively or otherwise—any sooner. His information had been incomplete and faulty.

In fact, his information had been far more accurate before Hazel herself had been called in to take charge of Emily's case. At least then all he'd had to do was read the story written in the earth, intuit a path that didn't lie, the way her own people had lied to her. He hadn't had her to waste his time and distract him, to take him away from his task.

She swallowed the lump of guilt pressing the back of her throat, forced herself not to think about it because down that road lay the recriminations that made for damaged goods among criminal investigators. Along that dirt track lay madness.

When the truck quit swaying and straightened out, Hazel leaned across the seat, laid her fingers on Guy's arm.

Started to say, Guy, at the same time that he said, "He's goin' to her."

"You don't know that," she objected quickly, but her heart sped with an undercurrent of hope.

With the fear that if he was, they wouldn't get there in time.

With the dread that he wasn't headed toward her at all.

"I do." He tapped the center of his chest over his heart. "In here, I know. He's blown. He's goin'. My bet is he thinks the only way to get the tribe to vote the way he says on the casino is if he comes out of this lookin' like a hero. That means he has to 'find' her and bring her home when we couldn't."

"But—"

Once again the radio *shurred* to life, interrupting her.

"Guy?"

He reached for the mike. "What've you got, Russ?"

"Mabel—" their elder sister "—called in. Couple of Russian 'hikers' tried to snatch Sasha. Everybody's okay, but Allyn had to put one of them down. She's not taking it…well."

No, Guy thought. She wouldn't. Allyn wouldn't go hysterical, she would be furious. And she wouldn't do guilt in a have-to, no-choice situation either, but once fury gave way to reaction…

He picked back up on what Russ was saying.

"Havasupai Tribal took care of the other. Jeth's on his way home now."

Guy swore and glanced at Hazel who'd gone a bit ashen around the gills. "I thought Klimkov and Sasha were out of this."

"Incoming power struggle apparently. Klimkov's on his deathbed. Somebody who wants his dying goodwill and his position figured to slip Sasha in to see him, use him as a hostage to get Klimkov released so he can die at home.''

"Son of a gun."

"Yeah, well," Russ agreed. "I got another one for you. Apache County dispatch says Dawavendewa's made a side trip to Newcomb, New Mexico, picked up a package and what looks like some Russian muscle then crossed the Arizona state line headed northwest. Danny Greene and the FBI chopper picked him up from there. Says it looks like he's headed on a direct course to meet up with the Poley truck. I did the map. If they stay on track they ought to cross paths out near Black Mesa sometime in the next couple hours.''

They spoke little. Snatches of shouted directions that couldn't classify as conversation, when necessary, when Hazel, as navigator, thought she spotted the next turn, a plume of dust, anything out of the ordinary.

Agent Greene kept them apprised of progress from the air, adding his directions to the ones Hazel found and using his bird's-eye vantage to aid in coordinating ops with the other area agencies that had responded to the manhunt in force. Other than that, the journey was a tense, bone-jarring, hell-for-leather race across terrain better suited for horses, balloon tires and ATVs.

For the first time Hazel appreciated the oversize tires that raised Guy's truck too far off the ground for her to step up into comfortably. She winced when her head banged the window for the third time and her seat belt jerked hard across her collarbone *again* when the truck fishtailed through a particularly deep rut. Might be nice to have a little more weight in the back, though, or to ride in something that didn't feel like it was about to take off for the moon every time they took a hill or hit a berm.

A sudden stream of profanity followed by a frantic, "Hold up...hold up...hold up!" issued from the radio. "They've stopped." Greene's voice. "We got us a meet."

"Where?" Hazel, trying to sound calm. To stay calm.

"Shanty ten minutes northwest of your location. Got a couple of mules waiting. Looks like they're getting set up to pack from there."

"They spot you?"

From Guy's side of the seat came a muttered snort Hazel preferred not to interpret. It probably meant something along the lines of "Amount of noise they make? What do you think?" although she hoped not.

Greene apparently concurred. "Don't bet against it."

"Right." Hazel thought about it a moment, glanced an unspoken question at Guy.

He shrugged. "Try it. They're either keepin' her in the shanty or they're goin' to her. No way to know which. Risk no matter what."

Risk. Exactly.

Hazel sucked air, blew it out slowly. Forced herself to step back and put distance between her and the personal aspects of this situation. Compelled herself to see this through her professional eyes, to ask herself what she would do if it weren't Emily out there. What she would risk trying for someone else's child.

Listened to the instincts and intuition that made her among the best at what she did, that had earned her the reputation for bringing almost 100 percent of the kidnap victims she went after home alive.

And no, she wasn't going to think about the "almost."

"Hey, Greene," she said into the microphone. "You see any of our troops closing?"

"Affirmative. Fifteen vehicles less than twenty minutes behind you, maybe more behind them."

"How many possible perps we got on the ground?"

"I count five. One with the Poley truck, Dawavendewa and the two musclemen, and the guy with the mules."

"Weapons?"

"Russians are carrying ak-aks—" Automatic weapons, probably of the AK-47 variety. "Dawavendewa's got a rifle, mule guy a shotgun. That's i—Holy sh—" The expletive was lost in the sudden sound of gunfire, the helicopter's abrupt retreat toward them.

"Talk to me, Greene," Hazel shouted.

"They just blew 'em away." Greene's voice shook. "They freaking put a gun to their heads and blew 'em away."

"Who?"

"The muscle guys. The Russians. Laughin' down there. Talkin' like there's nothin'. Walk around behind Dawavendewa and the guy brought out the mules and just do 'em. Like that. Like nothin'. Sh—"

Hazel interrupted him, her voice hard-edged, calm. "The other one, Poley—" Her seat belt slapped across the edge of her throat and neck with bruising force when Guy stopped the truck and leaped out. She coughed, released the catch even as she asked, "He's alive?"

"At gunpoint. They're going inside."

"Buzz 'em," she ordered, reflex at work. If Emily was inside, she wanted to keep as much space between her and the weaponry as possible. "Keep 'em outside."

"*Roger,*" Greene said.

The helicopter *whap-whapped* away. Hazel pitched the mike onto the seat, opened her door and jumped to the ground. Guy had already rounded the bed and opened the cap, was breaking out their own hardware: Handie-Talkies, Kevlar, her .45 and rifle, his 9mm and a shotgun.

"I hate these things," he muttered, checking the clips

for his handgun, loading the shotgun and pocketing extra shells. "I don't even want to think about havin' to need 'em around a kid."

"I don't know if I hope she's here or someplace else." Hazel slid into her Kevlar and shoulder holster, snapped her rifle together and loaded it. "Why the hell'd they have to shoot 'em? Why?" It wasn't a question; it was fury giving vent.

Overhead the helicopter buzzed rapidly toward the ground at a point out of sight from them and lifted almost immediately away, chased by automatic fire. It circled and repeated the maneuver, covering the sound of the cavalry's motorized approach.

Guy holstered his 9mm, held the shotgun easily, muzzle down in his left hand. "Fill them in—" He jerked a thumb toward Russ who'd pulled to a stop, taken note of his brother's armament and gone back into his vehicle for his own. "I'll do recon—"

Another burst of automatic fire followed the helicopter's retreat; it sounded farther from its original location, but was accompanied by the *whang* and whine of metal striking metal and shearing away.

"—give Greene some ground support if he needs it."

"No." Automatic, reflexive. She couldn't let him go into gunfire alone. Wouldn't.

It was stupid; it was too soon, but somehow he'd become a lifeline. Without him her life would continue the way she'd let it go on for the past twelve years and remain in that condition her grandfather referred to as *koyanni-sqatsi*—crazy, in turmoil, out of balance. Disintegrating. A state that called for another way of living. With him, as confusing as things were they had also begun to make sense.

"Wait." She made it a command. Impersonal. Assistant

Special Agent in Charge to BIA investigator assigned to her. Well, mostly. Because, of course, it was very personal. "I'll—"

Guy shushed her with a wry twist of his lips and a shake of his head.

"He needs to be filled in, Hazel," he reminded her quietly. "And I can do recon faster and safer on my own. You know that. Remember I'm not stupid, and I've got the H-T. We stay in contact. You'll hear from me before I do anything."

Unless there's no choice. Guy read the unspoken on her face, touched two fingers to her cheek. "Even if there's no choice," he corrected. "Then you'll just hear from me as I'm goin' in."

"Okay," she agreed. Unhappily. Then, "Guy..." She stopped, unwilling to burden him with more of her concern.

He winked at her. "Absolutely," he said, turned and was gone. He knew who she was now. Underneath the suit. A woman who couldn't let the man with whom she'd just discovered what it meant to really make love walk into danger alone. He understood that, because he didn't want her anywhere near the gunfire, either.

Chapter 15

He moved soundlessly through piñon and rock, easing into viewing range. On the ground in front of the shanty lay the Indians whose shootings Danny Greene had witnessed. Not pretty. Nothing to be done for them, clearly.

Emptying his mind of the sight, knowing full well that it would catch up with him again later in nightmare form, he shifted his position to get nearer, spotted the two men Greene had described, ducking and covering amid outcroppings of rock, between cottonwood trees and scrub pine. One of them jerked along a smaller man—no, Guy realized with a start. Not a man. Not Sam Poley.

Emily's adoptive mother, Dextra.

For half an instant he considered letting Hazel know who the third person was. But he discarded the thought almost as quickly as it occurred. She didn't need any more on her plate. And much as he might have liked to take a minute to curse his own instincts for being taken by surprise yet again, Guy simply filed the information away and worked his way around to the side of the shack.

From behind it he could hear the mules stamping nervously, occasionally braying.

Moving fast, he crossed the space between his last bit of cover and the shanty, crouched at the corner of the wall with his back to it as soon as he reached it and unclipped his H.T.

"How you doin' up there, Greene?" The question was low-voiced, barely above a whisper.

"Pull in the friggin' ground troops, we're taking fire and I'm gettin' seasick up here," Greene snapped—equally quietly.

"I feel for you," Guy muttered dryly, grinning. Greene was at his best when he complained of being seasick in the air. "See if you can herd your guys toward Russ 'n' Hazel. I know Russ, they'll start circling and closing. Gimme time to see if anyone's inside."

"Roger that," Greene returned, and the helicopter moved to follow Guy's suggestion.

Switching off and reclipping the H.T. to his belt, Guy slid along the wall until he came to a scratched and clouded plastic window halfway along it. A piece of greased paper covered a place in one corner where the Plexiglas had cracked and been broken out.

Unable to see anything through the plastic, Guy continued down the wall to the back corner, looked, ducked, looked again. Clear. There were no windows back here, but a screen door sagged off its hinges in the middle of the wall. Behind it a wooden door yawned open. Instantly Guy crouched and inched his way back to the window, easing his knife from its sheath as he went. Gently, silently, he sliced the greased paper and started to pull it out—

And flattened to the ground just in time to avoid the shotgun blast that roared over his head.

Occupied with coordinating efforts between Russ's ground team and the helicopter, Hazel whipped about when she heard the twelve-gauge discharge from the direction Guy had disappeared.

"Guy?" she whispered his name, terrified for him. Then she switched her Handie-Talkie to his channel and yelled it over the din of the helicopter and the ground fire as she darted between the parked Broncos, Blazers and Jimmies, heading in the direction she'd watched him go. "Guy, answer me!"

"Hazel, don't." Russ suddenly appeared and yanked her back under cover. "He's fine. I've seen him handle this sort of situation a hundred times. He was on his face when that thing went off."

"He switched off, damn him." She hated the dread in the pit of her stomach, the fist clenched in her chest that seemed to have grabbed her heart and begun to squeeze the life out of it. Hated how it weakened her. Didn't like what it meant.

And knew, damn him, that he'd gotten to her exactly as he'd promised and she'd sworn he wouldn't.

"He was supposed to call for backup."

"Number one he didn't want us blowing his location." Russ kept his voice quiet, void of the urgency he felt to check on his brother himself. You couldn't have an entire family of brothers together in law enforcement and not understand the risk to heart and mind. Couldn't have them all be younger than you, feel responsible for them your entire life and then keep your sanity if you didn't trust them to look after themselves once in a while. "Two, he doesn't need backup or, trust me, we'd have heard."

Furious, Hazel stared up at him. Damn him, he was too calm. Her baby and Guy were out there, and the ice that had melted inside her had left behind a kernel of hysteria that was trying to break loose. God, why couldn't she be calm?

It's not the fear but what you do with it that's important, an old army mate's voice whispered in her mind's ear.

"It's not SOP." Allowing apprehension to turn itself into a focused anger, she voiced the thought, only half realizing what she said—or who she said it about.

Russ snorted. "And anything else he's done since you met him is?" He shook his head. "No. Trust me. He's best served if we stay out of his way and corral our own perps."

Hazel's jaw worked. He might be right, but she didn't have to like it. "All Levoies say 'trust me' as often and with the same conviction you 'n' Guy do?"

He grinned. "Every single one."

"Figures." She grimaced. Gave it half a second's more thought than she could really afford. "All right. Fine. But."

Russ waited.

"You're wrong and he's not fine, you go down first."

Russ nodded once and offered her a tight grin. "I like you, too, little sister," he agreed.

Then together they slipped out to help take down Thomas Dawavendewa's murderer, Russ humming the 'Suicide is Painless' theme song from M.A.S.H. under his breath and Hazel trying to ignore the fact that he'd called her "little sister" as though they were related.

The instant the blast cleared, Guy rolled and came up moving when he heard the back door burst open, followed by the sound of running footsteps. He arrived at the rear of the shack in time to see a young Hopi man attempting to catch and board one of the mules. Without bothering to do

the "BIA, freeze," routine, he snaked around the mule and
tackled the youth—well, he was about Jonah's age—and
relieved him of his shotgun. Then he wrapped an arm about
the younger man's neck and dragged him out of the way
of the unhappy mule's hooves in the same move.

"Don't kill me, man," the kid begged. "Please don't
kill me."

"I didn't save your blasted neck to kill you," Guy
snapped, exasperated.

"You're not with them?"

"With who, the Russians?"

The kid nodded, frantic, trying to dance away from the
sound of the automatic fire that came from out front.

"No. I'm Investigator Levoie with the BIA." Guy didn't
want to, but he relaxed his hold a fraction. Couldn't get
answers out of a broken windpipe, and the way the kid was
struggling, that's exactly where they were headed if Guy
didn't release. "I'm here looking for a missing kid." Every
ounce of willpower went into keeping his voice calm.
"Kid's a little girl. Emma Poley. Your chairman's daughter. But since I see her mother's out here, too, I'd guess
you already know that."

"I didn't know they was going to kill anybody." The
boy was shaking so badly he could barely stand. "No way
we would've done it if we knew. We just thought the
money, you know, the jobs, from bringing in the casinos.
We all needed the money."

Guy nodded with understanding—and loathing. Because
he'd spent most of his life on a money-strapped reservation
and he did know. And he still didn't know anyone on his
rez who'd gone—would go—to the lengths Thomas Dawavendewa and Clint Youvella had.

"I hear you there," he said quietly. "What's your name,
son?"

Three or four years younger than him at most and he was calling him ''son'' as though a generation and more stood between them.

Perhaps it did.

''Barton...Bart Dawavendewa.''

''Thomas's brother?''

A frightened glance toward the front of the shanty accompanied by an almost imperceptible nod.

Guy's mouth thinned. He shut off the instantaneous vision of one of his own brothers down the same way Thomas was down. It had been bad enough the day Allyn had brought Jeth home to them half-dead from the gunshot wound he'd taken to the chest three months ago. The knowledge that it could happen in their line of work at any time was something you lived with, not something you ever dwelled on, let alone thought about if you wanted to keep doing what you were doing.

''Anybody else inside, Bart?''

When Barton shook his head, Guy hauled him to the door, pulling out his H-T to contact Hazel and Russ as they went.

''They wanted us to have it,'' the boy rattled on, confessing to nothing and everything, both too afraid and too relieved to be alive to be coherent. He didn't resist when Guy led him back inside, handcuffed him and sat him in the only available chair. ''They were givin' it to us. I wouldn'a done it if I knew. I wouldn't. No matter what Tommy said. Now look at him. They just did him. Right out there. No warning. They would've come in for me next, I know they would. I wasn't gonna let 'em...''

Outside, except for the waning *chur-chur-chur* of the helicopter, there was a sudden and acute silence. Alert to it, Guy pulled Bart back up out of the chair, shoved him into the corner behind the front door and raised a finger, warning silence.

"Guy?" Hazel, shouting. Guy thought he heard an edge of worry. "We're done out here and I heard that shot, damn you. Where the hell are you? You were supposed to call for backup. You'd better not be dead, because I'm the only one gets to do that to you."

Guy grinned, warmed all the way down. Yep, definitely worry—and pretty uninhibited worry for such a keep-it-to-herself kind of gal to exhibit it in front of fifteen vehicles full of various agencies' cops. Aside from her admonition that he'd better be alive, he'd noticed that she only tended to swear when she needed to keep fear at bay.

"Do I get turnabout on that?" he shouted back.

"On what?" she asked. If he wasn't mistaken she sounded disgruntled.

"Never mind. Tell your guys to stand down. I'm opening the door. I've got one prisoner." He listened for the order, then pulled open the shanty's front door. Hazel and Russ met him on the wooden packing pallet that served as a step. "You got Dextra?" he asked his brother.

Russ cast a glance over Barton Dawavendewa and nodded thoughtfully. "Russians tried to kill her at the last minute. We shot one. The other did the job for us. I'll bring her in."

He left.

Hazel looked at Guy. "She's not here?"

Guy shook his head, hating that he didn't have answers for her. "I haven't found her." He smiled unpleasantly. "Yet. But I know who to ask." He hauled his prisoner around to face Hazel. "Barton Dawavendewa, meet FBI Assistant Special Agent in Charge Hazel Youvella."

Hazel stiffened.

Barton paled visibly.

She glanced at Guy. Something dark and almost viciously feral sparked to life in her eyes, suffused her being. She banked the flame with effort. "Related?" she asked. Tautly.

"Baby brother," Guy confirmed—then wondered if it might not be better to stand between her and Bart, just in case the killer instincts he'd seen in her came fully to the fore and scared Barton to death.

Nah, he decided. Do the kid good to live in hell's flames a little while longer, impress on him the things that one did not do regardless of the circumstances.

A muscle rippled visibly in Hazel's jaw. "And Dextra?"

Guy eyed her shrewdly, watching for the breaking point. Ready to protect her from herself if she needed him to. To guard this special agent with his life if he had to.

And equally as ready to let her unleash her temper and play her hand as far as he dared.

He shrugged his lips. "Ask him."

"My sister," Barton volunteered uncomfortably before she could.

"God." Queasiness punched Hazel hard in the stomach. She'd worked some tough abductions before, witnessed kidnappings that pitted parent against parent, involved little kids lured off playgrounds for unspeakable reasons, but this one...

This one was new—and not simply because it involved her own daughter.

"God! Her own—" She bit it back. No mother worthy of the name did this. What a fool! She'd been played, suckered, had big-time, and her baby had paid for her stupidity. Was paying.

Without warning—without even knowing she was about to do it—she jerked out her .45 and planted the muzzle in

the center of Barton Dawavendewa's forehead—without
taking off the safety.

Yet.

"Where is she?"

The kid quaked, more petrified than he'd been when Guy
first found him. "Don't kill me, oh, God, don't, please. I
didn't know, I *didn't*."

"Judas, Hazel." Reflexively Guy stepped forward and
stopped as though afraid to set her off, apparently shocked
by her, finally.

"Back off, Levoie." Good, she sounded only minutely
shaky. Enough so maybe Guy would catch the gist of her
impromptu plan and play good cop to her extremely bad
one.

At least, he hoped that's all that was happening here.
Hoped she hadn't just gone over the edge and lost her ob-
jectivity completely.

"I'm done screwin' around with these people and my
daughter's life. Now he's going to tell me where she is or
he can join his brother."

"Not much use if he does, is he?" Guy pointed out.
Judiciously. Every inch the good cop.

Hazel risked an eye flick in his direction. He sounded
suspiciously mild. He raised a brow and made a vague head
move in the direction of the safety. Blasted man figured
out everything—and, no, never mind that she'd intended
him to. She didn't feel like being rational at the moment.
Too much was at stake.

"Of course," he continued conversationally, as though
pondering all the possibilities—some of which included
shooting their prisoner, "if he *does* decide to join Tommy,
we still have Dextra."

The corners of Hazel's mouth curled coldly but appreciatively upward. Ah, yes, at last a man she could work *with* instead of against.

The same way she could make love *with* him instead of merely having cold, unfeeling sex with someone she didn't care to work with, let alone know.

"Please," she heard the boy plead, "I don't wanna die, I didn't know, they were— Tommy said...he just found out about Emma. He said...they owed him for lying all those years and this was how...and—"

Hazel planted her feet more firmly and put her thumb against the safety, enunciated each word carefully, "Where. Is. She."

"I—"

Before he could say anything further, Russ ushered Dextra through the door. She took one look at her brother and gasped, "No, please, no. It wasn't supposed to happen like this, please. Don't hurt him. He only tried to take care of her, to hide her from them after they cut her hair and started to make worse threats. He took her from the place they had her. He kept moving her so they couldn't find her. Please."

"Tell me," Hazel bit out. Her arms were starting to ache from holding up her weapon. Any moment now they'd start to shake. They'd done it a bit late, but she was glad someone had at last seen fit to try to protect Emily. If they truly had. Still, until she saw for herself that her child was safe and unhurt...

No, she couldn't give in until she had it all.

She stiffened her resolve and flicked off her gun's safety. "Tell me *now*."

Shaking harder, Barton swallowed convulsively. "She's all right," he mumbled at last. "I hid her when Tommy came and said the Russians were on their way here. He thought they'd give him more money if—" He broke off. The *if* was irrelevant at the moment. "There's a trap door, if you move the straw you'll see it. She's under the lean-to off the mules' shed.''

The lean-to was actually neatly hidden behind the shed, dark and hay-dust smelling but surprisingly clean. Hazel entered it first, soaked in the sweat of trepidation. Guy came in on her heels and laid a hand on her shoulder, aiming his flashlight around.

''Broom,'' he said, flashing the light on a broad-based sweeper. ''I'll do it.''

She nodded. She wanted to call out, to tell Emily they were coming to rescue her at last, but her throat wouldn't cooperate. Nerves. Fright. Relief.

Hope.

So instead of talking to her daughter for the first time since Emily was a day old, Hazel held the flashlight and watched Guy shove the straw out of the lean-to.

''There.''

The broom passed first over hinges, then over the iron ring used to pull the door open. Light showed through the imperfect mating around the edges of the door. Guy looked at it and swallowed hard before dropping to his knees. He put out a hand toward the ring, pulled back, suddenly shaking. If she was in there, like Marcy...he didn't think he could handle it.

Not with Hazel here, at least. He wouldn't be able to bear what would happen to her if...

As though hearing his thoughts, Hazel approached and knelt beside him. He was, she realized with shock, sweating, pale and trembling.

She put out a hand. He gulped and shook his head.

''It's nothin','' he said hoarsely. *You could wait outside,* he thought, but refused to let himself say it to her.

Refused to let himself protect her from whatever lay below the door.

If there was ever going to be anything between them, he had to begin as he meant to go on. "I'll open it." He couldn't—wouldn't *ever*—tell her that he'd flashed on what it must have been like for his brother when Jeth opened an all-too-similar hiding place too late and found Marcy entombed within.

Trying not to think about it, he hauled up on the trap—

And sagged in relief when Hazel's daughter's face looked fearfully up at them.

Without thinking, Hazel let herself down into what turned out to be an entire room under the floor.

"Emma," she said quietly, "You don't have to be afraid anymore. My name is Hazel. I'm with the FBI and that—" she pointed up at Guy "—is Investigator Levoie. He's with the BIA. We came to take you—" She almost couldn't get the word out because she had no idea what it meant to either of them. "We came to take you…home."

The little girl studied her solemnly for a long minute. Then she nodded. "I know who you are," she said calmly—as though she'd known all along that not only would someone come for her, but that the someone would be Hazel. "Great-grandfather told me all about you. He showed me your picture. He said one day when the time was right you'd come for me. He told me to think of you if I ever needed anyone to save me, because you would do it. He said you had that spirit. Warrior Woman, he called you. He said I should watch for you. It's not very good yet, but I carved the kachina for you."

Staring at Emily, Hazel sank to her knees, afraid to blink. "What?"

Emily shrugged. "I can say this now. He told me I shouldn't until you came."

The little girl put out a hand, touched it to Hazel's face as though making sure flesh and blood existed before her. "My real name is Emily," she said matter-of-factly. "And you're my mother."

Chapter 16

Things came together quickly after that. Or as quickly as might be, given the fact that, after staring at her wordlessly for a full two minutes with tears streaming down her cheeks, Hazel finally put her arms around her daughter and hugged her with no apparent plans to let go soon.

Then, of course, there were the moments spent counting to make sure Emily was still possessed of all of her fingers and toes, that she bore no life-threatening scrapes or bruises.

Nothing that a mother who hadn't been allowed to be one could think of when she inspected her baby for the first time in eleven-or-so years.

Progress was impeded by tears that blinded, by snuffling laughter—and by the rescued-and-therefore-resiliently-practical Emily announcing that she was A, being smothered and B, hungry.

At which point a first-time-mother-frantic Hazel ordered Guy to lift them both out of the hole—simultaneously if possible, so she didn't have to let go of Emily—and to find her some food. Now, at once, posthaste, immediately and at the same time.

Which, with tears in his eyes and a silly grin on his face, he did, of course. Caught them both up and delivered them from the womb of mother earth streaked in dirt and straw, tears and laughter, relief and reaction, joy and something even less common and far more tenuous: second chances.

Found the now-safe, albeit-shaky and therefore immediately plaintive Emily some dried peaches, fry bread, Gatorade and trail mix in the first-aid kit Russ had retrieved from his Jimmy and tossed to him.

Because he couldn't do anything less and because he wanted to do much, much more.

Like put his arms around both Hazel and Emily and not let go anytime soon himself.

Crouching beside Hazel and her daughter, one hand idly stroking his partner's hair while the other ruffled Emily's, he gazed at his brother through eyes flooded with an emotion that was far more than thankful and far less than anything either of them could express.

The same sentiment that coursed through his veins when he looked at Emily flowed through Russ's, he knew. Because, though he hid it better, Russ had suffered the same terror he'd felt imagining what might lie beneath the straw-covered trap.

In a short while, Deputy Hogarth turned up with an EMT. The woman once-overed—and then twice-overed at Hazel's insistence—Emily while her anxious new-old mother hovered too close to let the other woman do her job until Guy hauled his petite partner bodily out of the way.

Emily bore the overattention with queenly grace, as though it were nothing more than her due, a child who'd been told a thousand stories about her heroic birth mother and who'd expected to be well-loved by her immediately.

Even though she was not, perhaps, used to having such rabid interest bestowed upon her all at once.

But rabid interest, awe and fascination were all that was on Hazel's agenda regarding Emily for the foreseeable future. She turned once or twice to Guy, held out a hand to him, clasped his tightly and even hugged him once—all without once taking her eyes from her daughter.

Because for her there was no longer any mistake, any if, any question: Emily was her daughter...not Dextra's. In Hazel's estimation, Dextra had relinquished any rights she had by ineffectually attempting to hide Emily after realizing who'd stolen her. And Hazel understood fiercely and without hesitation that no matter what happened to the Poleys, she would do whatever it took to make sure Emily's future lay with her.

Aside from doing whatever she asked, Guy kept to the background as much as possible. Never taking his own eyes off them, he gave Hazel the time and space she needed to simply accept that Emily was here, that she was well, that the future lay ahead.

For all of them.

He hoped.

But that moment was more distant than he should even consider at the moment, he knew. Hazel would need time to reconcile her past with her present, need time simply to discover her daughter.

Need time to learn to be.

Not to mention that right now the EMT said Emily was a bit dehydrated and should be transported to the hospital for a more thorough physical than she could perform.

Hazel was for doing this at once, at full speed and with sirens blazing, but Guy and Russ eyed each other across the top of her head, then Guy bent to quietly remind her of the scene still set at the front of the shanty. Paling visibly, Hazel nodded and agreed without protest that as long as they got more fluids into her, transporting Emily anywhere could probably wait for a little while.

So they moved her inside and kept Emily occupied and away from the front of the shanty. She was still young enough to appreciate being the center of concerned adult attention and so didn't notice that she was being distracted.

When Emily saw Dextra and Barton handcuffed and seated inside amid a sea of law enforcement personnel, she flew to her adoptive mother, threw her arms around the woman's neck and clung tight. Red and green fury and jealousy hazed Hazel's vision at the sight. If Dextra dared pretend for even one *instant* that life had not been irrevocably changed for Emily by Dextra's own hand, Hazel didn't know what exactly she'd do. Something decisive, that was sure.

And whatever it was, it wouldn't be good for Dextra.

Dextra caught the look on Anna Youvella's granddaughter's face; her head came up, challenging for a moment, before her chin dipped with defeat and she disengaged from Emily's embrace as best she could, shaking her head and murmuring, "Go to your true mother now, child. She'll keep you safe."

Bewildered by the rejection, Emily drew back to study Dextra's face. Whatever she saw there, combined with the handcuffs the adoptive-mother-who-was-really-her-aunt and her uncle Barton both wore seemed to change something in her. Something that wasn't quite understanding crossed her features and filled her eyes with pain, tore at Hazel's heart so that she nearly lost her resolve, uncuffed Dextra and told Emily that everything was all right. That what she saw here was all a mistake.

That they would work out anything that needed to be worked out between the two of them later in whatever manner Emily wanted it worked out.

Almost she did that.

Then Emily's face crumpled into a look of betrayal, and she turned away from Dextra with the speed and revulsion only an eleven-year-old can muster and mean. Without a backward glance she stepped across the intervening space to Hazel and glanced upward to find Hazel's eyes, pleading for truth.

When Hazel lowered her lids and swallowed hard, then gazed down at Emily and nodded once, the preteen stiffened and fingered her shortened hair. Twin tears tracked her cheeks, reached her chin before she sniffed once and slapped them firmly away with the back of one hand. The other hand she slipped laxly into her mother's and let it hang there.

Instinctively Hazel caressed Emily's cheek and squeezed her fingers, trying to reassure her that somewhere along the line, everything would come out all right once more.

Comfortingly close but not hugging again without invitation.

When, with a sudden, wrenching, heartbroken sob, Emily threw her arms around Hazel's waist, buried her face against her mother's breast and held on tight, Hazel wrapped her close. She let her cry until she was drained—and while her own face grew soaked with tears.

From somewhere to the side she felt rather than saw Guy move. Then rough arms gathered her up, too, hauled her close. A gentle hand pushed her face into the solid wall of his chest and held her there.

Outside the cocoon Guy had built for her and Emily, she felt someone with bound hands try awkwardly to touch Emily and heard a voice—Barton's, not Dextra's—offer the misused girl a beseeching apology.

She tightened her grip protectively around Emily, felt the equally protective Guy swing them both away from the plea.

Felt the ever-resilient, Warrior-Woman-in-training child in her arms lift her head and duck her chin out to snarl something in Hopi at both Barton and Dextra that could never be mistaken for forgiveness. And that, among other things, Hazel thought suggested the Dawavendewas needed a visit from Chaveyo, the threatening giant kachina, to dispense some heavy-duty disciplinary action against them. Or that they needed some of the ogre kachinas to steal *them* from their homes so they could see how *they* liked it.

If she hadn't been so busy crying and trying to translate the gist of the rest of what Emily spat at Dextra and Barton, Hazel had the strangest sensation she might have laughed, then applauded Emily's stand.

As it was, she experienced the briefest twinge of pity over the pain that suffused Dextra's face and caused the other woman's shoulders to droop.

However, the twinge was brief and passed quickly.

The silence that descended after Dextra and Barton were escorted out was long and speaking. Though he instinctively wanted to, Guy did nothing to attempt to dispel it. Really, there was nothing to say that he felt wouldn't sound either false or forced—which wouldn't come from the wrong person. In his gut, he recognized that it was Hazel, not him or Russ or anyone else, who needed to get Emily to talk.

It took a little while and a great deal of circumspection, but finally Emily told her story a little at a time.

It turned out that, though not well, she'd known "uncle" Tommy most of her life. When he'd stopped to offer her a ride on his way to see Dextra that day, Emily had thought nothing of it. Even when they'd detoured and hadn't gone straight home, Emily hadn't worried. Why should she? Thomas was her mother's brother and no one in her life had ever threatened her before, after all.

But then Thomas had given her to nonnative men with heavy accents, men she didn't know. Men who'd put her down in that kiva alone with the snakes, then cut her hair and threatened other things if she didn't behave herself.

She hadn't been terribly afraid of the snakes—they were part of her life, after all. But the men weren't kind and they'd frightened her, then made her angry when they'd cut her hair. It took an awfully long time to get it to the length she'd worn it—all of her life, as a matter of fact.

It had been the last straw when they'd told her that it was Mr. Klimkov—for whom she'd made kachinas— who'd ordered her kidnapping. She'd gotten angry then, said things only an enraged eleven-year-old can spit out. One of the men had slapped her and would have gone on doing so if Uncle Thomas and Uncle Barton hadn't turned up just then and rescued her.

Except then, instead of taking her home, they'd brought her here and made her hide beneath the lean-to.

Tongue loosened, safe now and warming to her tale and the attention she was being given, Emily jabbered freely about what had happened to her—unlike so many victims Hazel had met previously who folded into themselves and stayed there. The entire tale infuriated Hazel; she had to fight herself to control the urge to explode—had to step outside more than once to breathe her way through the fury and the heart-clutching relief that despite everything, Emily was here, safe, well.

And hers.

Permanently.

Which was, though Hazel didn't allow herself to think about it then, one of the most frightening revelations she'd ever had: she had a daughter. To love, protect, teach about life, care for and rear.

She, who barely understood how to deal with herself, suddenly and irrevocably had an eleven-year-old daughter to raise.

Whoa, baby. Hazel gulped down trepidation. When she thought about it, her jaw felt awfully slack, Jack.

But that didn't mean she didn't intend to face both insecurity and challenge face-on. There was, after all, no truth so great as the one you kept to yourself. And she damned well intended to keep the truth of her anxieties to herself as much as possible.

She risked a glance at Guy and knew he saw them as clearly as he saw everything about her. He twitched his lips at her in a kind of private salute; she raised her chin and glared back.

Determined to her core.

It took a while longer, but the coroner's van finally arrived and the bodies were removed. Even then Hazel hated having to take Emily out past what remained of the bloody site. It was bad enough that her daughter had heard the shots, listened to Dextra scream and imagined who knew what; bad enough that Hazel knew she herself would have nightmares about the incident without wondering how it would affect Emily, too.

Still, the bloody ground had to be passed. So with Guy and Russ's tacit help to keep Emily's view blocked, Hazel led her daughter to Guy's truck for the long trek out to Russ's office.

Where the already-long day grew longer.

And more emotionally intense.

Because Hazel had to decide in real life how to let Emily make the choice of whether or not to go home with Sam Poley, the only father she'd ever known, to stay with her—where, she didn't know—or to go to Hazel's grandparents.

It wasn't easy.

In fact it was the hardest thing Hazel ever did. Because she wanted Emily to choose her.

And after a great deal of consideration, Emily chose Sam.

Over the next many and interminable days, it seemed there were loose ends and pain everywhere Hazel looked.

Out on the reservation with her grandparents—her grandfather especially; with her parents, particularly her father; with Emily, Sam and, of course, with Dextra and Barton; and with Guy, whom she couldn't even think about now amid all the other confusion.

He didn't seem to mind her apparent neglect, though. He was, after all, Guy: big, strong, full of himself and capable of keeping her supplied with coffee or sodas or food or whatever else she required.

Like the simple nearness and physicality of his presence while she sorted through everything else and tried not to hold on to Emily too tightly at the same time.

Or to blame her for making a choice Hazel wished she hadn't.

Emily's preference stood to reason, after all—especially after the insecurity and upheaval she'd suffered. If Hazel had begun to doubt herself and her choices at fifteen when she was fully four years older than what Emily was now, how much more distrust must her daughter be experiencing? How many times had she said, "If only I hadn't...?"

How many times in the interminable interval did Hazel witness her child, her heart, suddenly close up and blame herself for "uncle" Tommy's death. Because if she hadn't gone with him that day, maybe he'd still be alive... And every time Hazel saw it, her heart broke anew.

She understood because she'd been there herself, that time would eventually become Emily's ally—though Hazel hoped with all her strength that time for Emily would not stretch into the years Hazel had turned her own, much-different guilt into.

At her insistence, Emily spent time with a child psychologist from Phoenix, and with a counselor from victim's services. The process wasn't quick, but it was steady, and that was all anyone could ask.

Regardless of how much more Hazel wanted to demand.

Okay, so while this major concern was sorting itself out, where else to start...?

The Russians. They'd been busy little bees from the beginning, finding out everything there was to know about Hazel, buying information and setting up phone patches so that Klimkov himself could contact her from prison, then using Thomas and his brother—well-known faces about the reservation—to maintain covert watch over the scene and Hazel's whereabouts and state of mind. The whole deal had worked a treat—until Klimkov's lieutenants got greedy and decided to do him in.

Word awaited Russ at the office that Grigor Klimkov had expired from his wounds. His death and the death or capture of the other members of his company guaranteed little, the Levoies knew, but at least it left Sasha free and clear and of no more use in mob power plays or hostage situations. It also left him the sole beneficiary of Klimkov's will—something that made Jeth gag and Allyn shudder.

On the other hand, it also made them extremely happy. Because no longer would they have to fear for Sasha's life at the hands of someone out to hold something over his biological parent. Their child was free to live and grow and be as happy as he'd become in the few months they'd had him, and they were free to love and cherish him—and free, as Jeth was impatient to do and Allyn was plenty ready for, to present their eldest child with siblings.

As many as possible.

At once.

Dextra Poley and her brothers. Dextra and Sam had been married three years before they discovered Dextra would be unable to bear the children she'd always wanted. When Hazel's grandparents had come to her and Sam as kin and asked if they would raise Dextra's niece without telling Thomas the child was his, Dextra had been overjoyed with the prospect of having a baby at last. They had always intended to tell Emily about Hazel, but Joseph Youvella had taken care of that for them. Anna had treated Emily as nothing less than her great-granddaughter, the joy of her life.

When, in Russ's office, Hazel asked why Dextra or Sam hadn't told her grandparents the truth about Thomas sooner, a decidedly strained Dextra had explained that Sam hadn't known all the details. He'd only known that Thomas opposed Sam's stance regarding bringing gaming to the tribe and was involved somehow with the casino venture.

She also hadn't told everything she knew to Hazel sooner because she was afraid of losing Emily either to the Russians or to Hazel. This despite the fact that Hazel being able to reclaim her daughter at some point had always been part of the deal. Then she'd kept the rest to herself out of misguided loyalty to her brother in part because neither Hazel nor Guy had thought to ask the single question that would have commanded the truth: no one asked who had introduced Grigor Klimkov to Hopiland in the first place.

The answer was, of course, Thomas Dawavendewa.

Yes, Thomas had some problems with the law in the past, had run with a gang when he was younger, but he was Dextra's brother. If he had found a way to become a whole, strong, upright man in his own eyes, she wanted to help him. But then he'd found out that Emily was his daughter and the whole terrifying plan had been set in motion. When it began to spin out of control, Dextra had tried to enlist the aid of her youngest brother to help her protect Emily.

Not that it had been good enough, of course. Thomas's life had disintegrated beyond all repair by that time, become *koyannisqatsi,* and he hadn't been able to pull out. To save himself.

Hadn't tried.

Clint Youvella. Even when she tried, Hazel couldn't bring herself to look at him. Intellectually she was pretty sure she might be able to forgive him eventually, but that day was a part of a future so distant she couldn't begin to see it yet.

Her grandparents. They had known about Emily. They had been part of the original lie that had taken Hazel's daughter from her in the beginning.

But.

But they were also the reason Emily knew who she was, had trusted that Hazel would find her no matter what. Because great-grandfather had likened Hazel to Warrior Woman.

And Hazel's heart spilled open and begged to forgive them. Begged to spend time with them so she could discover what she'd missed on her first visit to them.

And Emily… As she calmed and began once again to trust, she sought Hazel out and put her first in her trust even while she got to know her. She even promised to teach Hazel to carve her own Warrior Woman kachina.

Emily. What was there to say? Her daughter had been prepared to meet Hazel practically from birth, while Hazel thought Emily lost to her forever. She didn't know how to be a mother, she had a hellacious career too far from the reservation, and she was torn as to whether or not she should remove Emily from the only home she'd ever known despite Dextra's part in the eleven-year-old's disappearance.

But Emily solved that problem for her, too. After her first week home, she asked Hazel to move with her into the small house near Joseph and Anna's so they could at least be together for a little while. Emily understood from the stories that warriors couldn't always stay behind with their children, that sometimes they had to go into the world to slay their enemies. And that meant women warriors as well as men.

So, humbled beyond all thought by her child, Hazel requested a month's leave. She settled into reservation life as best she could with the daughter she would not only have died for, but for whom she'd been willing to kill.

Chapter 17

Hopiland, Three Weeks Later

She was afraid of him.

Not only that, but she didn't—wouldn't—trust him. Not with her heart. Not where it counted. As sure as he knew his own name and his place in the world, Guy knew this, too.

Frustrated beyond anything he'd ever felt in his life, Guy kicked a divot out of the scrub at his feet. From a healthy shouting distance of thirty feet, which was about as close to him as she'd let herself come in the past twenty-three days—Guy cursed himself for counting—Hazel tossed feed to the few chickens scratching in the dust at her feet. And intermittently eyed him.

With regret.

And longing.

Guy read both emotions in every nuanced expression,

every glance, every movement. What he didn't see any sign of was that Hazel had the slightest inclination to approach closer.

As though doing so would prove unhealthy for one or both of them.

For one uncharacteristically violent moment, Guy wrapped a thumb around a tight fist and considered every single one of the expletives his brother Jeth had once included in his vocabulary—and discarded them all. Venting his frustrations by spewing vituperative language to the wind or by giving in to the urge to smash something wouldn't cure anything. It wouldn't even make him feel better briefly. He knew himself too well for that. In fact, the only thing that would do any good here would be for him to solve the riddle Hazel had become.

He'd made a mistake telling her about the five other committed relationships he'd been involved in, that he was a commitment kind of guy. He understood that without having to think about it. Because Hazel, being Hazel, would turn his penchant for committed relationships into a grievous sin and a huge question mark. For which the question preceding went something like: "If you thought you loved five other women enough to possibly marry them, how can you possibly know that I'm not just another one of them? How do you know I'm the one? What makes me different?"

And "How can I trust you?"

To which—when he was allowed to answer—his standard, though clearly unhelpful, response was A, I didn't leave them, they left me and B, Trust me, I just know it's different with you."

Which she would counter with, "Wouldn't some other woman—*any* other woman—do as well?"

No, God bless it. Some other woman would *not* do as

well. Not unless she turned into Hazel herself, and even then he had his doubts. There was simply no substitution for the aggravation and challenge of the real thing. For the way it had felt to be inside her.

Not to mention he'd never before been willing to even contemplate giving up what he was considering giving up for Hazel. Heck, he'd even consider a posting to D.C. if she wanted it. He'd move for her.

What he felt was more than passing fancy or passion—grand or otherwise. Hazel was unique, special. No other woman who'd shared his bed for months had ever gotten under his skin, pulsed through his blood like she did.

But it was more than that, too. No other woman he'd ever known had faced the kind of fears Hazel dealt with daily with the kind of courage she exhibited. She was possessed of a strength and a vulnerability that made him long to possess and protect her at the same time it made him want to share his own strengths and vulnerabilities—his flaws—with her. Let her see some other side of himself than the charming, rarely serious man he'd presented to every other woman of his acquaintance.

He'd never realized before Hazel that despite his willingness to commit to his past relationships, they'd all been rather shallow—a form of serial monogamy, not unlike that practiced by his Havasupai ancestors. He'd let his former partners walk out of his life without a fight because by the time they left, even during the time that it hurt, being with them hadn't really mattered to him anymore.

He hadn't needed them the way he found he needed Hazel—emotional baggage, long-term fears and all. And if she was worried about whether or not he'd accept Emily, too, well, all he could say was that Emily was part of Hazel and therefore part of making the package whole. He wanted them both in his life. But he needed Hazel.

Which probably should have scared him, but didn't.

Of course, since she wasn't exactly listening to him or his protestations and promises these days, he was darn well going to have to show her, rather than tell her.

Which naturally meant that he'd have to enlist a little underhanded aid from Emily—who *did* have her mother's ear—and ambush Hazel by not only offering her his love, but by handing her his heart on a platter.

In other words, whatever it took he was going to seduce her, overwhelm her, one sense, one emotion, one fear at a time.

To that end he gave Hazel space and he offered her time.

Another two weeks. By which point her leave was supposed to be up, but at which time she pleaded extenuating family circumstances—no way was Emily ready to leave the reservation even if Hazel had been inclined to make her do so by now—and extended it.

Then Guy decided enough was enough and started to spend all of his free time on the reservation with her and Emily.

Deliberately invading the thirty-foot space she tried to keep between them—until, like the skittish horses he'd worked with as a kid, she forgot to start and run every time he drew near.

Learned to accept his presence as a simple matter of fact, even as she maintained her wariness. But since he didn't push the issue, she let him stay.

Wanted badly for him to stay.

Emily, naturally, fell in love with him with all the innocence and ease of prepuberty—which only seduced her mother all the more into finding herself more and more eager to see him and be with him.

And allowing herself to cautiously bask in his attentions and his intentions.

After another week, he began to ask her to dinner. And to movies where he oftentimes included Emily.

And out on dates where he only *sometimes* included Emily.

Who giggled.

And the minute she let him close enough, he started to kiss her.

A lot.

Everywhere—as long as it was above the collar or over the clothes when they were out alone.

And every place—as long as it was above the collar—when they were around other people, including, or perhaps especially, Emily.

With tremendous heat and leashed longing when they were alone. With affection, laughter and heat when Emily was watching.

But he didn't ask her back into his bed, regardless of how badly they both wanted him to. "Bed" could always come later.

When she knew what else she wanted of him.

Until she understood that she was different from anyone who'd gone before and, with her, he didn't plan to let go.

Because if he did, if he didn't fight to keep her and any *permanent* relationship he might have with her, well, he might recover. Eventually. But he wouldn't be whole, and he wouldn't be well and he'd damn sure be less than he might be if she remained a part of his life.

The declaration thrilled and scared Hazel no end.

On top of the decisions she had to make about her own and Emily's future, the risk he asked her to take terrified her.

Still, by the middle of her third month with Emily—and

Guy—Hazel was fairly certain she wanted a lot more of him. Or rather make that *with* him. She simply needed to quit being afraid of what she felt for him.

She was also certain there was no way she could leave Emily behind again, however briefly. Because loving Emily was as necessary as breathing. And despite how important Guy was to her, Emily took first precedence at this juncture in their lives.

So Hazel applied for a posting to the nearest FBI office to the reservation or, barring that, to be named liaison to one of the state, county or local law enforcement agencies not far from Hopiland. Then she made arrangements to have her spartan Phoenix apartment furnishings packed up and shipped north.

When a gleeful Emily confided this development to Guy, he immediately went out looking for a buyer for his one-person trailer and a larger trailer to put in its place. One with actual bedrooms—perhaps at opposite ends of the trailer. Or with at least one very private bedroom and a bed down the hall to accommodate a hopelessly romantic eleven-year-old who had designs on his heart that were only slightly less potent than the ones he had on her mother's.

Than the hold her mother had on his.

By this time he'd known for ages that Hazel was definitely The One, The Only. It was left only to convince her that she'd known the same thing about him for almost as long. So he requested and got Emily's blessing and finally set out to seduce three words and a promise out of her mother.

Over his special black bean and corn stew in his new trailer with the shower he'd gone to a lot of trouble to make sure could fit two—if one of the two was his size and the other was oh, say, Hazel's.

To which end, he dressed in his best jeans and a clean

black T-shirt and appeared to pick her up in his truck late one afternoon four months to the day after they'd met.

"Here, put this on," he said, handing her a bright turquoise blindfold when she appeared at her grandmother's door with Emily behind her.

She laughed at him. "What? Why?"

She'd started to laugh a lot with him, and he liked the way the sound fitted her, loved the way it crinkled the skin at the corners of her eyes and made her entire face light up.

"Surprise. Just put it on. Trust me."

Her face, her eyes softened. "You know I do." She took the bandanna from him. "Can I at least wait to put it on until after I get in the truck?"

"Sure. Go ahead. I gotta talk to Emily a sec."

She gave him bright-eyed but laughing suspicion and went after admonishing her daughter, "Don't keep great-grandfather up too late. You may not have school tomorrow, but he and great-grandmother are getting old."

"I heard that," Anna called from the kitchen.

Guy watched Hazel out of earshot behind the truck's closed door, then bent to Emily. "You do what I told you?"

"Yep." The girl nodded. "Brought my pajamas. You gonna do what I told you?"

"Yep back at you. She's not comin' home till she says yes."

"Good." Small houses left little room for privacy and little doubt among the children about what went on between adults within them. "And you'll tell her you love her?"

Ah, the romantic preteen heart and mind at work.

"Of course, absolutely." Guy nodded solemnly. Then he grinned. "That's the best part of it. She going to run when I do?"

Emily screwed up her face. "I dunno. I say it to her and she cries."

"Yes, but does she say it back?"

"Only about thirty-seven zillion times a day."

"Well, that's good, then. You're gettin' her ready for when I say it to her again tonight."

"Good," Emily said. "Because she needs *both* of us for her family, that's a fact."

She bussed him on the cheek while he was still chuckling at her emphatic turn of phrase. He was darned glad she agreed with him so fully. Made seducing Hazel's heart and soul, mind and body, life—past, present and future—all the richer and more rewarding. Gave him his shot at having his own instant family, and he liked the weight and feel of that tremendously.

"You better go," his co-conspirator whispered. "She's opening the door."

He glanced behind him, dropped a kiss on Emily's forehead. "Don't wait up, sport."

"Bring her home engaged to you, Guy," she retorted, and retreated into her great-grandparents' house.

"What were you two talking about?" Hazel asked when he climbed in behind the wheel.

He leaned across the seat and covered her mouth with his, murmuring, "I'll tell you later," against her lips.

She cupped his face between her palms, held him to her until they were both breathless. "Promise?"

He groaned. "Do that again and I'll promise you anything."

"Good," she whispered. Kissed him again with tongue and teeth and emotions that offered promises, demanded them in return—and that suggested it was time to make some—and eased back into her own seat before she lost her head completely in full view of her new world. "I'll hold you to it."

"Do." He collected himself, switched on the ignition. "Now put on your blindfold and keep it there until I tell you to take it off."

"Wait here a minute," he told Hazel when they arrived.

"Guy," she protested.

He cupped her face in one big hand and kissed her deeply. "A minute," he promised. "One. Count it. One *koyannisqatsi*...two *koyannisqatsi*..."

He left her laughing and trying hard not to tilt her head back to peek out from underneath the turquoise cloth over her eyes. It was no mean task. Guy's "surprises," while usually worth the wait, had a tendency to blow her away, steal her breath, bind her heart even more tightly to his than ever—and frequently bring them closer than she was ready to be. Not than she *wanted* to be, but only was ready to be.

Her heart, though healing, was still damaged goods, and more than anything in the world she wanted to be fair to him, to Emily, to herself. Had to be fair especially to Emily and him. She was pretty sure that the only way to be fair to herself was to let go and free-fall, have faith that Guy would catch her *and* Emily.

The way Emily was already positive he would—and had. Hazel knew this because Emily had said as much.

Which made Hazel decide that Emily had been listening too much to Joseph, who spun stories about the non-Hopi man whose heart was bigger than the whole land area of the Havasupai, Hopi and Navajo Nations combined, and who was the equal of Warrior Woman—and whose name was, coincidentally enough, Guyapi.

She heard the door latch click; the door opened.

"Come on," Guy said.

"How am I supposed to get down?" she protested. "I can't see anything."

"Trust me." His favorite phrase. The jury was still out on whether or not it was hers, because he tended to say it both when he was serious and when he was teasing. Right now he sounded a bit of both. "I won't let you fall."

"All right."

Sounding dubious but not feeling it, she felt for the steps Guy always let down for her—only to find air under her feet. She started to catch herself, then felt Guy close and let herself go. His arms closed around her; he swung her up against his chest.

"Told you," he said smugly.

She slung an arm about his neck. "Trusted you," she retorted—equally smug.

He brushed a kiss across her ear. "So you did," he said, and there was something oddly fluttery in his voice that made her want to see his face.

Before she could move to do anything of the kind, however, he strode away from the truck, turned sideways to mount two steps and stopped.

"Okay," he said. Was that trepidation she heard in his voice? "You can look now."

So she pulled off the bandanna and did. Looked and blinked and looked again.

Saw warmth and comfort and "coze" and colors that belonged both to Guy and to her.

Saw intimacy within confined spaces, saw roominess within them, too.

Saw a real living room and a dining table booth that invited. Saw a kitchen that was less compact than his old one but still efficient—still not exactly up her alley, but hey, she was learning. Saw and heard something heating in the programmable microwave.

Saw a single bunk against one living room wall, and a corner shelf that held an eclectic collection of Emily's kachinas—some carved, some sculpted, some made from toothpicks and embroidery floss.

Saw one of the quilts she'd helped Emily, her grandmother and some of the village women make covering the bunk.

"It's not huge," Guy said quietly, "but it's bigger."

"It's—" she could barely speak "—it's lovely."

He breathed something like relief. "There's more."

She looped her other arm around his neck and swallowed. Tucked her head beneath his chin and nodded. "I hoped there might be."

A breath and an increase in the tension in his arms. "Good."

Twisting and turning to edge them through tight spaces, Guy carried her across the kitchen and down the hallway at the back of the trailer. He paused outside a small door, indicated the bathroom.

"Tub *and* shower," he said. "Big enough for two. I measured."

She bit back a smile. "Trust you to think of that."

"Had to," he muttered. "I have fantasies."

"Am I in them?" It was blatant fishing, and she didn't care.

He traced her ear with his tongue. "You *are* them," he whispered hotly and everything inside her peaked, tightened, heated, pooled and went breathless with anticipation.

Tonight, her body announced, hungry for it.

Tonight, her mind breathed, half hoping, half afraid.

Tonight, her soul murmured with longing.

Tonight, her heart whispered, and knew with awesome clarity that *tonight* was absolutely right.

For everything. For free-falling and for being caught and for catching.

For promises given and received.

For not only becoming lovers but for loving and being loved in return.

In word and deed.

He took a step farther down the hall.

She snuggled deeper and more comfortably into his arms and said it plainly, without thinking. Without needing to think. Wondering why it had taken her so damned long to acknowledge and give voice to something that was bursting to be let out.

"I love you."

He stopped and his hold tightened about her. "What?"

She kissed his chin. "You heard me."

"Say it again," he ordered fiercely. "I have to be sure I heard right."

She leaned back and looked up at him. "I love you. You heard right."

"You do."

She smiled. She felt him holding his breath waiting for her answer because he was having trouble believing she'd said it even though it was exactly what he'd wanted to hear—what she understood without doubt that *he'd* longed to say to her for weeks. "Yes. I do. With all my heart. With all of me. So much that the only thing I'm afraid of about it anymore is not saying it to you as often as I can. As often as you'll let me. And if you want to say it back, I'm not afraid of hearing it as often as I know you'll say it. You want to say it. Say it, Guy. Tell me." She indicated the last door in the hall. "Show me."

He needed no further invitation.

"I love you, Hazel." Fervent, hopeful, tremulous, laughing.

He swept her into the bedroom, stood inside the door and let her look her fill at the big bed: the Hopi-style wedding quilt spread over it, the extra quilt folded at the foot of the bed to keep her warm when his shoulders tented the covers over her too much—the simple furnishings that made up his bed, his life, his heart.

Made him her home.

"I love you and I want you in my bed, I need you in my life always. Marry me. Be my wife, my heart, my woman, my life."

"Yes." She thought she'd be filled with trepidation when she answered, but she wasn't. It was simple. It was right. It was—her heart soared and filled, spread wide— *absolutely* right. So she said it again. With conviction. "Yes." Then, laughing with her newfound freedom. "Yes—yes—yes!"

She felt him relax. "Good." He strode to the bed and dumped her on it, came down on top of her. "When?"

"Now," she said softly, nuzzling his mouth. "Right here, right now, in the old way. As soon as possible in the new."

He grinned and kissed her deeply. When he raised his head they were both dazed and far more than half-gone. "I was hoping you'd say that because I wasn't sure I could wait for another five minutes to make love to you, let alone months."

"No more waiting," Hazel mumbled, working to get his shirt free of his pants, her hands on his skin. "Become my husband. Take me to wife. Now. Please, Guy. Don't wait."

He didn't.

And neither did she.

Epilogue

Hazel stood in their two-person bathroom and looked at the pregnancy test results. Her heart trip-hammered with an excitement she hadn't anticipated feeling, and she placed the "mom's hand" on her belly the same instinctive way she'd ever seen any pregnant woman do.

The way she'd done when she was pregnant with Emily.

She'd been relatively certain of her condition for almost three weeks, though she'd hoarded the feeling to herself and said nothing about it even to Guy; this was just the icing of confirmation. Now she wanted to tell Guy first, then find a doctor, then tell Emily.

Laughter bubbled from her. She was pregnant again, and it felt glorious because this baby had been cherished before it existed, wanted from the moment she and Guy had said yes to each other in their bed across the hall.

Of course, this addition might necessitate a few changes. At work, for instance, and soon. And here at home—she still couldn't get over the simple joy that tingled through her with the word. She had a home. Family. Emily.

Guy.

She shut her eyes and held him close in that most intimate and private place that was his and his alone inside her. Oh, yes, she had Guy.

Smiling softly, she returned to the matter at hand. They probably wouldn't have to make the changes here yet, but certainly, in a year or two. Emily was twelve now; she would need some space of her own soon whether that space entailed adding a room onto the trailer or something else altogether.

But that was part of tomorrow's planning. Today was for telling her *husband*. The mere word still filled her with awe—and with reason for celebrating. After Emily went to bed. She'd tell him then, when their bedroom door was closed and it was just the two of them.

She couldn't wait.

Just then, as if he'd heard her thoughts the way he so often seemed to, Hazel heard Guy's truck pull up under the carport beneath the cottonwood trees. Doors slammed, and Emily bounded into the trailer first, chortling about something. Guy followed her deliberately less quickly, letting her get ahead of him in whatever game they played today. The way they sounded, Hazel doubted she wanted to know what they were up to. Yesterday it was a heated debate over Navajo use of Hopi partitioned lands and vice versa with Guy taking the Navajo side just to be difficult.

The day before that they'd come in from Guy picking up their fifth-grader on his way home discussing the methods of birth control that he and her mother weren't using.

Hazel shuddered. She didn't even want to think about

Emily entering puberty and needing to know about birth control or anything else along that line, but Guy talked about it openly with her.

If Emily had a question, he answered it as plainly and simply as possible—and the more outrageous the question, the bigger a kick they both seemed to get out of the answer and resulting discussion.

Or argument, as the case might be.

A week ago they'd come in with Emily sporting tattoos on her ears and down the sides of her neck, and him wearing a sizable Warrior Woman depiction on his scarred right shoulder. Hazel had seriously considered killing him over that one—even after he'd let her wrestle him to the couch where he'd laughingly confessed that Emily's were only five-to-seven-day hennas, and his was of the forty-five-day East Indian variety. He'd wanted the longer-lasting kind, he said, because he was thinking of letting his cousin do him a permanent Warrior Woman.

Hazel had muttered something, though she was secretly tickled by the thought. Then she'd surprised herself by going out and letting Guy's cousin henna a small but long-lasting rattlesnake around her finger where it could be hidden by her wide silver wedding band. Guy had laughed himself silly when he'd caught her doing dishes without her ring and spotted the tattoo. That night, though, he'd removed her ring with her clothes and lavished his attentions on that finger until they were both crazed and she'd realized how deeply touched he was by the gesture.

Today, God alone knew what her husband and her child were up to—and God alone could keep knowing because she *certainly* didn't want to.

The noise in the other room subsided, and she felt rather than heard Guy come soundlessly down the hall.

"Hazel."

He was through the open bathroom door and had her in his arms practically before she knew it—before she realized she hadn't yet discarded the test stick. He picked her up and stood her on the stool where he could kiss her long and thoroughly without getting a crick in his neck. She slipped her arms around his shoulders, sank into him and tossed the stick toward the basket, hoping he wouldn't notice.

Yeah, right. As if.

"Mmm," he murmured. "You taste good." Then, when she thought she'd gotten away clean, he kissed her dizzy again, pulled back and looked over his shoulder. "Okay, now tell me. What was that?"

"What was what?" One of the marvelous things about kissing him was the way it made her unable to remember her name let alone think about anything else. Like lying to him on purpose just so she could tell him what she wanted to tell him in her own way later.

He slid his hands under her shirt, stuck out a foot and kicked the door shut. "That stick you didn't want me to see when I came in."

"That what?" She gasped and arched into him when he unhooked her bra, eased it upward and replaced it with his wonderfully talented hands. "I don't know. You know I can't think when you do that."

"I know." He was grinning and she heard it. He hoisted her around the waist and rubbed himself against her belly. "Put your legs around me," he urged. When she complied he moved over and locked the door, leaned her back against it, supporting her with one hand while he continued to stroke her breasts with the other. "Mmm." A low groan. "You feel good."

"Guy." A halfhearted protest, belied by the undulations of her lower body against him. "We can't. Emily—"

"Is doing her homework at the other end of the house," Guy said firmly. He pulled her away from the door and sat on the counter, started on the buttons of her shirt. His lips followed his progress, pushing aside her blouse as it opened, planting sizzling, open-mouthed kisses everywhere but in the ever-tightening and aching centers of her breasts. "Now tell me before I have to guess."

"Not now." She gasped when he unzipped her jeans and slipped his fingers inside the scrap of satin covering her body's secrets. Secrets he knew well. Secrets he kept for her and made with her. "Later. I had it all planned."

"But this was part of the plan, wasn't it?" Those incredible fingers were inside her now, hungry, stroking, plucking, easing deeper and taking her into that world shared only between them. "You and me. Alone. Like this."

"Yes!" The tension was unbearable, building inside her, springs tightening with the muscles of her belly, coiling around his fingers.

"Then it's okay to tell me now, isn't it. We can do whatever you had planned later, too, but I've been good. I've been patient. I've waited three weeks for you to tell me what I already know."

"You don't know." She was moving hard and fast against his hand now. She couldn't help it. He knew exactly how to do this to her, how to make her wait, how to take her to the brink and keep her there, how to send her over the edge within seconds. "You can't know. I wasn't even sure until today."

"I know," he said softly, then brought her close and took her mouth to catch her cries when he gave her release. She stiffened and pulsed around his fingers for a long time before slumping into his arms. Still stroking her deeply, he put his mouth to her ear. "I can smell it on you. It's different. Sweeter. We're pregnant, aren't we?"

"I—we—" Nonplussed that he could know so easily, she sat back. The movement changed the position of his fingers to one of exquisite torture. She hiked her pelvis forward and her insides contracted immediately, ready. So ready! But she wanted more this time. She wanted him inside her.

Without hesitation she lifted herself off his hand and wriggled out of her jeans. Straddled him, worked his shirt off and shoved him back against the wall so she could open his pants and take him into her hand.

His eyelids slitted with his concentration, his breathing went shallow. "Hazel."

She started to lower herself onto him. He caught her by the waist, stopping her. "Tell me first."

She shook her head and bent to nip his mouth, licked his lips with wanton abandon, rubbed her tongue against his. "When you're crazy inside me," she promised. "I'll tell you." Then she thrust her hips downward and impaled herself on him.

He groaned.

She took the sound in her mouth. And then she began to move. Hard, fast furiously. Because she knew him, too. Knew how to bring him to instant climax, how to make him insane waiting for her. How deep or shallow to take him, and how to distract him.

How to love him.

When she could feel the tension corkscrewing through him, could see his control slipping from his eyes, the way his breath came in serrated gasps from his lungs, she leaned forward to take him as deep as she could while she whispered it to him.

"Yes. I'm pregnant."

His response was a growl of satisfaction and a shift in position that let him share control of the outcome with her. And when she was delirious with her own release, he held her tight and filled her with his seed, whispering as he did so, ''I love you, Hazel.''

And she could only cry with happiness and say it back, over and over and over until he shut her up by kissing her hard and making love to her again.

Loving her for always.

* * * * *

If you enjoyed what you just read,
then we've got an offer you can't resist!

Take 2 bestselling love stories FREE!

Plus get a FREE surprise gift!

Feel like a star with Silhouette.

We will fly you and a guest to New York City for an exciting weekend stay at a glamorous 5-star hotel. Experience a refreshing day at one of New York's trendiest spas and have your photo taken by a professional. Plus, receive $1,000 U.S. spending money!

Flowers...long walks...dinner for two... how does Silhouette Books make romance come alive for you?

Send us a script, with 500 words or less, along with visuals (only drawings, magazine cutouts or photographs or combination thereof). Show us how Silhouette Makes Your Love Come Alive. Be creative and have fun. No purchase necessary. All entries must be clearly marked with your name, address and telephone number. All entries will become property of Silhouette and are not returnable. **Contest closes September 28, 2001.**

Please send your entry to: **Silhouette Makes You a Star!**

In U.S.A.	In Canada
P.O. Box 9069	P.O. Box 637
Buffalo, NY, 14269-9069	Fort Erie, ON, L2A 5X3

Look for contest details on the next page, by visiting www.eHarlequin.com or request a copy by sending a self-addressed envelope to the applicable address above. Contest open to Canadian and U.S. residents who are 18 or over. Void where prohibited.

Where love comes alive™

Our lucky winner's photo will appear in a Silhouette ad. Join the fun!

SRMYAS1

HARLEQUIN "SILHOUETTE MAKES YOU A STAR!" CONTEST 1308
OFFICIAL RULES
NO PURCHASE NECESSARY TO ENTER

1. To enter, follow directions published in the offer to which you are responding. Contest begins June 1, 2001, and ends on September 28, 2001. Entries must be postmarked by September 28, 2001, and received by October 5, 2001. Enter by hand-printing (or typing) on an 8 ½" x 11" piece of paper your name, address (including zip code), contest number/name and attaching a script containing 500 words or less, along with drawings, photographs or magazine cutouts, or combinations thereof (i.e., collage) on no larger than 9" x 12" piece of paper, describing how the Silhouette books make romance come alive for you. Mail via first-class mail to: Harlequin "Silhouette Makes You a Star!" Contest 1308, (in the U.S.) P.O. Box 9069, Buffalo, NY 14269-9069, (in Canada) P.O. Box 637, Fort Erie, Ontario, Canada L2A 5X3. Limit one entry per person, household or organization.

2. Contests will be judged by a panel of members of the Harlequin editorial, marketing and public relations staff. Fifty percent of criteria will be judged against script and fifty percent will be judged against drawing, photographs and/or magazine cutouts. Judging criteria will be based on the following:

   • Sincerity—25%
   • Originality and Creativity—50%
   • Emotionally Compelling—25%

   In the event of a tie, duplicate prizes will be awarded. Decisions of the judges are final.

3. All entries become the property of Torstar Corp. and may be used for future promotional purposes. Entries will not be returned. No responsibility is assumed for lost, late, illegible, incomplete, inaccurate, nondelivered or misdirected mail.

4. Contest open only to residents of the U.S. (except Puerto Rico) and Canada who are 18 years of age or older, and is void wherever prohibited by law; all applicable laws and regulations apply. Any litigation within the Province of Quebec respecting the conduct or organization of a publicity contest may be submitted to the Régie des alcools, des courses et des jeux for a ruling. Any litigation respecting the awarding of a prize may be submitted to the Régie des alcools, des courses et des jeux only for the purpose of helping the parties reach a settlement. Employees and immediate family members of Torstar Corp. and D. L. Blair, Inc., their affiliates, subsidiaries and all other agencies, entities and persons connected with the use, marketing or conduct of this contest are not eligible to enter. Taxes on prizes are the sole responsibility of the winner. Acceptance of any prize offered constitutes permission to use winner's name, photograph or other likeness for the purposes of advertising, trade and promotion on behalf of Torstar Corp., its affiliates and subsidiaries without further compensation to the winner, unless prohibited by law.

5. Winner will be determined no later than November 30, 2001, and will be notified by mail. Winner will be required to sign and return an Affidavit of Eligibility/Release of Liability/Publicity Release form within 15 days after winner notification. Noncompliance within that time period may result in disqualification and an alternative winner may be selected. All travelers must execute a Release of Liability prior to ticketing and must possess required travel documents (e.g., passport, photo ID) where applicable. Trip must be booked by December 31, 2001, and completed within one year of notification. No substitution of prize permitted by winner. Torstar Corp. and D. L. Blair, Inc., their parents, affiliates and subsidiaries are not responsible for errors in printing of contest, entries and/or game pieces. In the event of printing or other errors that may result in unintended prize values or duplication of prizes, all affected game pieces or entries shall be null and void. **Purchase or acceptance of a product offer does not improve your chances of winning.**

6. Prizes: (1) Grand Prize—A 2-night/3-day trip for two (2) to New York City, including round-trip coach air transportation nearest winner's home and hotel accommodations (double occupancy) at The Plaza Hotel, a glamorous afternoon makeover at a trendy New York spa, $1,000 in U.S. spending money and an opportunity to have a professional photo taken and appear in a Silhouette advertisement (approximate retail value: $7,000). (10) Ten Runner-Up Prizes of gift packages (retail value $50 ea.). Prizes consist of only those items listed as part of the prize. Limit one prize per person. Prize is valued in U.S. currency.

7. For the name of the winner (available after December 31, 2001) send a self-addressed, stamped envelope to: Harlequin "Silhouette Makes You a Star!" Contest 1197 Winners, P.O. Box 4200 Blair, NE 68009-4200 or you may access the www.eHarlequin.com Web site through February 28, 2002.

Contest sponsored by Torstar Corp., P.O Box 9042, Buffalo, NY 14269-9042.